ADVENTURES OF A ROCKING HORSE

# THE SAFFRON THREAD

THE SEQUEL TO 'A HEART BEATS WITHIN'

# LANA GAZDER

*This book is dedicated to my wonderfully brave friend*
*'Bless her' Caroliney, A.K.A Minty Cake*

*Also, with thanks to Helen Robbins and*
*Gillian De Vere for their input and patience.*

# CHAPTER 1.
# THE NIGHT-VISION

## 1990

How should I begin my story? Well, it all started with Charlotte's night-mare, or should I say, night-vision. She refused to call these nasty dreams by their usual name, as she said it was an insult to all females of the equine species. However, we are not actually real horses and before you get muddled, I had better explain. We are rocking horses. That doesn't mean we're not alive, a lot of us are and we have hearts and can communicate with one another through feelings and thoughts. Rocking horses all have one thing in common: we are capable of emotions and we adore children, often forming un-breakable bonds with our small people, even when they become adults. If we are loved, we come to life, it's that simple. And yes, we can dream.

Perhaps I ought to introduce myself and my two companions, so you get a clearer picture of who we are and where we live. I am now known as Blitz, a name I earned myself through the many previous experiences of my life. I was made in 1899 in the workshop of Mr Leach and I'm a traditional dappled grey English rocking horse of the highest quality, mounted on a swing stand. In 1900, I went out to my first home to start my career looking after children.

There in the attic nursery I met my dearest, oldest life-long friend Cobweb. He is a charming little bow-mounted horse who was made in the G&J Lines workshop (yes, we rocking horses have a sort of pedigree of who made us) and he is about 20 years older than me and is extremely kind and caring. We were separated for over 60 years, during which time we never forgot our friendship and missed each other very much. Having both survived two world wars in our own way, and having led very different lives, we were magically re-united in 1968. Our present people, June and Jacs, who are also life-long friends, rescued us from auction sales.

Then there is Charlotte, the wonderful, regal, ancient and most beautiful bow rocking horse I've ever met. She is like a wise and caring great-aunt on the one hand, and like a glamorous film-star who we idolise, on the other. To us mere youngsters, this rocking horse mare, who must be all of 140 years old, is a legend. Charlotte has been with us since 1973 when Cobweb's person, June, rescued her from dilapidation and sent her off to be re-born. By that I mean 'restored' but I prefer to name the process as being re-born. All three of us are dappled grey and very proud of being this wonderful colour. Over a century ago, when Queen Victoria bought one of us rocking horse toys for her children, she chose a dappled one, giving this colour her Royal seal of approval. Funnily enough, it's a colour theme that runs through our racehorse stud farm here, where we now all live. Both Charlotte (often referred to as the Duchess) and I have our original paintwork back now, discovered under layers of overpaint. This happy miracle occurred whilst we were being worked on by our family's great friend and restorer, Brenda. Cobweb is one of the lucky ones. Despite his age, he is all original – no-one ever sloshed horrid gloss paint over his beautiful dappled body. He never needed much doing to him as he survived all his years intact, within the homes of an extended 'well to do' family.

Charlotte has had the most bizarre and exciting life, almost more eventful than mine, but then she IS older than me… She has kept us enthralled with her strange tales of all the different homes she's had and the exciting years she spent in India during the 1920s and 1930s. Quite a stickler for good manners, etiquette and high principles, she has kept us on the straight and narrow. We bow to her great wisdom and are still in awe of her, even though we love her dearly. When annoyed, Charlotte's expressive glass eyes can change from a mellow claret-brown hue to a fiery, burning-coal red, which is very disconcerting. We tried hard not to upset the Duchess, as one look from her could shrivel the paint off your back! We certainly did not want to ignite those strange vermillion eyes of hers! At all other times she was the gentlest, most demure and patient soul you could hope to meet.

Charlotte and Cobweb live mainly with their people, June and David, at their large, elegant home called Wick House. I live just a stone's throw away in a quaint cottage named Airborne Lodge with my own wonderful family consisting of my beloved person Jacs (short for Jacqueline), her husband Eddie, their teenage son Sebastian and a little old cat called Fireworks. I say 'mainly' because Cobweb and I could be moved about between the two abodes, depending on circumstances. Both properties are on the large Holmwood Wick estate, which is in the county of Surrey and is owned by June's parents. The racehorse breeding business where we all reside is within this estate and is called Wick Stud. It belongs to our people jointly. Our two families are all the best of friends, just like us three rocking horses. We had all lived in such harmony and bliss for years, watching lovely little Sebastian growing up, sharing in the delights and successes of the thriving stud farm and... feeling safe. This is of the utmost importance to rocking horses, especially to those who have had to contend with a troubled past. Feeling safe in a loving, secure home is priceless. So as you can imagine, Charlotte's upsetting 'episode', that is her first ever terrible dream was a shock to both of us and extremely unsettling. Looking back, I feel life as we knew it started to unravel from that point on.

*'Nightmares take you deep into your soul to witness sights that you dare not view by day.'*

I will set the scene of Charlotte's awful night-vision. The three of us were dozing happily in the peaceful sitting room of Wick House, where I was staying temporarily due to renovations being done at my Lodge. It was a late winter's evening in November, pitch black outside with lashing rain drumming against the window panes. The room was dimly lit by the dying embers of a log fire. June and David had retired to bed as they always had an early start looking after the mares and foals on the stud. Outside, the wind howled menacingly, the trees were taking a battering and as I rested my eyes, my mind drifted back to times long ago, when I'd found myself exposed to the elements. These memories made me smile inside now that I was safe and I felt even more grateful to be indoors. Through the noise of this brewing storm, I suddenly heard the ominous creak of a rocking horse's bows being put under the strain of extreme movement. It was a sound I knew so well and I only say 'ominous' because it should not have been happening. It was dark, it was late and certainly no-one was riding any of us to set us into motion.

Now, I know I have good eyesight because although I say it myself, I have the most beautiful Victorian glass eyes; they are big, bold and shine like gemstones. They also give me very clear, sharp vision, as good as when they were first given to me over 90 years ago in the workshop where I was made. Considering my very mixed fortunes over the years, they and I have done well to survive. So, there was no mistaking what I saw – and it came as a shock. The usually composed, calm and dignified Charlotte was in complete distress. The storm had broken with thunder and lightning putting on a dramatic show in the night sky outside. She was rocking frantically, her majestic body glistening with sweat, which caused her varnish to shimmer unnaturally, highlighted with each strike of lightning. Her long mane and tail were thrashing about with every sickening lurch of her bows. Charlotte's liquid, gentle eyes were changed into orbs of terror, staring at unspeakable past horrors. Her forelock was being whipped to a frenzy around her delicate face and appeared dampened from tears she had shed during those horrible moments.

*Charlotte's gentle eyes were changed into orbs of terror*

I was beside myself with fear and concern for the beautiful Charlotte. My friend Cobweb, who stood next to me, also awoke to see this frightening sight. We tried desperately to wake her from her trance-like state and between us we both tried shouting at her until her rocking slowed and her eyes changed from looking haunted to just plain desolate. Poor Charlotte was visibly shaken but tried to make light of the incident and apologised profusely for causing us to worry. But worried we were, as she refused to talk about what had happened. We thought it prudent not to labour the point; we didn't push the Duchess to discuss what had happened that night or to disclose what she'd seen that was so terrifying. All of us thought it was an unfortunate isolated incident that would never happen again. But it wasn't, and it most certainly did...

1991. Christmas came and went. This had been a joyful time spent with my family whole again, as Sebastian had returned home. I was in my element as this lad was my whole world. I had developed a strong bond with him since he was born and had given him his first taste of riding during many early lessons. Seb had rocked on me since he was a tiny baby and his jockey father and I had taught him well. This handsome young man was now in his eighteenth year. Being athletic and neatly built, he was the perfect size and weight to fulfil his ambition to be a jockey. He'd been away for a couple of years with a Newmarket racehorse trainer, honing his talents in his chosen profession, to return triumphant. Sebastian had come home as a champion apprentice jockey. Soon after he'd arrived, he'd come straight over to me as was his habit and sat with his arm over my neck, gazing lovingly into my eyes. It was so good to have my boy back next to me again. Speaking softly, he'd told me all that had happened to him since we'd last met, his loves, his fears, his triumphs and disappointments. I'm sure I knew him better than his own mother!

In March, my family and I, including our elderly cat Fireworks, moved into Wick House temporarily to babysit and take care of the various canine occupants. This was to allow June and David to have the first of the staggered two week breaks they enjoyed once a year. March was a time when there was a temporary lull in business, enough to allow the running of the stud to fall on one half of the partnership whilst the other couple took a holiday. I was transported over to Wick House on the back of the stud's pick-up truck, a short trip that Cobweb and I had done many times. Wherever my people went, I was taken and now I would be with them at my second home, reunited with Cobweb and Charlotte. It felt good to be a valued part of the family and not be left behind. Many years ago, I'd experienced the devastating feeling of being abandoned and it's a painful memory. Nowadays, I was never left at home alone.

How wonderful it was to be back with my two friends as we hadn't seen each other for a couple of months. We instantly fell back into our comfortable ways, catching up on scraps of news and gossip that we'd heard whilst eavesdropping. This is an essential way of finding out what's going on around us. Not always done intentionally, eavesdropping just comes with the territory of being a rocking horse. Although we are much loved, we tend to blend into the furniture and become invisible when our people are deep in conversation. We are often privy to the most revealing conversations.

Of course, we rocking horses are great listeners and we have the power to bring comfort. Many a time, our loved ones have come to us to whisper and share their worries, secrets or their joyous news. All this is for our pricked ears only. We uphold the unwritten rocking horse code of complete discretion and confidentiality. But eavesdropping is a different kettle of fish. It can be a blessing or a curse; you may hear something rather good and cheering, or something deeply disturbing that causes great anxiety. However, we are generally problem-solvers. We only ever want to help and in the past, Cobweb and I have put our heads together and resolved some tricky matters, purely by eavesdropping. It's all about having integrity. We would only ever discuss what we had heard amongst ourselves. After all, we are all one big family.

Within a couple of days I began to feel uneasy. Things just weren't quite right at Wick House. I can't explain it, but a weird atmosphere of underlying tension and worry pervaded. Charlotte was a bit distant and seemed to doze a lot during the day, staring vacantly at the wall. My little pal Cobweb was not himself either, he seemed reticent, unusually quiet for him. My lovely person Jacs, who had always been my soul mate, seemed pre-occupied and stressed. Whenever she'd had a problem in the past, I would be the first to know. She'd always confided in me and used me as a sounding-board. Not this time...for some reason Jacs never came to sit by me and talk, she never even approached me.

When I noticed that Charlotte was yet again dozing off in the corner, I took my opportunity to ask Cobweb what was troubling him. He replied in a hushed whisper that he was worried about Charlotte. Oh dear; I had hoped the subject of that night vision would not rear its ugly head again, but apparently poor Cobweb had been dealing with it all on his own and I felt so sorry for him. He confided that Charlotte's bad dreams were not quite as violent as the dreadful vision she'd had on the night of the storm, but she was suffering with them more frequently. In fact, this explained her constant tiredness during the day: she was fearful about sleeping at night. I consoled Cobweb, assuring him that together we would try to talk to the Duchess before our people noticed anything was amiss. We didn't want to worry them; they seemed to have problems of their own. The very next day, whilst eavesdropping on a telephone conversation and then hearing Jacs' and Eddie's sombre voices coming from the kitchen, it all became clear. Good news travels fast, but bad news travels faster.

*'Eavesdrop if you must, but temper your findings with kindness.'*

From what we could gather, the business was failing. January was usually an exciting time on any racehorse stud as from this month on, the first crop of foals would be born. Occasionally there were losses, but this year several beautiful babies had been lost, which was heart-breaking for all the staff and owners. Many of the mares had fallen ill and the vets had been in and out, constantly reviewing the situation. Quite a few clients and owners had heard the stud's tragic news and were withdrawing their support. Some of the mares had been taken away, to foal in a different location. The surviving foals would be impossible to sell at a later date because of the huge black cloud that now hung over Wick Stud. Its wonderful reputation was being wiped out; years of hard work and many glorious successes were to count for nothing. This was the curse of eavesdropping... we learned the stud had been hit by a deadly equine virus.

That very word VIRUS strikes fear in the heart of all horse owners, especially in the breeding or racing industry. I won't go into boring detail but suffice to say the yard was put into quarantine, the smell of disinfectant pervaded. The paddocks, usually full of prancing young foals and content new mothers, seemed nearly empty with only a handful of surviving mares and foals turned out for short periods. It seemed the worst was over and those who had come through it would be fine, but the business had been decimated.

This whole dilemma had been hidden so well from us rocking horses, we knew nothing about it; everyone had tried to act normally and had soldiered on bravely, refusing to give up hope all through January and February. By March, David and June were completely exhausted and had been packed off to have a well-earned rest. Jacs and Eddie were left to man the fort. Sebastian had stayed on to lend valuable support. He hadn't returned to his old job after Christmas as the stud was locked down in isolation to prevent the virus spreading. It was all over now, but the devastation it had caused was only just beginning.

# CHAPTER 2.
# THE DAPPLE STUD

Well, we rocking horses fell into a sort of depression after hearing that news. Even Jacs noticed and asked Eddie if rocking horses could contract the virus because she thought we were 'off-colour'. I do know she was only joking, but it almost felt as if we had. We knew the importance of Wick Stud and that it supported our beloved home here. We'd always felt so safe. Now, everybody's future looked uncertain.

The business had started up just before we came to live here over 20 years ago and in that time, had done so well. Our people had earned themselves many accolades; they were breeders of a dynasty of successful mares who consistently produced winner after winner. The loveliest thing was (especially as our people were avid rocking horse fans) all the best winning stock were dappled greys! We had earned ourselves the nickname of The Dapple Stud. Many of the mares were home-bred from the original grey-coloured foundation mares, Flora and later Cobweb's Grace and Graceful Charlotte. Nearly every one of the dappled grey foals born seemed to turn out extremely fast, throwbacks to their illustrious forebears. Would that all be over now? It seemed we were in danger of losing everything.

## 'Long live good grey blood!'

Now I don't wish to bore you, because not everybody is as obsessed with dapples as we rocking horses are, but I think you'll find this bit of 'genetics' quite interesting. I gleaned this information many years ago, through productive eavesdropping. I had listened to Jacs and June doing what all serious breeders do, poring over volumes of books about racehorse pedigrees. They would spend hours tracing the speedy heritage of their best mares trying to find a husband for them, a sire whose bloodline would complement theirs to produce the best foals. Then one day, they discovered an astonishing fact. I had been listening casually, but their triumphant whoops of surprise and excitement made me strain my already pricked ears urgently. I didn't want to miss out on this news!

Apparently, a very important record-breaking horse with phenomenal speed was responsible for all their successes. They had traced back to a legendary horse called The Tetrarch. He was born in 1911 and guess what colour he was? Dappled grey? Not quite... he was a bit of a freak as he had been born a very rare and unique colour known as 'Chubari'. As a foal, he looked to be a chestnut colour but with weird black spots all over his body! However, over time, the chestnut faded into iron grey and the black spots turned white. If this isn't amazing in itself, then I'll tell you what made my people whoop with jubilation. The Tetrarch was an unbeaten, speedy youngster who captured the hearts of the public and earned himself the nickname of 'The Rocking Horse'! As our people are serious rocking horse lovers, this was joy to their ears! Later he was known as 'The Spotted Wonder'. Whether it had been luck or judgement, all the carefully chosen sires (husbands) that Jacs and June had used on their mares had doubled up on The Tetrarch's line. My clever people had stumbled upon something called a 'nick', an affinity of blood lines that produced winners. In breeding, when you find a winning formula like that, you have hit the jackpot!

Both of June and Jacs' best foundation mares went in a direct line back to this wonder horse through his best ever spotted grey daughter, Mumtaz Mahal, nicknamed 'The Flying Filly'. They excitedly read up all they could find about this incredible distant relative who had been responsible for them breeding so many winners and the famous dapple colour they were now well-known for. The Tetrarch himself had inherited his rare colour from his great grandfather Bend Or. He was chestnut with dark spots and a silver mane, who in turn had inherited it from his ancestor Pantaloon, born in 1824. It is said that if it had not been for these three strangely spotted horses breeding on down the line, the dappled grey colour would have probably died out in the thoroughbred horse. Also, practically every grey racehorse alive today can trace its pedigree back to The Tetrarch.

Well, my lot were ecstatic and I clearly remember a party springing up in the kitchen of the Lodge that night when the menfolk were told about their revelations. I think the cherry on the cake was the horse's nickname 'The Rocking Horse'. How perfect was that? Well, that was in happier times, unlike the gloomy days we were now going through since we heard the devastating news of the virus. Anyway, end of breeding lecture and I apologise for going on a bit.

During that two-week period while June and David were away recuperating, another very frightening incident occurred. It was a dreadful day that I hardly want to tell you about but it's part of the story so I must. They say people kick you when you're down and I fear that is true, because what happened next is an example of nasty people taking advantage of others' misfortunes.

It was about mid-morning when we heard a big lorry pulling up outside Wick House. Of course, the place was deserted as the stud staff had been laid off and Jacs, Eddie and Seb were working flat out at the stables to do all the extra work. Although the yard was only a few hundred yards away from the house, no one could hear or see what happened next. There was a knock on our front door but of course nobody in to answer it. Being the tallest of us three, Charlotte could see out of the sitting room window and reported back to us that the lorry appeared to belong to a removals firm. Then, horror of horrors, we heard people entering the house through our back door which, unwisely, was never locked. We watched in disbelieving shock as three men in khaki overalls approached, glanced round the wonderful antique-filled room and proceeded to carry out precious articles of huge value. They had by now un-latched the front door and next, hurriedly started to remove larger pieces of valuable antique furniture. Back and forth they went until the room looked quite bare.

My first reaction was one of overwhelming sadness. Oh, how had it come to this? Were things so bad that our poor people had resorted to selling their most prized possessions to keep a roof over our heads...but wait a minute, these were not antique dealers, they were removal men...and we certainly were not moving house! Then it struck me—we were being robbed, in broad daylight! A sharp memory raced across my mind. I remembered when years ago I had been stolen from the yard where I was being stored, waiting to be collected by my friends. Men in overalls had seen me and returned in the dead of night to bundle me into a waiting vehicle. A terrible anger was welling up in my belly and just as I was about to warn the others, Charlotte spoke. She too, had realised.

"Something is grievously amiss." She spoke in a cold but controlled voice. "These men are villainous imposters! Get ready, my friends, to fight for your lives, for I fear they will abscond with us, too!"

At that precise moment, our little cat Fireworks trotted in through the open back door looking mystified. "Whatever's going on?" he enquired.

I screamed at him to run and get help, I told him to try and alert Sebastian to the fact that there was a robbery in progress. "RUN, before we all get taken!" I was now so furious, I felt ready to do anything to protect my friends. Poor little Cobweb was quaking with fear; he had led a very sheltered life and just couldn't quite believe there were such evil men in the world. The Duchess was cold, calculating and ready to defend herself. Her eyes had turned a most awful shade of icy crimson.

The next five minutes were intense. There was complete pandemonium in that room and I don't think the men knew what had hit them, literally. They'd frowned at us through crafty, assessing eyes and I heard one say, "These are worth a few bob, reckon we should have them away an'all."

Another answered, "We ain't got room fer all of 'em, take the big'un, it looks the oldest."

Charlotte was marvellous; she waited until their hands were actually on her before exploding into action. Her muzzle dealt the first blow to the man at her head. A violent swing had her bows crushing several toes. Another forceful forward nod caught one on the cheekbone. They were swearing at each other, thinking one or the other of them had moved her at the wrong moment. Although nursing bloodied faces and bruised feet, they again tried to man-handle her towards the door. That's when I swung into action with my attack. I'd used my weight to shuffle myself within striking distance of the man clutching the back of Charlotte's bows. Lowering my head like a charging bull, with an almighty surge, my ears made contact with his backside and he fell heavily into her, yelling with pain and rubbing his shins. It was very satisfying. Unfortunately, despite our valiant attempts to foil the brutes, they managed to haul the Duchess up the ramp of their lorry, secure the tailgate and drive off.

Well, what can I say? It had been a traumatic experience. Cobweb was upset as he felt he'd been cowardly, not knowing how to fight back. I was beyond feeling desolate but tried to comfort my sobbing friend as Fireworks came rushing back with Sebastian close on his heels. One look round the room and realisation of what had happened had him phoning the police as he flew out the house, jumped into the stud's vehicle and gave chase. The lumbering lorry was careering down narrow lanes, trying to make good an escape.

We were left feeling numb with delayed shock, exhausted and sick with worry. An icy March wind was blowing through the house due to the two wide open doors. Everything was in disarray and Fireworks had climbed aboard my saddle for comfort. I could feel his little body shaking with spent emotion. He explained how he'd raced into the yard, meowing plaintively at Sebastian. Then, he'd hurried towards the house, looking frantically back over his shoulder to encourage the lad to follow him. Seb had got the message straight away. He was brilliant like that; always understanding us with an uncanny intuition. He'd shouted to his parents that something was very wrong and to follow on to the house when the horses were all safe.

Jacs and Eddie soon arrived to witness the awful scene. Their friends' front room emptied of all their valuables but much, much worse—Charlotte gone.

Jacs came over to us and with an arm over each of our necks, she comforted us as best she could. "Oh, you poor, poor boys, what a terrible fright you've had." Through stifled sobs she whispered, "Don't you boys worry, we'll get her back. Seb'll catch them. We'll make them pay...how can people be so vile. They must have heard June and David were away and thought the house was empty."

It all turned out alright in the end. Within ten minutes of tearing off in hot pursuit of the loaded vehicle, Sebastian had rung his parents to give them the good news. Unluckily for the criminals, a tractor had come trundling along and met the lorry at a particularly narrow stretch, allowing Seb to catch them up and make a citizen's arrest. It's funny how big tough men like that become snivelling cowards when cornered. They gave in meekly when faced with the burly farmer and my brave young hero. When the police arrived, the three admitted their crime and were carted off. A spare officer was left to drive all our possessions back home, including the most precious cargo of all, a demure and calm Charlotte. She was ceremoniously brought back into her home and received a tearful, grateful reception. The Duchess took up her rightful position near the window next to us and seemed none the worse for her terrifying adventure. However, I suspect she was more shaken than she let on and this incident just added to her existing troubled frame of mind. When everything was accounted for, replaced back in its proper location and police paperwork duly filled out, we were left with a stark warning to make sure everything was securely locked in future and to be on the look-out for any 'unusual activity' in and around the estate.

Later that night with us all gathered round safely, my family sat by the roaring log fire. Eddie and Jacs said they deserved a stiff drink and even Seb had a glass of wine. The day's events were mulled over several times and the conclusion was that we had been very lucky. Fireworks had saved the day with his prompt actions and got well-deserved praise. Seb teased him and told everyone that he'd been like the doggy movie star in a 'Lassie' film, when he'd arrived in the yard to warn them of the robbery. Fireworks looked smug when Seb said he was more intelligent than a collie dog. Then, the lad came and stood by us three and gave us a long knowing look. Turning to his parents, he told them something that made us all rock with laughter.

"D'you know what? I almost felt sorry for those blokes... They all had massive bruises and cuts on them. One had a shiner coming; the other was hopping around saying he'd broken all his toes.

The third man had lumps as big as eggs on both shins and a big fat lip. And they said a strange thing. They said... 'Those blasted rockin' horses shouldn't be allowed anywhere near kiddies, they're bloomin' vicious'!"

Sometimes, good things can come out of bad. That 'good thing' was that Charlotte finally admitted, in part due the shock of her abduction, that it may help her if she talked to us about her 'problem'. We all tried to get some sleep that night, hoping the morrow would bring answers. As Jacs bid us all goodnight, wearily climbing the stairs to bed, her throwaway comment was, "Oh well, things can't get much worse..." I really hoped she wasn't tempting fate.

★★★★

# CHAPTER 3.
# CHARLOTTE'S LAMENT

It was now the end of March and four months since the first of Charlotte's disturbing bad dreams. Since then, life had generally gone downhill for our families at Wick Stud. We'd endured terrible luck with our people's business being hit by the dreaded horse virus. The long-term repercussions meant that none of the mares had been able to visit their husbands, so there would be no new foals born next spring. This meant no income in the future. Also, there had been that attempted robbery on one of our homes. Even though the Duchess had been rescued quickly from the theft, it had left her feeling vulnerable and overwhelmed. She now felt ready to accept some help from us, her closest friends. David and June had returned from their two weeks away to learn about the break-in and the depressing developments with the stud. They had insisted that Jacs and Eddie should now have their turn for a much-needed break.

So, I was still staying at the big house and it was the perfect opportunity for the three of us to talk. Well, four of us actually, because Fireworks was involved as well and was a huge help. Cobweb and I broached the subject by telling Charlotte that whatever her worry was, a problem shared is a problem halved. Cobweb added that seeing as we were three, it would be the problem 'third-ed'. Of course, Fireworks, who has always been a bit of a wordsmith, immediately corrected the little horse, saying in a prim tone, "I think you'll find the correct term is 'trisected'. But as there are four of us, your problem will be quartered, Charlotte, so spill the beans and you'll feel so much better!"

*'Nightmares speak about the un-speakable.'*

The Duchess addressed us with a sombre warning. "Be careful what you wish for, my friends, for what I am about to tell you may invade your peaceful slumbers and haunt you, as it has me." We assured her we would take that chance if talking about it helped to unburden her. So she began her tale of woe, and as she spoke, her ever-changing eyes now took on an eerie, dull, blood-red hue to match her mood. Being quite ancient and having spent decades locked away from society down an air-raid shelter, Charlotte still spoke in a rather flowery way, a remnant from her days living through the Victorian era. Many years later, her family had fled from their house during the Second World War, leaving her behind, stored underground. Eventually, she was discovered and brought up to the old house when it was sold. That was when she was rescued by June. As a result of her isolation, her language was old-fashioned and sometimes hard and tiring to follow, so I will relate her long story just as she told it, but in an everyday way.

"Well dear companions, the reason for my recent distress is because during my night visions, I've been re-living awful events from the past. Many years ago, I was unlucky enough to witness the brutal murder of my beloved mistress."

If our glass eyes could have stretched open any wider, they would have! From that moment on, she had our full attention and sympathy. Fireworks leapt on my saddle and tucked his front paws under him, crouched and ready to hear the worst.

"It's a long story and I'll have to go back in history to place you within my life at that time. In the late 1920s, the children of a very rich family had sat astride me whilst having their photographic portraits done, and had desired me from that moment on. Their parents had no choice but to purchase me from the studio owner for their beloved children. I went to live with the family at their mansion situated in the beautiful county of Yorkshire.

"When young, my new mistress Lady Teresina, was the childhood friend of another woman, Lady Josephine. She was the daughter of an aristocratic family who had connections in the horse breeding and racing world, not unlike our people today. They owned a large, successful thoroughbred stud farm and both friends grew up surrounded by beautiful horses. In the 1900s, as young women, they attended many lavish balls and this is where they both met their eventual husbands. Teresina's friend Josephine married Lord Giles Matchem-Styles and Teresina fell in love and married Rustom

Ferozshah, a good friend of the Aga Khan. He was a wonderful, kind and generous man, educated and living in England when the couple were married. Originally, his ancestors came from Persia but had moved to India many generations ago and he still had family living there. The couple had escaped the ravages of the Great War by travelling to Rustom's ancestral home in India, but returned to England to start their family. They had a son and daughter named Cyrus and Tehmina. These are old Persian names, I just love them, as I did those children. This is when I entered their home, to be a nursery playmate for those delightful siblings. The family were back in Yorkshire and re-united with their old friends.

"This group of companions, Josephine, Giles, The Aga Khan, Teresina and Rustom were all passionate about and heavily involved with racehorses. In 1922, The Aga Khan bought a dappled grey filly bred by the stud, who turned out to be the very best seen in many years. She was named Mumtaz Mahal and became a famous sprint champion, nicknamed 'The Flying Filly'. Everyone was so excited about this amazing filly; they kept abreast of her progress all through her career, even when she retired from the track to become a brood mare. The Aga Khan kept her at his own stud farm and carefully chose her future husbands. This illustrious mare, Mumtaz Mahal, had been named after the famous wife of Shah Jehan, an Indian ruler. A tragic love story tells how he built the magnificent mausoleum, the Taj Mahal, in her honour after her death. This is how I got my name. Being a dapple grey and bought at the exciting time of her illustrious career, my enamoured children wanted to name me after the 'Flying Filly' and so they named me Mumtaz. As they sat upon my back, I would rock them as fast as that famous racing mare and in their minds I was galloping them up the race track to the winning post. I was nicknamed Mumty (pronounced

Moomty). Oh, how they doted on me."

Here, I must admit, I interrupted Charlotte's story. I just couldn't help it. Ever since she'd mentioned that name 'Mumtaz Mahal', my mind had been racing as I knew I'd heard it before – it sounded so familiar. And then it struck me. It was the name I'd heard many years ago when eavesdropping on our people's conversation in the kitchen as they had discovered their own mares' ancestry. She was The Tetrarch's best daughter! This was strange, odd enough for me to mention it now. I piped up with an apology. "Charlotte, I'm so sorry to stop you there, but do you realise our connection to all this? Our stud's mares are all related to you! Or your namesake, I should say...."

The Duchess turned her sad, deep, red eyes towards us and answered softly, "I am aware, and I think all the talk about breeding during my years here and the mention of my old name is what has triggered my memories...horrible visions that I had buried."

I told her that at one stage in my past I, too, had been thought to bear close resemblance to a Derby winner called Airborne and how wonderful it had made me feel. Charlotte was not surprised and said she thought many of us rocking horses may have been named after famous horses of the era, especially those of us owned by horsey families. After a deep sigh, she continued...

"Well, I had been a loved member of the Ferozshah family for many years, travelling with them on their trips back to their magnificent palatial mansion in Bombay. It was an idyllic life out there; we had a full complement of staff, loyal employees who had worked for the family for years. My master Rustom was often away on diplomatic business and Teresina missed him dreadfully but had many friends in the city. These ladies would come over for dinner parties or card evenings, and my mistress was a wonderful hostess. I remember the evening entertaining was always held outside in the glorious grounds that extended just beyond our mosaic-tiled veranda. Often, I would be placed there during the balmy evenings so the children could play in sight of everyone. When the youngsters went to bed, I would take in that heady night air laden with the perfume of evening-flowering jasmine and 'Lady of the night' that grew all around. I remember the soft gas lighting, the wafting aroma of sandalwood incense mixed with those delicious-smelling Indian snacks that were served up and the happy chit-chatter of my mistress and her friends. I can picture those tranquil evenings as if I was back there now... the happy times when life was good. I had many adventures while looking after Cyrus and Tehmi and enjoyed living with a loving couple who adored each other.

"Then it all went horribly wrong. My master Rustom Ferozshah's elderly father died. It was 1937, I do believe. The whole family was summoned to Rajasthan in north India where he and his wife had been living, and of course, I went too. It was a long, dusty and exhausting journey. The children had adored their grandfather, who was a great lover of horses.

"Over the years, he had told them many tales and legends about the fabled Marwari horses. This unique breed of Indian horse came from Rajasthan and was famed as a courageous war horse of great loyalty, only allowed to be ridden by warriors of high caste. Marwaris had been schooled in all the athletic moves that were needed to fight their foes in battle. They performed what is now termed Haute Ecole. Later, they were used for festivals and weddings, and would 'dance' to music, doing elaborate dressage moves. They are very special as they're the only horses in the whole world to possess 'lyre' shaped ears, ears that curve inwards and touch at their tips. The children had a special bond with their grandfather through these stories and were fascinated by the Marwari horses. They knew they would now miss him terribly.

"Everyone was in deep mourning for this lovely old gentleman. We were all so sad, and despite his grief, poor Rustom had to deal with the formalities and arrange the funeral, which was a massive affair. Before returning home to Bombay, the family solicitor read the will and solemnly handed a small package to Rustom, declaring he must take the greatest care of its contents. Apparently, it contained a family heirloom that was worth a fortune. He valued it so greatly, he described it as 'priceless'. The solicitor advised Rustom to hide it most securely, not to even trust banks or vaults with its safe-keeping. He was even concerned about their journey back to Bombay, in case of highway robbers. No one except my master seemed to know what was within the innocuous package. However, he was so heart-broken by his father's death that he could hardly be bothered with it. This is why Rustom entrusted it to his beloved wife and from that day on, my mistress Teresina had the huge responsibility of keeping this treasure safely hidden and secure for the future.

"We all headed back to Bombay and arrived safely without incident, but there was a change in the family. That heirloom, whatever it was, had almost become a curse on our happiness. My mistress had the burden of guarding the precious thing and it weighed heavily upon her. Rustom was distracted and in mourning, with the worries of the world on his shoulders. Even the children were unhappy living in this tense atmosphere. Teresina felt she could trust no one except the ancient gardener, Mali, who was the oldest and most loyal of their staff. He had known Rustom since he was a child. Mali knew all the family secrets and had always proved to be her closest friend and ally during her husband's absences. Being worried about where to hide the package, she confided in Mali who understood the enormity of the problem. He came to her a few days later and announced he'd had a clever idea.

"'Memsahib Teresina, are you soon to return to England?' he enquired. My mistress told him that in a few weeks they were due to board a steamer ship back home. He then asked if I, Mumty, the children's beloved rocking horse would be going too, and Teresina replied that of course I would as I was adored by all the family and went everywhere with them. 'Good, then my plan will work!' he said triumphantly. Now, I was in the huge sitting room with them, listening to everything that was being discussed. Lady Teresina fetched the tiny package from her bedroom and together they carefully opened it to reveal something of splendid and breathtaking beauty. Wrapped around this treasure was a delicate scroll of paper. It was inscribed in Sanskrit, the ancient form of the Indian language. Written in beautiful copperplate handwriting, it told of the heirloom's provenance. 'My idea is to hide this treasure within your elegant English horse. But, I strongly suggest you write a note of your own, preferably in the Hindustani language, to document what you have done in hiding this thing of such value. Also, it will prove beyond doubt, your ownership.'

"Well, I presumed they would drop the 'thing' into my belly via my pommel hole. I was sure most people knew about this secret hiding place that all we rocking horses have, accessed when our side-saddle pommel is removed. The hole drops deep into our hollow bellies and is the perfect place for stashing treasures. But for something so valuable, this hiding place seemed to me to be rather naïve and a little too obvious. I'm afraid I thought it a frivolous plan.

"I shouldn't have worried because Mali was a shrewd and wise old man who knew the conniving ways of common house thieves. He had kept that household as safe as a royal palace over the years. No street vendors, magicians, fortune-tellers or workmen had ever managed to steal a single item from the mansion. But it's not always strangers you must be wary of, as I later learned…Anyway, his plan was to hide the treasure somewhere else in my body, somewhere that no thieves would ever think of looking. Mali's idea had to involve his son, but he too was loyal and trustworthy. This man was a skilled carpenter and a craftsman with wood. In the past, he had made seamless repairs to the family's intricately carved antique rosewood furniture. So, his son did the 'work' on me quickly and quietly in secret, and caused me no pain. It all went beautifully to plan and from that day on, I became the keeper of the treasure… but now the burden of responsibility had become mine.

"The evening of my night-vision begins now, so I must gather myself together before I continue… It was a week before we were due to travel home to England. My master was away on some final business, settling up money matters concerning the crippling death duties that had resulted from his father's passing. Teresina received a message from an old friend of her husband's from England, a European man who had been educated with Rustom and had known the family for many years. He said he was coming to visit her, to convey his condolences. This character, Sacha Wafudovic, was a man that my mistress had never taken to. He was extremely conceited, had a high-handed manner about him and had often given her over–friendly looks when they were alone. She didn't trust him, but had always put on a show of polite acceptance, purely because he was an old family friend.

"He arrived that evening and after accepting a glass of wine, he said he had actually been sent by her husband. He was to collect the 'package' and had been instructed by Rustom to deposit it in the bank's vault for security reasons. Lady Teresina instantly felt great fear. She knew full well her husband would never have said such a thing. Anyway, she'd told Rustom all about Mali's idea, which he had absent-mindedly agreed to, saying it was a brilliant plan. He had congratulated her ingenuity and apologised for lumbering her with the responsibility. Now, she didn't know what to do. Thinking quickly, she made the excuse that she would just telephone her husband to check. This caused panic in the eyes of her guest, but she hurried out before he could rise to stop her. He had forgotten that, being a diplomat, Rustom had a telephone line installed which connected to the central exchange and it would be quite easy for Teresina to contact him. My mistress had no intention of phoning her husband, but ran straight to her bedroom to retrieve a small mother-of-pearl vial. Earlier in the week, with the help of Mali, she'd written the secret note in the Hindustani dialect and added it to the scroll, rolling them tightly together and placing them within this vial. Now, she clutched it in her hand and returned to the sitting room to face her villainous guest. Her plan was to drop this essential information into my pommel hole for safety, so he would never find it.

"When she returned, she was met with a scene of total disarray as she caught him in the desperate act of ransacking the sitting room.

He had rummaged through ottomans, sideboards and cupboards containing the family's china and silver. He'd even broken open her husband's desk to search frantically for the package. I had watched all this with horror and sensed his anger and frustration at finding nothing. I knew he was dangerous and feared for my mistress when she entered the room. She was so brave; she stood her ground and accused him outright, saying her husband had not authorised him to take anything from their house. She told him he must leave immediately before she called the police. Teresina had nerves of steel and faced him with a steady look of determination, while slowly backing up to lean against me with her arms behind her back. Then, with a deft sleight of hand, she slipped the vial through my pommel hole, unnoticed. She demanded to know why he was trying to rob his oldest friend. Sacha was furious and retorted that he was in serious debt and if he didn't repay the monies owed, he would be killed by the money-lender's henchmen.

'"Rustom has always had it all. A beautiful wife and children, property and racehorses. He won't miss the money, your families are minted, your sort make me sick!' He spat the venomous words out with such hatred that it contorted his face.

'"If only you had asked him, Rustom would have helped, he would have given you any amount of money...' My poor mistress couldn't finish her sentence because the scoundrel lunged at her, grabbed her viciously and put a knife to her throat, demanding that she give him the package. She bit hard into his hand and wrenched free, causing the knife to drop to the floor. As they were standing right by me, I managed to swing my bow onto the dislodged knife, to hide it. Sacha chased my sweet Teresina around that room till he caught her. She ran to my side and desperately clung on to me. I tried so hard to protect her...but it was too late. With his murderous hands around her neck, he tried to squeeze the very life out of her. I felt her body go limp and she slipped down my side until she lay lifeless on the floor."

At this point, Charlotte completely broke down at the painful memory. Huge droplets fell from her anguished eyes and splashed onto her beautiful, fine grey forelegs. To be honest, we were speechless. We fell silent for many minutes. Fireworks, in an attempt to comfort the poor mare, transferred himself from me on to Charlotte's saddle. Once she had re-gained her composure, the Duchess continued.

"That dreadful man then fled the scene and escaped. As you can imagine, I was beside myself with grief and anger. I rocked so violently that I crashed into the sideboard next to me to alert someone. The noise of smashing glass brought the housekeeper running. She screamed and all hell broke loose with people trying to revive the mistress and rushing to call for help. When the police arrived, they told everyone to go, and sealed the room off as a crime scene. Later, the doctor said Lady Teresina had actually died of a heart attack as the attempted strangulation had not killed her. I think she died of fright. I know I'll never forget that horrendous night and it haunts me still. But you, dear friends, are right, I do feel cleansed, now I've told you the whole awful tale. But I feel exhausted. Please let me recover myself and I'll tell you the rest tomorrow."

Cobweb and I had many questions, but we daren't ask Charlotte outright. We knew about the vial because when June had sent Charlotte to be re-born, Brenda had found this beautiful, mother-of-pearl container within her belly. She had given it to June who had decided not to open it because she felt the mystery of its contents should remain in the past. It was Charlotte's secret to keep. For years, we had wondered what was in that vial. Now we knew. But what had been the treasure within the package and where had it subsequently been hidden in Charlotte's body? We knew we shouldn't ask. If she wanted to tell us, perhaps she would…one day.

# CHAPTER 4.
# THE ROCKING FOAL

U nfortunately, a couple of days later I was due to return to
Airborne Lodge as Jacs and Eddie were returning from
their break. Although very happy to be going home with
my family again, it did leave me feeling worried about Charlotte.
She had not wanted to continue telling us the rest of the tragic
story, but promised to finish the tale to its bitter end when she felt
stronger. Before his parents came home, Sebastian had come to
us the day after Charlotte's revelation. We must have all seemed
a bit shell-shocked, digesting the horrors of the story we'd heard.
Squatting down beside us and looking directly into my eyes, he
said in a perplexed voice, "Whatever is up with you three horses?
Even Fireworks looks sick and didn't eat this morning. Perhaps
you HAVE picked up a rocking horse virus, huh! Seriously though,
whatever is amiss, it'll be all right. If it's worry about our future
or something you've heard, please don't fret. I promise I will fix
it and you lot are safe while I'm around. I give you my word." I

was touched by his concern and knew he would have helped if he could, but this was rocking horse business and too complicated to convey to my lovely Seb. We would sort it out ourselves and return to being care-free, happy horses once Charlotte had exorcised her bad memories. I returned home to the Lodge with my people and bided my time for a few weeks.

Eventually, the three of us found ourselves together again, as the stud's partners had to attend an important horse sale and were away for a few days. They left Wick House in the care of Mirabel, our stud's head groom. She was Eddie's childhood friend and the daughter of June and Jacs' friend Isabel, generally known as Izzy. I had known Izzy since she was born as I had been her horse for many years and loved her dearly. Her wonderful mother Grace, who is sadly no longer with us, was my oldest, dearest friend whom I originally met when she was a six year old girl at my first ever home in 1900. Cobweb and I were her and her brother's nursery horses. Of course, Cobweb and Grace had adored each other. Her passing on had left my gentle friend grieving for many months. It makes me feel very old yet privileged to have had Grace, her daughter Izzy and granddaughter Mirabel upon my back, rocking them all through the years.

Please don't assume my life had been straightforward, though! Over those 90 years I had many crazy times; years when I was separated from those I loved, often fearing I would never see them again. Somehow, things turned out well for me. It was due to a strange sort of magic that seemed to run through my life, allowing me to be re-united with friends and for them to find me, wherever I had ended up. I always feel my luck changed the day I met a brother and sister called Manfri and Sinni. They were Romany gypsy children who had been left at the orphanage where I lived during the Second World War. There, we struck up an unbreakable friendship, which has grown in strength and continues to this present day. I looked after them through those sad years and later, they repaid me. They saved my life once, and found me twice.

That was all in the past and I must not digress, as I need to continue with my story. So, Mirabel came to look after us all and keep an eye on both properties. No chances were being taken with security after that break-in and my people refused to leave me home alone at the Lodge. So, back I came on the pick-up truck to be reunited with my friends. I was placed next to them in the sitting room and, as usual, we got chatting. I was delighted to hear that the Duchess had suffered no re-occurring bad dreams since she'd talked to us, and that she and Cobweb had been sleeping well. Charlotte's whole demeanour had changed; she seemed brighter and stronger and was willing to continue with her tale. We had plenty of time to talk as poor Mirabel was up early, dashing around feeding various dogs and cats plus having to work on the yard, only popping back for a quick snack before rushing out again. On the second day, it was Charlotte herself who offered to tell us the rest of the saga. Fireworks, Cobweb and I gathered around her in anticipation, steeling ourselves for possibly some dark moments within the story.

*'Family ties are the threads that
bind us together in life'*

"I have now come to the conclusion, dear friends, that my night-visions were, in part, caused by guilt. Re-living the incident has cleared my conscience. I now realise there was nothing I could have done to prevent the murder of my beloved mistress. I no longer blame myself and it's a weight off my shoulders, so I thank you for listening. I will now relate what happened next.

"That awful villain, Sacha Wafudovic, ran from the house knowing he was now a wanted man. As he emerged in the street looking dishevelled and panic-stricken, he was seen by an old Chinese gentleman called Fu Ling Yoo. Well, that was his 'stage' name, for he was a well-known and respected magician. This lovely man had visited our house countless times, employed to amuse the children, always on hand to entertain at birthday parties and the like. We never knew his real name, but Fu Ling Yoo was an honest street magician who lived locally and was trusted and liked by all. Soon after spotting the fugitive, he heard a great commotion within our house, so rushed up to our front veranda to be greeted by the police, who stopped him entering but listened intently to his story. They were extremely interested in his account of what he'd seen earlier. They were anxious to have him as a reliable witness, as he knew the name of the perpetrator and had actually watched him flee the property.

"The next week was dreadful. Everyone was distraught and many tears were shed. My master was hit the hardest by the death of his precious and adored wife. He retreated into a deep, sorrowful state, unable to even talk to his children. They needed my company now, more than ever. I tried my best to comfort them, but they were devastated by the loss of their mother. All Rustom wanted to do was catch the next steamer ship back to England, to escape the misery he now felt in that house. Everything was hurriedly packed up in the huge trunks used on our sea voyages. All we knew was that there was a country-wide search in progress to locate the murderer and bring him to justice. The evidence against him was overwhelming. With the magician's testimony and the fallen knife found on the floor, it was an open and shut case. Rustom did not wish to be around for the man's capture, trial and conviction. In all his haste, I'm sure he forgot that his worldly treasures were hidden in my body. It was only because of the near-hysterical insistence of Cyrus and Tehmi that I even came home with them. They certainly forgot to bring my family back with us…"

A huge sob emitted from deep in Charlotte's throat and a solitary teardrop fell to the floor. Whatever did she mean by 'her family'? Cobweb and I glanced at each other with a frown. Fireworks came straight out with it. "Charlotte, what do you mean? Surely you were WITH your family, sailing back to England?" he enquired gently.

Another stifled, gulping sob came from the Duchess as she whispered, "No, I mean my rocking horse family…I had a husband and my very own foal…"

We weren't expecting this unbelievable twist to the tragic tale and just didn't know what to do or say next. I had no idea there were other rocking horses living with her in India….and I'd NEVER seen or heard of a rocking foal in all my 90 years. We were all quite stunned. Eventually Charlotte cleared her throat and continued bravely.

"Yes, I had my own little family back in India. I will explain how this came about. You see, the Ferozshahs were avid followers of their friends' racehorses who were doing so well in England. Cyrus and Tehmi were older now and very interested in Mumtaz Mahal's foals and their subsequent careers. In 1933, their grandfather had given them a wonderful Christmas present. He had commissioned the making of a beautiful rocking horse stallion, modelled on the brood mare Mumtaz's chosen husband for that year, the magnificent bay-coloured Rustom Pasha.

"This rocking horse was expertly carved by Mali's son and was based on my shape and style. He had taken careful measurements and done many sketches of me to produce a rocking horse as fine as any English-made horse. This rocking stallion had one specific difference, though. He looked just like a racehorse but had the ears of a Marwari. His magnificent arched neck and finely fashioned head were crowned with the shapeliest curved ears. The very tips of his pointed ears actually touched each other. Oh, he was so handsome, I was proud to call him my husband. Their grandfather arranged for the local saddler to bedeck him in the finest traditional Indian-style tack and regalia, fit for ceremonial display. He even wore leg-bands of velvet with tinkling bells attached to them so he jingled whenever he was rocked, just as the desert Marwaris did when they danced. He was placed next to me and the children announced, 'Mumty, this is your new husband, Pasha, just look at him! His ears curve, he wears battle dress! Oh, you will love him as much as we do, we love you both so much!'

"The children who were now older but still small and light, would sit on him very carefully, least they ruin his wonderful ornate decorations. Pasha was more for admiring than riding. Around the top of his neck he wore strings of ceramic beads, a row of bells and beneath them, a string of amulets made of many tiny pure silver squares. This stallion had a hollow body made of rich brown mango wood, but his head and legs were chiselled from Indian rosewood, which was so dark it was almost black. However, this made him rather heavy, so he was never moved on to the veranda as I was, but I returned to his side every night.

"Soon after he came to us, we were married by a priest. Teresina thought it would be a nice touch to honour his arrival. The children were so delighted by the lovely ceremony held for us. There were many flowers, prayers and the heady smell of incense, as the priest tied sacred coloured thread called Kalava, around our ankles. Pasha wore red and yellow threads above his right hoof and I wore yellow and white on my left ankle. This signified that we were married, and it also protected us from all evil, giving us joy, energy, strength and power. In the New Year, Fu Ling Yoo had come to do a magic show at our house party, thrilling the children by incorporating me and Pasha into one of his tricks. Then, as he finished his performance, he presented both the children and us with a sacred saffron-gold coloured thread that he solemnly wound around their wrists and our feet on top of our marriage threads, promising that it would bring us all luck and fortune. He told everyone in the room that the saffron thread would unite us as a family and draw us together if we were ever separated.

"I and Pasha were devoted to one another. I grew to love him more than anyone else I've ever cared for. He had a strange character, very much like the Marwari war horse whose image he was carved in; he was proud, fiercely loyal and solemn yet sensitive. It is said that when a Marwari hears music and the roll of the drum, his

*Fu Ling Yoo tied a saffron thread around our ankles*

ancestral soul causes his pulse to quicken, his neck to swell and his sharp hooves to slice into the earth as he rocks to the drum-beat, preparing to leap into battle… Yes, Pasha was indeed magnificent, alive with the soul of the Marwari breed. He was a complete one-off, a king among rocking horses.

"You can imagine everyone's excitement when, a year later, the news of Mumtaz Mahal and Rustom Pasha's foal was born in Ireland. The Aga Khan had sent a telegram to his dear friends in Bombay, stating his total joy at the birth of this baby and that he would name the filly foal Rustom Mahal! So of course, Mali's son was again tasked to make a wooden rocking horse foal for me, Pasha and the children. A description of the filly was faithfully followed by Mali's son and she arrived a few weeks later to grace our mansion and live with us. She was perfection, leggy and tiny with an exquisite, feminine face and of course with her father's curvy lyre ears. The foal had been beautifully hand-painted; she was a work of art. I would describe her colour as charcoal, very dark grey with pale milky-white dapples all over her elegant little body. A fluffy black mane and a short and curly scut of a tail completed the picture. We noticed that she, too, was wearing a golden saffron thread, like a bright little bracelet, on her left foot. Her wooden bows were deeply arched, allowing her plenty of movement when she frolicked and cavorted upon them at the slightest touch. It was love at first sight for all of us. This sweet foal felt I was her mother and, at first, always kept close to my side. The children named her Pashmina, due to her silky soft hair. They played with her all day long and she soon began to enjoy their company. Being small, she was often taken out into the garden and Pasha and I would watch their antics, as proud parents do. Every night the three of us were together again, enjoying our own family time. I think those were the most blissfully happy years of my life, until it all ended. My mistress was brutally taken from us, we had to leave in a hurry and I was torn away from my dear husband and foal, never to see them again. On the long voyage back to England, I wept for my loss and cursed that saffron thread for not doing its job of keeping us safe and together, but when I looked down at my foot…mine was gone. I fear it got torn off as my dear mistress fell against me on that awful night…"

Charlotte turned herself away from us, so we should not witness her misery. We three just couldn't speak. It was so terribly sad; words of comfort would have been trite. I suppose we felt guilty that we'd forced poor Charlotte to re-live a terrible time in her life. All we could do was to be there for her and offer our friendship, if she could forgive us.

★★★★

*Pashmina was perfection*

# CHAPTER 5.
# DIVERSIFY!

That summer of 1991 was a lean time for Wick Stud. With the mares carrying no foals for the following year and our resident stallion standing idle due to a lack of outside mares visiting, the stables were ominously quiet. Once the few surviving babies had been weaned, their mothers were turned out to graze for the rest of the year. Nothing had been bought or sold at the spring sales and our people had returned in low spirits. Grey Refrain, Wick Stud's only stallion, could not be used to breed with our own mares as he was too closely related. He had won top class races and carried wonderful bloodlines, but after the news of the virus, no outside mares had wanted his services. In the past, he'd proved very popular and had bred many winning sons and daughters. After a lot of thought about his future, the partners had decided to lease him out to another stud to be used for producing show horses. It was a heart-breaking decision but the best outcome for him. Our people were very sad when he was collected and left home for the first time in his life.

In July, it was decided that moping around would not solve anything and so a meeting was called. Everyone associated with the stud came to Wick House for what they termed a 'brainstorming session'. The plan was to put many heads together to try and come up with some ideas on how to revive the failing business. Our own families were present with Mirabel and her mother Izzy, too. Also invited were Izzy's best friend Ethel, Eddie's mother. As the meeting was held at June's, I felt rather miffed that I wouldn't get to hear what was said. Cobweb and Charlotte promised to remember every detail of the conversations and fill me in when we next met. I had not seen much of the pair since Charlotte had divulged her dreadful tale of family tragedy. I had left Cobweb to deal with her recovery. Happily, she had bounced back from her depression and returned to her old self, as graceful and calm as before. She hadn't suffered one bad night's sleep since she'd opened up to us and had made a point of thanking us for listening, which was cheering.

Luckily for me, I managed to get the whole gist of what was said at the brainstorming meeting. This was because although the gathering started at Wick House, later that afternoon everyone made their way over to Airborne Lodge, mainly because my old, dear friend Izzy wished to see me! Having once been her and her mother's horse, she had grown up with me and had even taken me with her during the war, when she'd been evacuated. Now in her early seventies, Izzy was extremely fond of me and never missed an opportunity for a visit and a hug. I know we are only wooden toys, but we rocking horses are very special and have deep connections with our old friends. She and I and had always been very close.

It was slightly crowded in Jacs' cosy sitting room, but everyone happily gathered around the circular mahogany table. With tea and cake in front of them, they began discussing ideas that had seemed viable. I also heard some of those voiced at Wick House that had been rejected, as they went back over these too.

One particular thought had come from June and had been unanimously vetoed, but I liked it very much. In fact, I thought it was brilliant. She had suggested that she should diversify from stud affairs by taking up rocking horse restoration! It would entail spending time in Dorset with Brenda, the family's knowledgeable rocking horse expert, to learn the skill. June and David had always loved antiques, collecting, buying, selling and even restoring them for healthy profits in the past. She felt sure her knowledge and passion would stand her in good stead and imagined herself scouting around at auctions, looking for sad horses that needed rescuing. Apparently, everyone had shouted her down, saying it would be too long a process, a big initial outlay, and worse still, she'd never have the heart to sell them on to make a profit. They concluded that the house and probably even the empty stables would be crammed full of 'saved' horses that would be deemed too precious to ever leave home. "We'd end up completely over-run and bankrupt within a year!" David had concluded pessimistically. She had been out-voted but I still think the idea had 'legs'. Lovely, wooden outstretched legs!

One of the better ideas voiced by Eddie, was concerning properties situated on the estate. June's elderly parents owned the whole of Holmwood Wick, which included their own home Holmwood Hall, Wick House, three lodge cottages and the stables. Jacs and June were childhood friends and her parents had always considered Jacs as an adopted daughter. When she and Eddie had married,

June's parents had gifted them one of the dilapidated cottages. They were allowed to live there as long as they remained partners in the stud business. The couple had renovated it themselves and it was now our wonderful home. Eddie had said excitedly, "Why don't we do up those other two derelict lodges on the estate and rent them out as holiday homes? They're only lying empty; it's a terrible shame. The income would tide us over till we get back on our feet." He thought he'd come up with a clever plan, but June had worried that the middle of Surrey was miles from the sea and not exactly a holiday destination. Jacs had argued that actually it was perfect for anyone who loved riding as Surrey offered glorious, extensive countryside all around. The idea had then suddenly blossomed into endless possibilities, people coming to stay, bringing their horses as well so they could enjoy the beautiful local rides. Perhaps they could offer holiday accommodation to hikers or off-road bikers or even dog-walking fans. The excitement died down quickly when Mirabel pointed out that house renovation was expensive, and all this would cost money that they just didn't have.

After a deflated silence, June said thoughtfully, "Hold on though…I know we never wanted to involve my parents with our problems or borrow money from them, BUT – surely if we renovate their properties, we'd be improving the estate for them, adding value to it. Accommodation is always wanted, whether for staff or to rent. I honestly think they'd be delighted at the idea and would want to help with costs. We could put a sort of business proposal together for them and see what they say!" This appeared to have the makings of a solid plan. With a lot of hard work and financial help, the estate and the partners could both benefit. Once the buildings had been made habitable and modernised to a good standard, their multiple uses could be discussed later.

Seb had had his own thoughts. He suggested the stud could offer to look after resting or injured racehorses or those that had retired from the track. He pointed out there were many empty boxes that would remain so until the following year. Looking after other people's horses would generate a healthy income. There was a snag, though. The others were worried about outside horses being stabled with their own mares, in case they brought in another virus. Seb then suggested using the furthest lodge house with meadow attached, for the people who might bring their own horses for holidays. It was far enough away from the stud not to be a threat. This seemed more acceptable. June then piped up with a comment that had everyone groaning again...she remarked that all those spare stables would make perfect storage and ideal rocking horse workshops. She added, "At least our lovely wooden horses don't bring in viruses! And they don't eat us out of house and home!" Then Izzy quipped, "I almost wished they did...then they might do a few droppings. Imagine. Rocking Horse Droppings! We'd be famous, our money troubles would all be over!" Everyone crumpled up laughing at this old cliché and the meeting was declared finished. They all went home smiling and happy to have found a workable idea concerning the lodges, which could just save our stud.

*'When the going gets tough, the tough get going'*

Properties it was then. The partners went ahead and drew up plans and a proposal to present to June's parents. They, in turn, welcomed the idea and offered to pay for all materials needed, if our families organised and paid for the labour. This would be tight and would drain the business's resources, but if everyone helped, it was deemed possible. So, in late summer, work started in earnest and the two beautiful, ornate Victorian lodge houses began to come back to life. Once essential yard work was done, all willing hands headed off to the new building sites to do hard manual labour. They all worked so hard from dawn to dusk, returning home late, in a state of near exhaustion.

Word of the stud's plight had travelled fast. Izzy had informed our wonderful Romany gypsy friends, Manfri, Sinni and her son Roybin, who were only too happy to offer help. I'd known the brother and sister when they were small children left in an orphanage during the war. I'd looked after them then and they'd helped me in my hour of need later in my life. In desperate times, true friends can always be relied upon. Manfri was much older now, but very fit and healthy for his years. Although carrying a distinct limp sustained through a war injury, he was the same handsome man I remembered, who in the past had helped me escape some life-threatening situations. He was one of my most treasured friends and I was excited when I heard he was coming up with his nephew Roybin and Roybin's young son.

It would be wonderful to meet up with these two again and Sinni's grandson, whom I'd not yet met. The gypsy families still lived in the New Forest and worked locally down there, but had dropped everything to offer labouring help on the estate. They arrived one afternoon and, as planned, would be staying at the larger property, Wick House. Of course, I knew they would want to see me and I wasn't disappointed. As soon as initial greetings were over, they dropped in to visit me at the Lodge. My lovely friends gathered round me and Manfri whispered, "Well, I had t' come an' see me old mate 'Bokky'. Youz is lookin' well. You'n me both has been through enough 'stuff' ta last us a life-time!" He turned to his nephew's son, and introduced us. "Joe-boy, this here is the famous liddle hoss we all talk about, Blitz. Mind, I always calls him by me old name for him, Bokky." (Bokky means lucky in Romany.)

What a fine strapping lad Roybin's son was! He laid a rough hand on my neck and said, "Honoured ta meet ya, Blitz. I've heard all about ya. Ma and Da told me all the stories when I were a chavvie (young lad)." I knew straight away that Joe-boy and I would hit it off; he was a chip off the old block, he knew I was special, that I had a heart and soul. He knew all about my past. We felt connected. 'Grey' blood and gypsy blood are powerful and similar in many ways. Joe-boy even talked in the Romany tongue, which I had learned whilst living among this family in the past. It was music to my ears and threw me straight back into memories of happy times long ago. They talked softly between themselves and I gathered Manfri had just come to drop them off. He would be heading back down to the Forest the next day, but would return with more help. He knew people with various skills who were willing to offer their services in the construction tasks. It was heart-warming to know everyone was pulling together to get us back on track.

# CHAPTER 6.
# ONE STEP FORWARD...

**W**hat a workforce we had that autumn. Our two homes were now full of optimistic, enthusiastic people willing to get the essential labour done before bad weather set in. Seb was around as much as possible, but he'd taken a part-time job to help with finances. Although his career as a jockey was temporarily on hold, he'd managed to find work exercising racehorses in the early mornings for an Epsom trainer. Seb and Joby (Joe-boy's nickname) had struck up a great friendship even though Joby was older and not really into racing. They enjoyed each other's company and worked well together. Joby turned out to be a marvellous carpenter who in his leisure time sculpted beautiful little model animals, walking sticks and small paper-knives. Seb was fascinated by his talent with a knife, so Joby started teaching him some whittling skills or 'chinning the kosht' as he called it in Romany (literally 'cutting the wood').

As Airborne Lodge badly needed some damp work addressing before winter arrived, it was decided that while labour was available, Seb, Eddie and Joby would bunk down at the Lodge and attack what needed doing there, whilst I and Jacs moved back to Wick House with Roybin, June and David. That suited me, as I would be able to enjoy the company of Cobweb and Charlotte again. The partners had also hired an electrician and plumber to do the more specialised jobs on the lodges and things were moving along nicely. As evening light started to fade, Jacs, June and Mirabel would leave the renovation work and return home so they could prepare a welcoming supper for the troops. With the log fire started, the gang would return, wash up and sit down to enjoy a massive feast with a huge pot of tea on the table. Every evening was spent like this; it became a comfortable routine. Everyone would relax for a few hours, tired but happy. They would laugh and joke, discuss the day's work, throw new ideas around and tease each other in an atmosphere of real camaraderie. With bellies full and souls content, they'd all retire to their beds, exhausted but looking forward to the next day. It was a really happy time. We rocking horses just loved being a part of it all, hearing all the plans and progress, and seeing our people less worried than they had been for months. They hadn't been so cheery since before the troubles had started in the New Year. It was almost too perfect... Then, near the end of October, disaster struck.

*'The good thing about hitting rock-
bottom is you can only rise upwards.'*

By mid-October, both Victorian Lodges were completed to a high standard. They looked quaint and characterful, yet offered comfortable, modern facilities. The furthest one from the stables, North Lodge, boasted an adjoining post and railed meadow containing a field shelter-cum-stable. It would be perfect for paying guests who wished to visit with their own horse. The other, East Gate Lodge, had no paddock but a beautiful, large and well-fenced garden around it, ideal for guests who may have dogs or children. The skilled workers had been paid and had departed. All their work had cost the stud dearly, but it was now expected that the lodges would start to pay for themselves and bring in some much-needed funds. Plans were being made to get the two properties advertised for holiday breaks. Airborne Lodge was now watertight for the winter and Roybin, Seb and Joby had just completed the yard repairs. They had painted everything, mended paddock fences and tidied up the stables ready for the mares and youngsters to come back in for the winter. In fact, it was nearly time for Roybin and Joby to return to the New Forest. Everyone had thoroughly enjoyed the last few months and it was going to be sad to see them leave. On their final night with us, June and Jacs had cooked a really special meal for the whole gang. Beer, cider and wine flowed freely, with everybody toasting their joint effort and celebrating the end of a long, hard job. Although the excitement of that jovial evening had kept them up late, everyone was keen to get some sleep. That's when they noticed how the weather had changed. The mild autumn night had suddenly become eerily dark, heavy and quiet. As Seb, Eddie and Joby headed back the short distance to Airborne Lodge, they glanced up at the strange fast-moving sky. Suddenly, large, heavy drops of rain began to fall and the leaves on nearby trees rustled ominously.

"Reckon ther's a whopper of a storm brewin'," Joby remarked grimly.

Eddie called back to Jacs and the others, "Batten down the hatches, folks, we're in for a rough night, me thinks!"

"See you all tomorrow!"

Little did anyone realise that one of the most ferocious storms of the year was about to wreak havoc on our lovely estate.

The storm broke and raged all night. Fireworks had scarpered under the sofa and I, Cobweb and Charlotte were quaking with worry, dreading what dawn might bring. In the early hours of the next morning, extensive damage was apparent all over the place. Driving rain and gale-force winds throughout the night had weakened many of the huge ancient beech tree roots. Many trees had fallen, causing destruction and ruin in their wake. Just after 6 am, Mirabel had run up from the stables to Wick House in floods of tears. She reported that half of the yard was destroyed with a row of stable roofs caved in. A near-by beech had fallen sideways, just reaching the stabling. She was shocked and devastated but relieved that there had been no horses actually in the boxes. "Our lovely mares could have all been killed. It doesn't bear thinking about…" she gulped, through her tears.

The three men sleeping at Airborne Lodge had been rudely awoken before dawn by a crashing noise as a branch had landed on our roof, smashing some of the clay tiles. Eddie had climbed into the loft and placed buckets under the incoming rivulets of rainwater. They had hurried over to June's house, which had luckily escaped any damage. Everyone donned waterproof clothing and headed out to estimate the extent of the devastation around the estate.

Once the mares and youngsters out in a far paddock had been checked over and found to be nervous but un-harmed, Mirabel was told to go home and not to worry. She announced she'd had trouble negotiating her way from her house to the stud earlier, due to fallen tree trunks blocking her usual route. She'd had to divert around to find other lanes open. The main road was shut but already the hum and buzz of chainsaws could be heard, as local workmen were trying to open up the highway. Mirabel refused to leave, wanting to help wherever she could. She headed off with the men to inspect the beautifully re-furbished lodges. These had been our one and only hope of saving the stud business and everything was riding on them generating essential income. It was not good news.

A bedraggled and bitterly angry group returned to Wick House to report on the storm damage. It was mid-morning as the families sat down in the sitting room to discuss all of our futures. Their plans and hopes for reviving the stud had been dashed in one night. All their efforts over the previous few months and the last of their precious finances had drained away with the storm. Charlotte, Cobweb, Fireworks and I listened on with a feeling of dread and disbelief as our inconsolable people listed the awful devastation that had been inflicted on the estate. Jacs and June told the men that most of the stables' roofs would need extensive repairs costing thousands, even some of the paddock rails would need replacing. Eddie announced that North Lodge was fairly intact, but toppled trees had flattened the meadow's stable and most of the fencing. East Gate Lodge had not escaped so lightly and would need repairs to a wall and two windows. David had checked Airborne Lodge and said, sadly, it would need half its roof re-tiled before we could live there again. The clearing up process would be long and tedious, involving the sawing-up and removal of all fallen timber.

Someone tried to make a half-hearted joke about there being enough firewood to last for many years, until June said, "That's if we're still living here to have a fire…"

My dear, lovely Jacs tried her best to encourage everyone by saying defiantly, "Look, we must just plug on. We can and will do the work ourselves. It will take time and it's a massive set-back, but we MUST keep going. We just can't give up now and lose our wonderful stud and homes. We'll ask for help, get a bank loan, we'll do whatever it takes!" But the awful truth was we needed money quickly to re-build. With winter approaching, our horses would have to be sent away to another stud until the yard could be used, the lodges could not be rented out until more work was done on them. Everything could be salvaged with finance, but the partners had spent every last penny on the property project. Money was the only answer and the one thing they just didn't have.

Seb got up slowly and thoughtfully from his seat and came over to sit with our little group by the window. Fireworks hopped on his lap and curled up into a tight ball, more depressed than I'd ever seen him. Cobweb and I were speechless at the grim news, but I noticed Charlotte was miles away, deep in thought as if she had not really been listening. Seb looked at us sadly and said flatly, "We seem to take one step forward and end up ten steps back. I don't know about just needing money…what we need is a blessed miracle." At these words, the Duchess seemed to jolt back from her thoughts and I noticed her eyes, which had been so calm and mellow of late, suddenly change in an alarming way. I don't think anyone else noticed, but Charlotte gazed straight at me with her eyes now a sparkling crimson and glowing in a strange way. They had taken on a clarity and brilliance I'd never seen before. Mesmerised, I looked into those bright, gleaming orbs and realised what had just happened. Charlotte had come up with an idea, one so momentous that it was no longer just an idea. It could be the miracle we needed.

★★★★

# CHAPTER 7.
# THE PEARL WITHIN...

I had felt so utterly devoid of any hope for our future after listening to the sombre post-storm meeting. But then I'd seen a change in Charlotte's demeanour. The way she had held me with that penetrating stare, I knew she'd had a sort of epiphany. Obviously, we couldn't discuss anything until we were alone and able to talk quietly among ourselves, but I felt strangely energized. I'd just have to be patient and wait till our people retired to bed. Fireworks also sensed something good and exciting was afoot. The Duchess had an aura about her. For once, he decided to climb aboard her saddle to receive comfort from her instead of giving it, as he usually did. Cobweb whispered he'd not seen Charlotte looking so happy and confident since before her night-visions and hoped she had good news for us. "She's thought of something, that's for sure," I whispered back.

It was a sad group of friends who had bid farewell to each other on the doorstep later that day. Roybin and Joby needed to return home as planned, due to work commitments. Despite the disaster, they had no choice. Father and son both promised faithfully that they would be back as soon as possible, with an army of friends to help with the clear-up. Jacs, Eddie and Seb went back to the now soggy Airborne Lodge to pack some essentials as they would have to stay temporarily at Wick House. That afternoon, the men had managed to climb on the roof and secure a tarpaulin over the rows of smashed tiles to prevent any more water damage. When they could actually afford to mend the roof properly was anybody's guess. After many miserable phone calls, June had arranged for the mares and youngsters to move to nearby stables where Mirabel could visit daily to look after them. Another call to their insurance brokers had left them downhearted as they were told only half of the damage could be covered through a claim. No one had actually got around to insuring the newly renovated lodges before that storm hit, so there would be no pay-out on them. Our poor people dragged themselves up to bed that evening, looking as glum as I'd ever seen them. And, they hadn't said one word to us. Only Seb had given us a sad backward glance as he'd followed them upstairs.

Soon enough, we were on our own in the sitting room. Although dying to hear from the Duchess, we knew we must wait patiently and not pressure her to reveal her recent thoughts. I guessed she'd been wrestling with an inner battle, but had now reached a decision. I think it had something to do with our future. It was when Seb had stated that we were in need of a miracle that her whole demeanour had changed, it was as if a light bulb had switched on in her head.

*'Take heed of nightmares for sometimes they contain the answer to set your dreams free.'*

"Vial, vial, vial...VIAL!" Charlotte suddenly uttered, and made us all jump.

Fireworks was off her back in a flash, gazing up at her as he enquired "Vile? What's so vile, Charlotte?"

She smiled slowly with a satisfied expression and continued, "No, my dear friends, not vile at all. I mean V.I.A.L. The answer to all our troubles lies within the vial, the container that was found and retrieved from within the depths of my belly. It is made of mother-of pearl..."

Here Fireworks butted in. "Do you mean it's valuable? The one Lady Teresina hid in you?"

"Yes, but not for the reason you think. What are oysters made of? And what do they contain?" Charlotte asked, beginning to enjoy teasing us with this riddle she'd created.

Cobweb then piped up with his guess. "Oysters have mother-of pearl on their insides and pearls in the middle! But we know that vial didn't have pearls in it, only scrolls of paper. That's what you told us..."

"Oh, dear, stupid friends, those scrolls of paper are worth more than a thousand precious sea pearls! Those scrolls tell the finder what the great Ferozshah treasure is, and more importantly... WHERE it is. And the amazing answer is of course – it's in ME!"

I'd never before heard Charlotte laugh, but now she let out a joyous guffaw straight from her belly and it was so infectious, we all started laughing. We still didn't understand the true significance of her mysterious revelation but were swept along with the joy of that moment, and we laughed and rocked and laughed for a full minute. I think it was through sheer relief that we'd been given a bit of hope for our future. Charlotte was offering us a miracle!

*'Miracles happen when you allow your dreams to overcome your fears'*

Of course, it wasn't that simple. Making a miracle happen is never simple. It takes careful planning, a sound strategy and a huge dollop of luck or maybe even some magic to get everything to fall into place. So, we started plotting. The Duchess first told us of her huge personal struggle with the decision to reveal her secret, her 'moral dilemma' as she put it. We completely understood as we knew she was faithful to the rocking horse code of conduct: 'One never breaks a confidence. One keeps secrets for ever. One guards valuables with one's life. One does the very best for one's people.'

Charlotte explained that for many long years she'd kept a secret, guarded a treasure and now, she felt it was time to look after her people. She was aware that this valuable heirloom was not hers to give away lightly, and that had been her dilemma. Because her past people were no longer in her life, she now felt loyalty to her present people. After a lot of thought, Charlotte decided the original owners, the Ferozshahs, wouldn't have minded giving their treasure away had they known it was to help a stud farm survive. After all, they too had been like our people, wrapped up in horses and racing. Teresina was gone and probably Rustom, too. It was so long ago, she lamented, there was no one left who would remember that she even had the treasure. I felt I had to ask her about the two delightful children, Cyrus and Tehmi Ferozshah. Here, she looked very sad and whispered, "They never came back for me. I don't even know if they were aware I'd been hidden in the air raid shelter – but they never came back. I think they returned to India at the start of the war. Perhaps they're dead. How can I know what befell them? I DO know that Cyrus and Tehmi never knew about the family heirloom or that it was entrusted to me. Only four people in the world knew – and they are probably all dead and gone now."

Charlotte confirmed she wished to help our families in their hour of need by releasing her valuable assets to them. The big question was how to achieve this goal. We still didn't know the intriguing details, but we respected her too much to ask. We knew it would be exciting just planning to have our people discover that Charlotte was about to offer them a miracle! The first burning question was – where had June put that all-important vial? Everything revolved around this crucial information. They all turned to look at me expectantly.

"What?" I exclaimed defensively. "Why are you all looking at me?"

"It was you, if I remember rightly, who was eavesdropping on June and Jacs at your Lodge when you heard them discussing the vial," accused Charlotte, who then fixed me with a glassy stare. "So, what did they say and where did June put it?"

I tried to defend myself. "Hold on a minute, we're going back to when you first arrived. That's got to be over 20 years ago and I'm sure it wasn't just me, Cobweb was there too…just give me time to think."

Ah, it was all coming back to me now. We'd all been in the parlour at Airborne Lodge. Yes, both I and Cobweb (who had been staying with me) had listened in to the conversation about Brenda finding the beautiful iridescent container whilst restoring Charlotte. It had been handed over to June and we'd been disappointed to hear that after much thought, she had decided against opening it, saying, "Maybe secrets should be left as exactly that." The two of us had been disappointed and so curious about its contents that when we next saw the Duchess, we'd asked her what it contained. I do remember she had not been amused and had always refused to divulge her secret until recently when telling us her sad tale. Cobweb now remembered the incident clearly. He said he was sure that June had told Jacs she was going to put the vial back into Charlotte's body, through the pommel hole. "Well, she didn't!" exclaimed the Duchess. This was a setback.

We all fell silent, racking our brains, trying to imagine where June would store such a lovely item. She would surely have taken it back to Wick House if she'd planned to return it to Charlotte's belly. Where would she have stashed it, even temporarily? Now it was Fireworks' turn to be scrutinised. He was the only one of us who could move about freely from house to house and had access to every room in the place. Three sets of eyes landed on the little cat. We urged him to think carefully. Where does June put things? Does she have a special, particular place for valuables or trinkets? Has she got a drawer or cupboard she uses for important items? Is there a safe hidden anywhere in the house?

The pressure proved too great for poor Fireworks and he fled from the room, asking for some time to think. We just hoped something might trigger his memory, and in the meantime, tried our best to get some rest. But of course, none of us could sleep as it had been an emotional rollercoaster of a day. That night, all we could hear was a worried little cat prowling around the house, muttering to himself as he searched high and low for that cylindrical vessel. The umbrella stand, telephone table drawer, coat rack shelf, any surfaces he could reach, all got inspected thoroughly but yielded nothing. Next, he peered in every ornament, bowl, dish or plate that might hold a small precious object. He had hoped for inspiration, but none had come. Admitting he had no clue where June may have put the vial, Fireworks eventually gave up and returned to us, extremely downhearted. What's the good of a miracle waiting to be released to help those in desperate need when the key to it is lost? By now it was too late to sleep, only a matter of hours before our people would be stirring, but we passed the time in fitful dozing, hoping the morning would bring answers.

Amazingly, that's exactly what happened! Now that there were both our families in one house, life was bound to get hectic. Seb left at the crack of dawn for his job in Epsom, but returned after the horses' morning exercise routine. Everyone else headed out early to do jobs dotted around in various locations. They all gathered in the busy kitchen at mid-morning to grab a quick coffee break before tackling the daunting task of clearing up after the storm. As work was being allotted to each person, David remarked that they hadn't even named the three foals that had been born at the start of the year during the virus. "We really must do that soon; they'll all have to go to the sales if we're to survive this. We have no option this year." This was a blow to the stud as the partners always kept back at least one dappled grey baby to keep their bloodlines going. Then later, the carefully chosen youngster would be to put 'into training' as a racehorse to hopefully have a successful career. Now there would be no finance available to cover the training fees.

"I've hardly had time to even see those babies this year..." Jacs bemoaned the sad fact.

Mirabel had dealt with them all year and had reported that the two dapples and one chestnut were flourishing. They had turned out excellent individuals and were apparently 'growing like weeds!'

June added despondently, "I don't even want to see them if we can't keep one. It's all too heart-breaking."

It was decided that Jacs must drive over to the stables where the mares and foals were now lodging, to hand over their passports to the office manager. "But I'm telling you now, I agree with June. I'm not going to even look at them when I get there!" she added vehemently.

Jacs asked June where she'd find the passports, after having rummaged unsuccessfully through kitchen drawers.

"And I need the workshop key to get the chainsaw out. Where the heck is THAT?" demanded David, not finding it among various other keys on the designated hooks.

Seb then piped up with his request. "If you want me to get back on the phone to the insurance people, June, I'll need the paperwork. It's not by the phone…"

Warding off accusations of being dis-organised and keeping a messy kitchen-cum-office, June calmly stood up and declared that she knew precisely where everything was. "I can lay my hands on anything you want, easily and efficiently. Everything is stored in one accessible and safe place. My filing cabinet," she announced proudly.

Four voices rose in unison. "But you don't have one!"

She dramatically raised an arm and, with a flourish, gestured to the magnificent, antique scrubbed pine Welsh dresser. It was larger than most and had originally come from the kitchens in the servants' quarters of a huge country house. It was one of June's most treasured pieces. Its capacious shelves, cubby holes and compartments were capable of holding many years' worth of receipts, important documents and other paperwork. It was also home to various items of rare handmade pottery, valuable ornaments, figurines and beautiful china tea sets.

June then directed individuals to their respective items in a rather smug voice. "Seb. Insurance paperwork? Behind the Staffordshire flat-back shepherdess. Jacs, foal passports? To the right of the Crown Derby tea pot, the Old Imari one. David, stud workshop keys are in the Minton jug. Eddie, want to know where I keep the crown jewels? Out of luck, I'm afraid."

Oh, if only she realised what she'd just said. That vial could be as precious as the crown jewels! Fireworks, of course, had been present, making a show of innocently swirling around people's legs but eavesdropping in earnest all the while.

David then retorted, "Oh, I don't know, I reckon you have thousands of pounds worth of rings and jewellery hanging off that poor Art Deco ballerina's outstretched hand! Every time you wash up, you take off your bling and load her with it!"

"Yes, it's a nice safe place for valuables and because I'm tall, no one else can reach anything!" She added triumphantly, "All my treasures are on the highest shelf."

Fireworks grinned from cheek to cheek; he'd cracked it! As if to prove June's point, Jacs, who was tiny, dragged the kitchen stool over to the dresser and stepping up, stretched high enough to retrieve the neatly placed passports, exactly where they should be. Everybody scurried about taking what they needed to complete the day's chores and left the house. All but Seb, who remained to do battle with the insurance company on the telephone.

Fireworks was so excited and eager to relate his splendid eavesdropping news to us, that he crashed headlong into the lad. He'd skidded flat out from kitchen to sitting room without looking, just as Seb was making his way to the hall phone. The impact sent them flying and both ended up on the floor in a heap. Seb picked himself and the cat up, gently cradling him in his arms. "What's got into you, you're acting like a spring lamb stung by a wasp! You, my boy, are 17 if you're a day and too elderly to be rushing around. I really hope your eyesight isn't failing and you're not going do-lally…" He carefully placed a very indignant Fireworks on my saddle and marched back to the hall to make his phone call.

# CHAPTER 8.
# NORTH FACE OF
# THE DRESSER

We listened carefully as the victorious cat assured us he now knew exactly where he could locate the vial. "June keeps all her treasures on the top shelf of that massive dresser. My problem is, I don't know if I can get up there. I certainly won't be able to get down again, even if I risk life and limb clambering that high…"

We gently persuaded Fireworks that he just had to be brave and find a way up to the top, somehow. The whole plan rested on him locating and freeing up those scrolls in the vial. Time was of the essence. If he did the dreaded deed soon, while Seb was still in the house, he would be rescued quickly – if he made enough noise. We knew it was almost 'mission impossible' and a huge 'ask' of the little cat.

"You had better describe it to me. I've never actually seen it. I don't even know what I'm looking for," he added lamely, losing confidence by the minute.

Only I and Cobweb had laid eyes on this beautiful item and although we remembered it well, it was nearly impossible to describe.

I started clumsily, "It's sort of shiny, but not. It's long and tube-shaped and can just fit into our pommel hole. Yes, pommel hole sized, long and thin. Sparkly, but in a dull way..."

Then Cobweb took over. "Look for something that's a funny colour, a bit pinky-off-white and sheeny and smooth!"

Fireworks had always been passionate about words and was extremely good with them, unlike us. I think his frustration at our bumbling attempts to describe the object was acting as a good distraction from his dread of the impending climb. In a withering tone, he said, "I think what you are trying to say and failing miserably, is that it's small and tubular. Funnily enough, the shape of a typical vial. As for colour and texture, I presume it is like all mother of pearl, opalescent, iridescent with a nacre-coated, multi-coloured, light-reflecting lustrous sheen, possibly in the Orient colour, favouring tones of peach and ivory with a silvery silken finish?"

Cobweb and I were used to these descriptive outbursts and usually shouted the poor cat down. Now we were awe-struck at this accurate picture he had created. "Exactly!" we answered together, feeling quite inadequate.

'Bravery without fear is commendable;
bravery with fear is pure courage.'

With the weight of the world (and the miracle) on his shoulders, the little cat walked slowly as if to the gallows, in the direction of that huge looming dresser. We watched nervously and began to feel rather guilty that Fireworks had drawn the short straw and was being made to risk his life. I have to say, I felt sorry for him. He looked hopelessly small standing next to the imposing lump of furniture. Thank goodness Jacs had left that stool close by because it gave him a springboard to leap from. With eyes fixed on his target, he took a good gulp of air and sprung up gracefully to reach a shelf halfway up. There he sat and proceeded to wash his face. We were incensed by this apparent lack of urgency. We could just about see him on the dresser through the open doors and couldn't understand this strange behaviour. We hissed at him to hurry before Seb went out, or he would be stranded. Fireworks answered coldly, "You have no idea how imperative washing is. Mere horses can't appreciate what effort it takes to scale a sheer vertical obstacle like this. Washing is a way of psyching oneself up and drawing on one's inner cougar."

Well, the cat was magnificent. How he reached those dizzy heights was truly heroic. With careful calculations, he sprung and clung from foothold to impossible foothold, almost defying gravity. We were terrified for him as it seemed that at each level, he could have toppled backwards, fallen and broken his neck. I now have huge admiration for the athleticism of the feline species. Once he'd arrived at the very summit of the dresser, the job was easy. There, lying innocently in a Japanese Hamada plate, was the vial. Now,

*It was a huge ask of the little cat.*

Fireworks knew the plate must be worth thousands of pounds but the contents of that vial were more valuable by far, so it was no contest as to which had to be sacrificed, if it came to it. But only a cat could pull off what he did next. With perfect dexterity, he scooped and flicked out the vial and as the plate toppled precariously near to the edge, he caught it with a curved paw and dabbed it back to safety. The mother of pearl container fell half the height of the dresser and came to rest safely on the wider pine top beneath. There was no way that poor elderly cat could now descend without a fatal injury and he knew it. His plaintive, blood-curdling pleas and cries were quite genuine as I think the enormity of the task had drained away every last vestige of his courage.

Thank goodness for wonderful Sebastian. We heard him slam the phone down mid-sentence as he heard the frantic calls for help and saw him rush to the kitchen. With horror etched on his face, he spied his precious cat perched dangerously high up, in obvious distress. Thinking quickly, he told Fireworks to stay completely still while he fetched a ladder. Then, placing the ladder against the dresser's solid frame, he climbed up and reached carefully for his cat. Fireworks knew the job was not quite finished as he had to somehow get the vial to hit the floor, so it would be noticed. It was pure genius how he managed to fake a panic attack when he was level with it and a scrabbling foot accurately knocked that vial cleanly to the ground.

"Steady up, ole boy, you're safe now. Whatever has got into you today, eh? You've NEVER gone up there before in your life. And don't tell me you saw a mouse. Even mice would get vertigo up there!" Then he spotted the iridescent container which had suffered a crack along its length from hitting the flagstone floor. He picked it up, placed it on the table and rambled to himself, "Oh well, it's very pretty and I hope it wasn't too valuable, not compared to you anyway, cat! I'm sure your Aunty June will understand. It was a question of life and death…" Seb plonked Fireworks back on my saddle, telling him to behave and not to get into any more tricky situations while he was out.

"Stage One of our plan completed. Job done!" the cat declared, happily basking in our heartfelt praise and admiration. Now that we'd succeeded in the first phase, all we had to do was wait and hope that June would find and open the blessed thing. Charlotte mentioned that she could see another problem, 'a fly in the ointment' as she put it. "Once they discover the scrolls, they won't be able to understand what's written there…unless any of them have a degree in Sanskrit based languages!" I pointed out that surely their curiosity would urge them to investigate further, but Cobweb reminded us that although in normal times this would be the case, our people were not acting normal due to an overload of stress.

Fireworks then made a clever observation, being as he was a 'student of the written word' and a lover of etymology. He suggested that if we could 'arrange' for Manfri to be present when our people read the scrolls, he felt sure our gypsy friend would recognise at least some of the words as the Romany tongue was very akin to Hindi and Sanskrit, being a closely related language. He added nonchalantly that this is because all genuine gypsies had originally hailed from Northern India. We turned to look incredulously at our little font of knowledge and marvelled at his sheer depth of stored information. I couldn't help but tell him how much he reminded me of his grandfather, which pleased him enormously.

Yes, Fireworks was indeed the grandson of my most revered friend, the old ginger cat, Diesel. This tom cat and I had lived together in the 50s when I worked as a carousel horse on a roundabout at a fun fair. It's a long story, but suffice to say that it was there I met two exceptional characters, Diesel, and the love of my life, Jacs. That feline was the cleverest, most knowledgeable, intelligent, interesting and educated cat I'd ever met. Jacs was the kindest, sweetest and most loyal person I had the pleasure of meeting. And still is. But sadly Diesel died, leaving a ginger daughter who then gave birth to a lookalike ginger kitten who grew up to be uncannily similar to his grandfather. This kitten was then gifted to Eddie and Jacs 17 years ago as a wedding present from Roybin, who worked at the fair where Diesel had lived. Maybe that's why I love that now grown-up kitten so dearly; he is Diesel personified.

We couldn't wait for evening to come, when our folks would return to Wick House and discover the all-important vial. After all, we had gone to great lengths to bring it to their attention. We were filled with a mixture of trepidation and excitement. Obviously, June would be heart-broken and perhaps angry that her beautiful mother of pearl keepsake had suffered damage. However, it would all be worth it when she realised that inside the container was a possible answer to all the stud's troubles. We imagined our people joyously celebrating and being able to return to their happy selves with all life's worries lifted from them.

Unfortunately, it didn't work out like that at all. Everyone came home in dribs and drabs, each with their own depressing account of how their day had gone. David and Eddie limped in first, made themselves a mug of tea and flopped down with us in the sitting room. They started moaning about the various injuries they'd sustained whilst labouring, and worrying about their painfully slow progress with the clean-up. They hadn't even noticed the vial.

Next, Jacs arrived back from delivering the passports to the new stables where their horses were lodging, with a very glum face. She'd been offered to go and see their foals, which she'd flatly refused to do as she knew it would upset her. Then the stable owners had showered her with sympathy, remarking on the stud's awful luck that year and to rub salt into the wounds, they said they were very interested in buying the chestnut filly. They added it was the most perfect specimen they'd seen in a long time and could she please discuss the offer with her partners.

David answered, "Well, I suppose we have to consid..."

"DON'T!" Jacs had shouted and left the room in emotional turmoil. She had entered the kitchen, too upset to notice the vial.

When June arrived back laden with bags of shopping and started to prepare a meal for the dejected partners, she DID notice her little broken treasure lying in the middle of the table. She had slowly and sadly picked it up, turning it over in her hand to assess the damage and then, with a tired sigh, placed it resignedly into a saucer on the dresser. Oh, this wasn't going well. Not the reaction we were expecting from June. Now, all we could hope was that Sebastian would return and revive some interest in that blasted vial.

The lad had blustered in, apologising profusely to June about the breakage and explaining about how he'd had to rescue Fireworks from the very top of the dresser. He added lamely that he guessed the vial had fallen off during the scuffle with the terrified cat.

"Was it very valuable, then?" he enquired tentatively.

June answered that it was more of sentimental value to her, although she guessed it was a rare piece. "It was found inside Charlotte actually, but I don't know if you were even born so you'd not remember. That's how long it's been here, and I don't have a clue what it is. It must have meant something to someone…only Charlotte knows that secret!" June actually managed a smile when Seb offered to mend it as soon as he found a quiet minute. "Yes," she said kindly, "we'll do it together when things calm down. And don't worry, Seb. It was an accident."

I did warn you that miracles could be tricky customers. They often don't just happen, but need a bit of a nudge. Quite a sizeable nudge, in our case!

★★★★

# CHAPTER 9.
# WORD GAMES

I t was a long, tiresome and frustrating week before we saw any progress with our plan. I say frustrating because we could see our people were exhausted, struggling under a gloomy cloud and completely unaware that we had an answer to their problems. We had given them Charlotte's miracle on a plate, literally! We had put it right in front of their noses, or at least, on their table. Now the pretty little lustrous flacon languished in a saucer on that oversized dresser, waiting to be mended…and, hopefully, opened.

Despite our exasperation, we rocking horses are patient souls at heart and have learned that all things come to fruition in the fullness of time. So, we remained cheerful and optimistic. Our deliberate breaking of the vial had saddened June, but it had been a necessary part of the scheme and the Duchess simply called it collateral damage. "You can't make an omelette without first breaking eggs," she'd announced cheerfully. In fact, there was a marked and wonderful change in Charlotte's whole demeanour since she'd made the decision to give up her treasure. I think she'd wanted to reward our people for all their love and care over the years since rescuing her, and she felt a burning desire to secure all our futures. This had turned out to be a happy and lucky home for her, everyone loved her deeply. Nothing is more rewarding for a rocking horse.

By the end of the week, two events happened to speed the plan along. Friday had turned out to be fairly quiet, as all the lighter jobs had been completed around the estate. The heavy and skilled work was on hold, awaiting manpower to arrive from the New Forest as promised. So that afternoon, June and Seb found time to sit down and attempt a careful repair on the beautiful mother of pearl container. They had investigated which specialist jeweller glue would work best on its calcium-rich, shell-like surface. Clearly being an exquisite object of great antiquity, it was rather brittle and extremely delicate. They would have to be very careful not to worsen the large fissure, which ran along its length. Its ornately carved stopper had also been loosened by the fall.

June, always passionate to learn more about the wonderful curiosities she collected, had done a lot of research that afternoon. She had been fascinated by what she'd learned and was keen to tell Seb all about the strange substance called 'nacre' that lined certain shells in an effort to protect the pearls that grew within them.

"The funny thing is, Seb, this nacre or mother of pearl is an ancient organic gemstone of the oceans and is supposed to attract prosperity and relieve stress! We really could do with some of that magic around here right now, eh! Perhaps I'd better wear this thing round my neck, once it's mended," she'd said with a hollow laugh.

The two had meticulously sanded, cleaned and joined the cracked edges together, when that little stopper popped out from the top of the vial, exposing a roll of tightly furled paper.

"Oh, look at that, there WAS something inside it all along!" exclaimed a surprised June.

Well, you can imagine how relieved we were to hear those words spilling from her lips. We'd waited with bated breath all afternoon for the discovery to be made. Cobweb was really enjoying our unfolding plot and in a collaborative whisper he announced, "Ooh, Stage Two successfully accomplished!"

The impending arrival of our friends from the New Forest the following day gave us hope of being another step closer to our goal. This had been confirmed by a phone call that evening, after the discovery of the strange hidden notes had been made. Through our crafty eavesdropping, we heard June tell Manfri how excited she was with her find. She was fascinated to know in which language the scrolls had been written and she described the sheer beauty of the handwritten script on the older of the two tiny documents. She explained how she and Seb had painstakingly smoothed out the fragile pieces of paper and secured them between two sheets of clear acetate to protect them. "We'll have to get them looked at properly and translated by an expert. Even if we are broke at the moment, it's worth doing. But have a look at them tomorrow and see what you make of them. I'm dying to show you because they're just amazing," she concluded.

Everyone was on good form that night. They sat lounging around with us in the sitting room, looking more relaxed than they had for a long time. June was full of enthusiasm and told everyone all about her newfound knowledge on 'MOP', her newly coined acronym for mother of pearl. It was as if the MOP vial was working its magic already, spreading its stress-relieving qualities, ahead of its promise of prosperity!

Fireworks climbed contentedly onto Seb's lap and stretched out luxuriously. The lad looked at him and said to the others, "We have him to thank again, for knocking that container off the dresser when he got stuck up there. And because he broke it, we found those mystery notes. They may mean nothing and the vial may not be worth a fortune, but it's cheered us all up. Thinking back, he was acting very oddly that day…it's almost like he planned the whole thing!"

Jacs added, "If you ask me, they're all up to something. Those three horses have been acting decidedly cheerful and I've caught them rocking about for no reason. They've certainly got their mojo back! With all this bad news at the moment, it's so nice to see them happy." My sweet Jacs then came over to me and hopped on my back for a relaxing rock. She hadn't done that for months. Oh, things were looking up.

The next morning, the troops arrived in force. Manfri had brought not only Roybin and Joby but also two of their cousins. Full of enthusiasm and purpose, it was all hands on deck, with the men eager to finish the clearing and begin the re-building. Joby's cousins were general builders capable of all the construction tasks that would be needed. Even more wonderful was that they'd refused any payment, saying all they needed was board and lodging and a good get-together at the end of each day and that would be payment enough. The boys assured June that it was a pleasure to help out mates in need, and they were sure the favour would be returned if in the future, the boot was on the other foot. Oh, the kindness of these people whom we hardly knew was heart-warming. How lucky we were to live in such a lovely place, surrounded by true friends and our wonderful family. All this was absolutely worth fighting for. Our people had been hit with one disaster after another this year, and if anyone deserved a bit of good fortune now, it was them.

While the others went out to start work, Manfri and June had other plans. They headed to the kitchen where June carefully took the mysterious scrolls from the dresser drawer and laid them on the table. Manfri was intrigued. He bent over them, scrutinising every sentence, word by word, his handsome, weather-beaten features expressing total concentration. We of course, were stuck in the sitting room hardly able to hear anything, so you can imagine how we strained our ears until they almost touched at their tips, Marwari style! Fireworks had the advantage. By using his usual pretext of rubbing up against legs, he was able to hear every word said from his position under the kitchen table. He badly wanted his prediction about the similarity of the two languages of Romani and Hindi to be confirmed.

After a long and agonising wait, Manfri slowly looked up at June with a perplexed frown but his dark eyes bright with excitement. He spoke in an incredulous whisper. "Well, June, I ain't no scholar as ya knows – but I'm tellin' ya now, I understands some o them words!"

June was shocked and asked him how that was possible and did he recognise the language? "Nope, not a clue. I juss know wot some of them words means. They're so like 'the old language'. More on the newer lookin' bit o paper, mind."

At this point, Fireworks let out an ear-piercing shriek of triumph and scooted back to us in the sitting room, whooping with joyful meows. "The cat was correct…just saying!" he announced smugly.

"Oh lore, did one of us step on his tail?" June inquired with a worried frown. "He's acting most peculiarly lately…"

As June started to prepare an evening meal for the returning workers, she furnished Manfri with pen and paper, and instructed him to jot down all the words that he thought he recognised. She could hear him mumbling laboriously to himself as he pronounced possible connections between the two differing tongues. After a while he announced he'd completed the task to the best of his ability, adding, "Tis hard to remember the pure old 'Romanes' wot Jed and the Lovells spoke. They was our uncles and an aunt, our old folk. We's was only kids then, an me an Sinni spoke a sorta slang wot we call 'poggered jib', than means broken tongue. But even so, some o these words are almost the same as wot we'd use! Juss change a few letters and you can get the gist alright! Tis very strange…"

June came over and scrutinised Manfri's jumbled list. He'd made three columns, one of words he'd vaguely recognised from the note, another, his interpretation of them into Romani and finally, a translation to English. It was a conundrum. The puzzle was how to piece this all together to make any sense of it, to form meaningful sentences. He'd understood and worked out a few phrases and quite a few individual words. It read something like: My name is – Teresina Ferozshah. Hidden – husband – money, jewellery or treasure – in my big – horse – go to big – horse and look in eyes (this bit he was very sure of) – big red – hidden – names are (here he recognised the word for 'blood', ' heart' and 'star') followed by the names Manjri and Gwalior. There were also familiar-sounding words for 'rare' and 'big value/money'. At the end of the note was a repeat of the family name, Ferozshah. I have written dashes for the words he didn't understand.

Just at this point, a cheerful little Jacs appeared in the doorway. Seeing the two absorbed faces, she rushed over to the table to stare in surprise at the random mix of words and half-finished sentences. She asked what was happening and June explained that Manfri had understood some of the words in the scrolls.

"Well, that makes sense; Romani must be like some Indian dialect. After all, it was found in Charlotte and she was probably in India during the war, just like Cobweb. It stated that in his family history you got from the sales paperwork at the auction. Wow, Manfri! You've written a list, let's have a deckers!" she said excitedly.

On hearing this, the old man burst out laughing at Jacs's casual use of the slang word 'deckers'. "Youz lot don't even realise when ya use our words, so many of 'em have come inta English!" He explained to the women that 'dik' or 'dek' means 'look' or 'see' in Romani and he'd recognised the very same word within the tiny note. In effect, Jacs had said, "Let's have a look-see!"

My clever Jacs then had a brainwave and said she was going to phone her old school friend Shymala, whose parents had come over from India in the 60s and had settled here. She was sure that if she read the words to her, someone in the family would understand. She grabbed the list and headed out to the hall phone. She was gone a fair while.

Well, things got very exciting after that call. Jacs came into the kitchen looking pleased as punch. Everyone had now returned for the evening and had all crowded around the table waiting for an update. She told them that she'd got some answers, but the best bit of news was that Shymala's brother had recently graduated with a degree in ancient languages. He was fascinated to hear about their discovery and asked if he could visit them the next day to try to decipher the scrolls. No payment necessary, he'd said, he would volunteer his services free for the privilege of gaining experience in a field he was passionate about. Good luck suddenly seemed to be flowing freely around Wick House since Charlotte's decision.

Seb had been thoughtfully reading through the notes again and turned to Jacs saying, "I knew it rang a bell yesterday. Mum, doesn't the name Ferozshah sound familiar to you? I can't believe you've forgotten! He's one of the most successful trainers in Newmarket! They're the people we sold one of our dappled grey yearlings to, the baby that 'Graceful Charlotte' foaled in 1985. Surely you remember them, they own a massive breeding farm called Gwalior Stud."

"What did you say?" interrupted June, intrigued at hearing mention of names that had cropped up on the scroll.

Seb explained to June and Jacs that the Ferozshahs were wealthy, successful breeders and trainers of some of the best bloodstock in the country. The women replied that of course they knew of the family and remembered selling them a Wick Stud baby, but surely this couldn't be the same people that were named in the old notes.

"Why ever not?" declared Sebastian with a huge grin on his face. "There's not many Ferozshahs floating about in England with a stud farm called Gwalior, the same name as mentioned on your scroll! If it is them, they were HUGE back in the old days! Best buddies with the Aga Khan and owned loads of classic horses!"

June and Jacs looked at each other with their mouths open...Jacs spoke first. "And you know who The Aga Khan owned? The Flying Filly, Mumtaz Mahal! Oh my goodness, THAT explains why they paid such a hefty price for our yearling...her bloodline must be so precious to them, it goes straight back to the Aga Khan's best ever mare."

June looked directly at her friend and whispered, "Weirder and weirder, this can't all be a coincidence! Somehow, this is all connected to Charlotte. I think Charlotte may have belonged to this family..."

The two women were so overcome with excitement that the men left them in the kitchen, poring over old breeding manuals listing horses and owners from the 1920s. They dished up June's pre-prepared supper for themselves and the hungry workers all filed into the dining room to gratefully fill their bellies. It had been a good day concerning work done on the stud, but the men didn't really understand why June and Jacs were getting so worked up over those old scrolls. They were quite prepared to wait till the morrow to hear what an expert made of the scribbling. No point getting excited over what was only conjecture, hit and miss guesswork at best. The guests decided to retire early to be ready to tackle more heavy work in the morning. Roybin, Joby and his two cousins Billy Bob and Oxo, headed off to bed-down at the empty Lodge, while Manfri was content to sleep on a camp bed set up for him with us in our sitting room.

Eventually, overwhelmed and exhausted by the discoveries of the last two days, Jacs and June headed upstairs to grab some sleep. Their heads were spinning; they knew sleep wouldn't come easily. It was that exciting prospect of unlocking the hidden secrets in the scrolls that would keep them awake. How does one clear one's mind and resist trying to guess?

Similarly, Cobweb and I were doing an imaginary jig of delight. The day had ended well, better than we'd dare hope. Our plan was galloping forward and the miracle being nudged along nicely! Although Charlotte seemed rather pensive, we weren't too worried. We just assumed the mention of her old family had stirred sad memories. However, the rest of us felt excited and I was bathed in a feeling of optimism for our future. There was still a fair way to go, but there was light at the end of the tunnel. It was late now, and we needed to rest to prepare for tomorrow's visit from our linguist friend. Fireworks mumbled sleepily, "Stage Three accomplished and the cat's assumption proved correct, thank you all, it was nothing, really..."

# CHAPTER 10.
# MORAL DILEMMA

Despite being a Sunday, our willing workers had made an early start to make the most of the unseasonably mild November weather. Shymala's kind brother Zairaj arrived at Wick House on the dot of eleven as arranged. He cordially introduced himself to June, Jacs, Seb and Manfri, and when June reciprocated, letting slip that their dearest friend was a Romany gypsy, the man's eyes lit up with nothing less than pure joy!

Zairaj extended his hand warmly towards Manfri and said in the most perfect manner, "Sar shan, prala? Mande cams to rokker the puro jib!"

Well, the older man's face was a picture. He hadn't heard such a polite and formal greeting since the old folk of his family had passed on. Hardly anyone spoke the old language nowadays, and Manfri was pleasantly surprised and taken aback. Zairaj had actually said,

"How art thou, brother? I love to talk in the old tongue." This obviously led to them chatting away among themselves for the next few minutes, much to the amazement of the others. Eventually our expert linguist said he couldn't wait to get down to business, Manfri had explained the matter to him, and he was very keen to see the papers in question.

June invited him to sit at the table with pen, paper and Manfri's scribbled notes in front of him, while she busied herself making coffee for everyone. The scrolls delighted Zairaj, he gazed at them appreciatively and started translating immediately. After an hour of diligent work, he announced he'd finished and produced a neatly written transcript of both pieces of paper. He said in a serious tone, "Well, what I have disclosed here is of grave importance and a big shock to me, IF it is to be believed..." He added cautiously, "If what's written here is true, it will have a big impact on your lives. Shall I read it to you?"

Although everyone had been so keen to learn the contents of the vial's notes, now the moment had arrived and with that rather alarming caveat, nobody spoke.

At last, Seb looked round the room and back to Zairaj saying boldly, "Yes please, we would LOVE to know."

The linguist said he'd start with the declaration first, the letter apparently written by the owner's wife in Hindustani. The translation went something like this:

"It is the year nineteen hundred and thirty-seven. My name is Memsahib Teresina Ferozshah, wife of Rustom. I have hidden my family's heirloom treasure within my big swaying wooden horse. Go to the largest of my wood horses and look at her eyes. Behind her eyes are hidden/stored two large blood rubies, one in each eye. One ruby is named 'Heart of Manjri' and the other, 'Star of Gwalior'. They are old and rare Persian rubies of great value and belong to the Ferozshah family. Signed T. Ferozshah and witnessed by Mali Chaiwallah."

There was a deathly hush in the kitchen and in the sitting room too, for we had been listening intently. It was an awful moment for Cobweb and me because we'd expected our people to be expressing great joy by now. Instead there was a cautious silence. Fireworks was sitting on Charlotte, who had become very still and pensive. He could feel something was amiss with her, too. However, everything made sense now we knew Charlotte had rubies stored behind her eyes! What a clever place to hide them and of course it explained why those orbs would gleam and sparkle in a strange crimson-red manner whenever she was roused. I fully expected everyone to rush to Charlotte's side and gaze deeply into her valuable eyes, but no one moved. It was as if they were rooted to their chairs.

As our people digested this incredible information, Zairaj picked up his second transcript and asked if he should continue, stating that the older Sanskrit note was of even more importance as it told of the rubies' provenance. He had found it quite a labour of love, ploughing through the ancient script, but one he had enjoyed immensely. Proudly, he read out the gist of his translation:

"It is dated from 1809 and tells of the Ferozshah family heirloom. These are two large blood-red rubies extracted from the family 'FEROZAH' mines in Persia. It is stated here that three precious gemstones were mined there, turquoise (called ferozah), spinel (called la'l) and rubies or yaqut, but we are concerned with the rubies. Known as 'Raatnaraj Yaqut' which loosely translates from ancient Sanskrit as 'The King of Gems – the blood-stone ruby', this term applies particularly to the heirloom rubies in question. They are described here as being 'angushtari' rubies which means they are of the highest quality, suitable for jewellery-making. The rubies are named. One is 'The Heart of Manjri' and the other is 'The Star of Gwalior'. They are legitimately and solely the property of the Ferozshah family, to be passed down through the generations."

"So, your rubies are big, rare and extremely valuable…and I take it you didn't even know you possessed them?" Zairaj enquired gently of his stunned audience, adding quizzically, "Oh, and whatever is a 'swaying horse'?"

This caused Jacs to giggle, which was a great ice-breaker for the tension that had built up. "It's a rocking horse, obviously!" she said, fondly gazing out towards us in the next room.

We had heard an audible intake of breath from Manfri at several words Zairaj had read. Now the expert turned to him and said with admiration, "Well, my friend, you did a wonderful job of recognising many words. You are a clever man to have spotted many similarities. Are you aware that your Romany race originally hailed from North India and that Romanes is a sister tongue to Sanskrit? I have studied this in depth." This started another conversation between the two as they discussed the finer details of the etymology involved. Fireworks had re-located to the kitchen and was listening avidly. Of course, this was right up his street because he too had a passion for words.

Zairaj took his leave just after lunch. He thanked June and Jacs for inviting him, adding it had been a privilege to have viewed and transcribed the scrolls. He assured everyone that he would act with discretion concerning their contents. Before leaving he gave them some advice. He told them they should have a gemologist test and certify the rubies. But above all, see if there was any record of them having been lost or stolen. His parting words were sombre: "If they were mined by this family and never left their ownership, there will be no records. Any surviving family members may have no idea of their existence. What you do next is up to you, but it leaves you in an unenviable position. It's a moral dilemma."

The whole strange affair had turned out somewhat of an anti-climax. After Zairaj's departure, June, Jacs, Manfri and Seb were plunged into deep conversation, huddled round the kitchen table trying to decide what the best course of action should be. They were still in shock and felt they really needed to discuss it all with the men on their return. Charlotte looked completely deflated. We asked her how she was feeling and her answer was morose.

"Until yesterday, I didn't realise the Ferozshahs were still alive. My children, Cyrus and Tehmi, may now be adults, living in Newmarket. That means I am giving away their heritage, their treasure. I feel like a traitor. Those rubies I've kept safe for over 50 years are still a curse. But now they will curse our poor family. I should have kept quiet and suffered the night-visions…" And tears began to fall from her beautiful, luminous, ruby-red eyes.

★★★★

# CHAPTER 11.
## 'FINDERS, WEEPERS...'

The rest of that Sunday afternoon dragged on, everybody going through the motions of getting their chores done, unable to concentrate as their thoughts kept returning to the astounding piece of news they had received earlier. Charlotte had composed herself but refused to talk once she had made it clear she wanted nothing more to do with our plan, a plan that had gone badly awry from her point of view. We had to respect her decision as we knew she was torn with emotion, she felt guilty of treachery. But, I reasoned, at the end of the day we're only rocking horses and our motives and intentions had been good. I didn't feel guilty; after all, we were only trying to help...

At last the menfolk came home in a jovial mood, teasing and jesting with one another. It had been a productive day and high spirits prevailed. Having got themselves washed and changed, they were looking forward to a good meal and a relaxing evening. As they entered the kitchen, they immediately sensed the peculiar atmosphere and said jokingly, "What's up? Someone die? You lot look like you've seen a ghost!"

"You'd all better sit down in the other room. I'll make us a pot of tea and then we have a lot to discuss. We have HUGE news to tell you..." Jacs trailed off, her face giving nothing away.

Manfri and Seb shrugged non-committedly when the men turned to them with inquiring faces.

"Let the women explain," Manfri said cautiously.

The workers headed into the large elegant sitting room to sit with us horses, beginning to feel uneasy. June started by explaining the information Zairaj had uncovered within Teresina's declaration note.

"Wow, that's incredible!" David shouted, leaping up and dashing over to gaze disbelievingly into Charlotte's eyes. "So how is this bad news?" he inquired.

Next, Eddie exclaimed, "You're saying we're the proud owners of two whopping rubies, worth a fortune, that may be the answer to all our problems, yet you look like something awful has happened. What's the snag, then?"

This is when Seb pointed out that the oldest scroll had stated the rubies were a family heirloom, to be passed down to the next generation. Roybin then chipped in saying that if there was no record of them, who was to know? He added, "Finders keepers, losers weepers, in my book!" But Seb argued that he DID know the family in question, maybe not personally, but they were very influential in his industry. The Ferozshahs were well-known and highly respected racehorse trainers and breeders. He added that Wick stud had even had business dealings with them in the past.

"We've talked about it," June added; "it would be immoral not to tell them. It would feel like stealing if we kept those rubies. And anyway, how could we possibly sell them without raising suspicious questions?"

"Oh, that'ud be easy," piped up one of the cousins, "yer find yerself a 'tame' jeweller and get 'im to break 'em up an knock out smaller pieces of stuff like rings, necklaces an' things. Easy t' do." Jacs gave him an old-fashioned look and asked what a 'tame' jeweller was, exactly. "One wot does wot yer tells 'im to. No questions asked!" he answered, grinning widely.

The next ten minutes were tense and fraught with everyone voicing their opinions. Differing points of views and theories were being aired, all rather loudly. Cobweb and I glanced at each other nervously. Oh dear, whatever had we started here? Charlotte remained stonily impassive and Fireworks had scuttled off to another room. He hated raised voices.

"I know, let's take a vote on it and see who thinks what," declared David.

"Right! Who's for keeping them, then?" asked Eddie, raising his arm in unison with David, Roybin and one of Joby's cousins; the other admitted he could not decide.

"Who thinks it's only right to tell the Ferozshahs the whole story?" demanded Jacs, looking round for support. Seb, Joby and June already had their hands up. That left Manfri sitting quietly in the corner saying nothing. Oh, I loved that wise and gentle man, my oldest, dearest friend who'd known me for most of his life. Now he was the voice of reason and calm, just what was needed to take the heat out of the discussions.

Everybody turned to Manfri, as he had the deciding vote. He quietly stated that before getting carried away, we should be certain that there actually were rubies hidden in Charlotte. He continued that if any valuables were found, surely the final decision should be up to June as it was she who had bought and rescued the horse. Then he admitted he thought it would be wrong to keep them. "I couldn't juss take 'em. It juss wouldn't sit right, 'tis thievin' an' no good will come of it, mark my words..."

Everyone stopped and thought for a minute. June suddenly jumped up and headed out of the room saying that Manfri had a good point and she urgently needed to talk to Brenda. As Charlotte's restorer, she thought her friend may remember something that could shed light on the matter. June made the phone call, even though it was a Sunday, apologising to her but emphasising the urgency of the question she was about to ask. Brenda was most curious and offered to help in any way she could. June quizzed her about Charlotte's arrival in Dorset many years ago, to be restored. Her friend answered that yes, she could still recall the awful state the horse was in. She added that she distinctly remembered Charlotte was missing an ear and an eye. When asked to elaborate on the eyes, she answered, "Well, the good glass eye was exceptionally bright and a strange deep red colour, quite beautiful. When I went to replace the missing one, I noticed that someone had stuck a red glass bead there, temporarily I suppose, so she wouldn't look odd and completely lacking an eye on that side. I thought about taking it out and chucking it, but it was set in really deeply and I didn't want to damage the socket. Anyway, I left it there. Once I'd tested the new plain colourless glass eye over the top of the old red bead, it matched so perfectly with the other side that I decided to go ahead and put the new eye in over it. I realised the other one was exactly the same. A matching pair, if you like. It is odd, though. I've never seen eyes done like that before, with beads behind them..."

There was a long stunned silence at the other end of the line. June was trying to digest the overwhelming confirmation she'd just heard. It was like hearing you'd won the lottery...but you'd lost the ticket only to hear someone else had claimed your prize. She stifled her excruciating disappointment and with a long sigh she told June a shortened version of the story, how they'd found the mystery vial Brenda had given her years ago and discovered the scrolls inside, that told of the hidden gems. She ended the conversation by saying, "Thank goodness you didn't dig out and throw away those 'old red beads'. Do you know what they turned out to be? The most priceless, rarest Persian ruby gemstones, worth a small, no, a very large fortune!"

Brenda could not believe her ears. "Wow, I'm delighted for you! After the year you've had, this must be a huge relief! You can sell them, I take it?" she added excitely.

June answered in a flat tone, "No, Brenda. We must give them back to their rightful owner. I just feel it would be wrong to keep them. So...there you are, no good news for us, I'm afraid. We are still doomed with the business here. I'll ring you later and explain everything then."

When June returned to the sitting room and reported that Charlotte did indeed have two valuable jewels embedded behind her eyes, there was a thoughtful hush. Suddenly Seb exclaimed in horror, "Oh Lore, I've just thought of something. Those men! The ones who tried to steal her, back in March. Do you think they knew, when they took her? If they didn't know, they would have been sitting on a fortune without realising it. Thank goodness we got her back…not just for the rubies, I didn't mean it like that," he added lamely.

Everyone agreed the thieves could not have possibly known and it was pure coincidence that she'd been targeted, but an uneasy feeling had descended on the house and everyone in it. They all agreed that the sooner the jewels were extracted from the Duchess, the better. June had made her decision to return them and that was the end of it. David had remarked sadly to no one in particular, "Oh well, I don't know about 'Finders, keepers' – it's going to be more like 'Finders, weepers' for us."

Now they knew they must return the heirloom to its rightful owner, the general consensus was that they should get the valuables off the premises as fast as possible, the quicker the better. Those rubies had become a liability, a burden for their keepers. For a second time round, their very presence in the house felt like a curse. We had trusted the rubies to bring us a miracle, but they had failed miserably.

# CHAPTER 12.
# ROCKING HORSES
# AND RUBIES

After that emotional weekend, Manfri decided he must return home. It was sad to see him leave as we all loved him dearly. He was like a kind old grandfather to us all and his very presence was a comfort. Early Monday morning he drove back to the New Forest, leaving behind our wonderful helpers. Our families felt they had failed to show the guests good hospitality due to the dramas of the last few days, so now, everything would be done to make their stay more pleasant and to show them appreciation. The women made sure the workers came home every night to a roaring fire, a hearty meal and as much beer as they wanted. The whole household made an effort to shrug off any negative feelings. The partners owed their friends so much for their cheerful, willing labour and were forever grateful to June's parents who had generously paid out for extra materials. As the estate came back to life, it genuinely had everyone celebrating. My home Airborne Lodge had a new roof, the other lodges and grounds were fit for purpose again, and the stables and yard were nearly ready to welcome home our mares and the three older foals born early that year. Plus, we had enough logs to keep our home fires burning for many years! Repairing all that storm damage had been a challenge and a gargantuan task.

June had phoned and given Brenda an in-depth account of what had occurred over the last few days and had requested she undertake the delicate job of relieving Charlotte of her treasure. Brenda said there was no need to ship the Duchess all the way down to Dorset as she was happy to put some tools in her car and drive up to Wick Stud. Now that the Lodge roof was fixed, there would be plenty of room and she could stay overnight. When she arrived on a mild November evening, it was decided to have an impromptu al fresco meal. Food was prepared and David lit the garden's fire pit. Chairs and spare logs were dragged to form a circle around the blaze and with lanterns lit, it was a welcoming sight. Spirits were high that night. Cobweb and I gazed out of the window, relieved and grateful to hear our people truly back on form. They sang, chatted and celebrated the estate's re-birth late into the night.

Charlotte had also rallied magnificently. Once June had made the decision to return the heirloom to its rightful owners, she had swelled with pride and had said quietly, "I really love my June. She's got moral fibre. She is my sort of woman." Now this was very unusual for Charlotte as she was not a demonstrative or emotional mare. Other than when she'd talked about her rocking horse family and admitted she'd dearly loved her children, she never spoke about feelings. I think her mistress Teresina's murder had affected her deeply. She'd never allowed herself to get too attached to anyone since.

"Aren't you nervous about your operation?" we asked incredulously, gazing at a calm and serene Duchess. It was the next morning and Charlotte was scheduled to have the precious gems extracted from her eyes.

"Absolutely not. I welcome their removal. It will be a relief after many years of carrying this tiresome responsibility. And I trust the esteemed Brenda to do a sterling job," she remarked casually.

The procedure was carried out with careful precision, and June, acting as assistant, helped her friend skilfully extract the rubies without inflicting damage to them or her patient. They had thought long and hard about whether to put back glass eyes only or to replace the missing gems with an alternative. Brenda had bought two similar claret-coloured custom-jewellery cabochons at a car boot sale before coming to Surrey. The women tried them out during the operation and they fitted perfectly into the deep crevices left by the rubies. The swap was completed. With clear glass eyes over the replacement stones, nobody would have noticed any difference as Charlotte had her amazing carmine eyes back. Very carefully, they wrapped each ruby individually in soft spectacle-cleaning cloths to prevent them from being scratched. They were incredibly beautiful, their quality obvious even to a layman's eye. The sheer depth of clarity and purity of colour was astounding, each glittering with their own individually-cut facets. One resembled a shining star, the other a gleaming heart.

"I bet we could buy the whole of Wick Stud with these..." June remarked wistfully.

"More than likely you could buy every stud in Surrey with just one of them!" Brenda retorted hollowly. Then June reached on tip toes and placed them in her Hamada plate at the very top of her 'filing cabinet', along with the now empty vial.

Brenda left for Dorset that evening feeling pleased and satisfied with her handiwork. Her friend thanked her profusely and as she climbed into her car, she whispered, "Good luck with it all. I know it's harsh on you, but I think giving them back is the right thing to do. You never know, they may give you some reward money."

June was adamant and replied, "I wouldn't take a penny. I didn't want to return them for that reason. We don't need charity; we'll survive this with hard work and determination. We'll fight to the last, Brenda."

The next question, which was playing on everybody's mind, was how to approach a very busy, famous racehorse trainer to tell him an unbelievably strange story and then hand over to him something of immense value. Who was best placed to approach the Ferozshah family? Should the extraordinary news our people were about to impart be best received by letter, phone call or in person? These were some of the decisions that had to be made, and in a hurry. Everyone wanted rid of the rubies. They represented finances we desperately needed but couldn't have; the wherewithal to save the business and our homes. They were like salt in a wound.

Poor, young, sweet Sebastian drew the short straw. My boy was chosen to speak to the illustrious trainer as there was a tenuous connection through him having spent time working and riding in Newmarket. The plan was for Seb to phone Mr Ferozshah and set up a face-to-face meeting. They all had different suggestions as to what the reason for a meeting should be, for he would surely ask. In the end his mother Jacs told him to 'wing it'.

"Thanks, Ma, my whole career could be affected by this! I don't want him to think I'm a time-wasting idiot," he trailed off, feeling genuinely apprehensive at the mammoth task he'd been lumbered with.

"Don't be silly, Sebbi, wouldn't you like to be given the news he's about to receive? Pretend you're him," Jacs said encouragingly.

"Huh, in my dreams!" he answered sulkily. After several attempts to make contact via the office secretary, Seb eventually managed to speak directly to the great man in person.

Well, what a pleasant surprise that phone call turned out to be! Nothing as bad as Seb had feared, although he'd felt somewhat foolish. We eavesdropped (as usual) on Sebastian's conversation, willing him to be impressive and bold. He did a splendid job and the gist of the call went something like this:

"Good afternoon, sir. You don't know me, I am Sebastian Marland and I'm so sorry to phone you like this, but I need to speak to you on a matter of great importance…"

Here he was interrupted. "Oh hello, of course I know you; you're the son of that good jockey Eddie Marland. You're not a bad little jockey yourself. Weren't you champion apprentice last season? I've been keeping an eye out for you this year, but you seem to have fallen off the radar. Are you after a few rides from me, son?" the trainer asked kindly.

"Oh no, sir, I wouldn't dare ring you for that...I've had to put my career on hold because my family and the stud needed my help here, after we had a few disasters..." Sebastian faltered, when the man again butted in, "Oh dear, yes, I did hear. Terrible shame. Awful luck. I hate to see such a good small establishment like yours struggle with the troubles you've had this year. I'm quite a fan of your 'Dapple Stud'. You have such fine bloodlines and wonderful young stock. What is it then, have you some youngsters to sell, something you think would interest me? If there's anything I can do to help, I certainly will. The last filly we bought off you has done so well, we've kept her for breeding."

Seb, now emboldened by the compliments and full of confidence, ploughed on while he was ahead. He was surprised how at ease he'd felt talking to this personable and pleasant man. "No, sir, we're not asking anything from you, it's more what we can do for you. We have found something belonging to your family and we want to return it. It's complicated and I really feel you should meet with my family and the partners to discuss it. It just can't be done over the phone," he finished in a rush.

"Well, now I'm intrigued. Could you please elaborate? Is it really important?" the trainer said, his tone changing slightly.

Seb, now feeling pressured and out of his depth, answered, "Yes, sir, it's absolutely vital! Please Mr Ferozshah, it will be in your interest, please meet with my parents and they'll explain everything."

The man told him he would be coming to Surrey to see a horse within the next few days and he would ring to arrange a time to visit Wick Stud, while he was in the area. He added firmly, "But I would appreciate it if you would tell me what all this is about."

By now my poor lad was flustered; he just wanted to end the conversation quickly. He stuttered and blurted out the only thing he could think of on the spur of the moment saying, "Well, er, it's, erm to do with er, rocking horses and rubies, sir."

There was a horribly long silence on the other end of the line but eventually the man replied rather distantly, "I'm totally baffled now, young man. Absolutely vital, you say? Well, thank you for speaking to me and tell your parents I look forward to seeing them and clearing up this perplexing mystery."

Seb sat out in the hall for a couple of minutes until his hands had stopped shaking before he went back to the kitchen to report to the others.

"Oh hells-bells, that was awful…it was all going so well, I think he'd have offered me a job if I'd asked but then he kept saying 'what's it all about' and ' can you elaborate' and then I said something really stupid and he sort of went a bit cold on me. Anyway—he's coming. He'll ring…" Seb made himself a strong mug of coffee and apologised to his audience. Jacs told him he'd done very well for even managing to speak to the busy man, leave alone arranging for him to visit. She then asked him gently what he thought he'd said that was stupid. He looked down at the floor and mumbled, "He must think I'm absolutely bonkers…I told him he must come, it's absolutely vital and it's to do with rocking horses and rubies…"

### 'Laughter is the best medicine'

"Rocking horses and rubies?" Jacs repeated incredulously and then burst out in peals of laughter. That set everyone else off. They all laughed till tears streamed down their faces and repeated the phrase several times.

"Well, whatever is the poor man supposed to make of that? He must be totally discombobulated after that weird conversation. It's just hilarious!" croaked David, holding his stomach in an attempt to stop himself laughing. June announced giddily that it would be a great name for a racehorse, but Eddie mused that it may be too many letters.

"OK, perhaps 'Rocking Ruby' or 'The Ruby Rocker'?" she suggested, feeling quite intoxicated by the humour of it all. At this point Seb, grateful that nobody thought he'd made a hash of his phone call, joined in with a relieved smile.

Then Jacs brought them all back to reality saying, "Yes, it's going to be an interesting but awkward meeting now. I'm afraid Mr Big Shot Trainer must think we are all off our rockers. Rockers! Did you hear what I just said there? Rockers!" And she and the others fell about giggling all over again.

Back in the sitting room, the four of us looked at each other in bewilderment. It was nice to hear our lot being so happy, but for the life of me I couldn't fathom what they'd said that was so funny. What had amused them so? We decided to put their mass hysteria down to stress. They'd been through a lot recently...

Three days later on the dot of 4 o'clock, a top of the range midnight blue Mercedes car rolled noiselessly up the estate's gravel drive to halt outside Wick House. Everyone had worked flat out to smarten up the previously storm-torn properties and stables. With a massive push from the entire workforce, the place now looked pristine, worthy of a royal visit. Roybin, Joby and cousins had departed the previous day after having been showered with thanks and with an invite to come over for a Christmas party. "IF we're still living here by then," they'd said half-jokingly.

The partners had carefully worked out their strategy. They had decided to start the proceedings off within the large welcoming kitchen, sitting the trainer down comfortably with an offer of tea and cakes. There, they would relate the whole story of how the vial and subsequently their contents had been discovered. Then, June planned to produce the scrolls for Mr. Ferozshah and invite him read them for himself. Lastly, they planned to move to the sitting room and show the man a rocking horse that Jacs and June suspected may well have belonged to the Ferozshah family at one time. It had crossed their minds that they may be offering up their badly needed treasure trove to the wrong family, but plain common sense prevailed. In their hearts they knew they were doing the right thing.

As we all know, the best-laid plans can be de-railed in a heartbeat. Unfortunately, this is exactly what happened. The Duchess, Cobweb and I gazed out across the sitting room to the front of the house with a view of the drive. Fireworks was not with us as he had darted off to position himself under the kitchen table, ready to listen to all that went on. It started to go wrong when not one but two people emerged from the sleek car. Charlotte started to tremble with shock as she realised that the couple approaching our front door were her beloved children Cyrus and Tehmina, not as she remembered them but now transformed into gracious, sophisticated adults. Cyrus was tall, suave and distinguished, his sister elegant, poised and startlingly beautiful. I was worried for my dear friend as I knew this surprise meeting would bring up many painful memories for her. But I also knew she desperately wanted these two to have back their rightful inheritance.

Our people were also taken aback but they welcomed their guests and did the formal introductions. Coats were taken and Jacs was directing them towards the kitchen, listening to Mr Ferozshah's explanation. "I do hope you don't mind, but I took the liberty of bringing my sister with me. Young Sebastian did stipulate it was a family matter of great importance. To be honest, we are totally baffled by the whole mysterious matter and..." He didn't have a chance to finish his sentence because this is when it happened. I know the sitting room door was supposed to have been shut but Fireworks had rushed through and it had swung open. Open enough for us to be in full sight. We are an eye-full at the best of times, especially if the viewer isn't expecting to see such a delightful group of us, but what Tehmina saw had come as a total shock. She stopped dead, stared and then audibly gasped as she entered and made her way across the room towards Charlotte, almost in a trance. Despite her wonderfully tailored, elegant cashmere suit and high heels, she dropped to her knees and stretched a manicured hand out to touch Charlotte, kissing her gently on her nose. It was if she had been transported back through time and was a child again. "Mumty, Mumty, how can you possibly be here? Where have you been all these years, my beauty?" she whispered, quite overcome with emotion. "And where is your saffron thread? Look, I still have mine!" Tehmina fingered absentmindedly at the vivid, twisted thread which lay under a very expensive ruby bracelet upon her wrist.

It seemed we were all under a frozen spell of shock for a long moment. Then Cyrus lurched forwards to grab and gently lift Tehmina to her feet, putting a protective arm around her. "Tehmi, are you alright?" her brother asked with concern and turned to the others to apologise for her emotional reaction. He explained that this had been their nursery horse from when they were very young until they were teenagers, very loved and precious and had been sadly missed for many years. He added guardedly that there was a very tragic story attached to 'Mumty', the name they called Charlotte, concerning the death of their mother, hence Tehmina's present state of grief. His poor sister stood there with tears running unashamedly down her lovely face, looking pale and rather shaken. Jacs took her by the hand and invited her to sit on one of the Chesterfield sofas, offering her a tissue. She gracefully dabbed at her tears and, smiling wanly, apologised yet again for her sudden outburst of emotion.

We of course knew the whole horrific story and willed the Ferozshahs to tell our people what had happened, so they may understand how the vial came to be in the Duchess. However, we'd forgotten that they actually knew nothing about the treasure, the vial or its contents. They would have to read the scrolls to understand.

Cyrus then made a shocking assumption. "So, I suppose you got in touch with me to return our family rocking horse? But however did you know she was ours? I'm sure my sister is grateful for the effort and trouble you've gone to and she'll be delighted but…personally, I don't want anything to do with rocking horses. They hold such sad and painful memories for me, a lost childhood that ended in such misery…and other family tragedies…" his voice trailed off, laden with emotion.

June's and Jacs' faces were instantly awash with panic and horror as it dawned on them that the trainer was expecting them to give Charlotte back to him and his sister. Jacs couldn't contain herself and blurted out, "OH NO, we were never going to give you our wonderful Charlotte, we just couldn't…we didn't even know for sure if you were the family that had her in the past. I'm so sorry but that's not why we invited you here. Oh dear, this is all a horrible misunderstanding!"

Luckily, David stepped in to do some damage limitation and be the voice of reason. "Look, let's start all over again and we will explain why we asked you here. Full disclosure, I promise," he murmured in a calm and soothing tone. He turned to his wife and prompted her, saying, "Over to you, June."

So June began her story, how she'd bought Charlotte in a terrible state of neglect and sent her off to be restored. She explained how Brenda had found something within the horse's belly. It was a mother of pearl vial which she had kept for many years, un-opened. When it recently fell and broke open, two tiny notes were discovered hidden inside. They had asked a friend to translate these, and they revealed that a Ferozshah family heirloom had been placed secretly in Lady Teresina's rocking horse. Subsequently the treasure had been located and removed from Charlotte. Now, she and her family felt they should return it to its rightful owners. She concluded by saying, "This is the reason we asked you here today. We want to return your inheritance to you."

June and Jacs then dashed off to the kitchen, rather embarrassed by the whole earlier misunderstanding. The two women made teas and coffees and put an array of small French patisseries on a platter to offer to their guests. June then retrieved the scrolls and vial from the dresser to show to Cyrus and Tehmi, but decided to leave the wrapped-up rubies till later.

When they entered the sitting room, laden with refreshments, the atmosphere had softened and lightened considerably. Cyrus was seated next to an over-awed Sebastian, chatting happily about some good up-and-coming horses in Newmarket, and racing in general. Tehmi seemed to have recovered herself nicely, serenity returning to her delicate features. She had seen Fireworks stroll in and remarked what a beautiful little chap he was. Always looking to give comfort and sensing she was in need, he'd wound around her shapely legs until she'd invited him upon her lap.

"Oh. You'll get covered in hairs," Eddie had warned, but she said she really didn't care, cats were precious souls and he was very welcome.

As June placed the tray on the coffee table, Cyrus turned to her with a look of genuine respect. He graciously thanked her for inviting them, clearing up the mystery and for her altruism. She was not completely sure of that word's meaning, but smiled sweetly as she handed him the scrolls and vial.

Tehmi gasped and held out her hand eagerly. "Oh, Mama's little bottle! How lovely to see it again," she said with a sad sigh.

Cyrus produced his spectacles from a breast pocket and began to read the notes out aloud to his sister, the words flowing easily with the fluidity of one very familiar with the language. "Well, this is a huge surprise and frankly, I'm speechless," he announced when he'd finished. Apparently they knew nothing of the heirloom and had no idea their mother had hidden these rubies. Above all, he just couldn't believe the honesty shown by our two families. He remarked that it all rang true as his grandfather's ancestors had always owned mines in Persia and that was how they had originally amassed their wealth. They had been famous for their 'manek-lals', or red rubies. "Rather like you are famous for your wonderful 'Dapple Stud'," he said kindly, looking up and smiling with genuine warmth.

They proceeded to tell their sad story, how their mother had been cruelly murdered and they'd been forced to leave for England. Their father had died a year later, from a broken heart, Tehmi said. Relatives had taken them back to India at the start of the war as they had no money here. All their wealth was in India and could not be taken out of the country. Charlotte, or Mumty as they called her, was abandoned at the country house. Tehmi was heartbroken and every time she saw a rocking horse, it made her feel sad. Throughout the time they were there, I noticed her and Charlotte exchanging little glances, looks full of deep affection. We rocking horses are very aware of these things. Tehmi then added, "June, I'd never have taken Mumty from you. She's got a wonderful home here. You've given me the gift of seeing her again and knowing she's safe. That's enough. By the way, she looks just as she did in the old days, just like her namesake Mumtaz Mahal."

As they prepared to leave, rubies stored carefully in Tehmi's handbag, the couple stated that the heirloom was more precious to them than any amount of money. The rubies would never be sold but would be passed down to their grandchildren as their grandfather had wished. They expressed a desire to reward the family, but June adamantly refused a monetary gift. "It's not why we did it," she replied firmly.

Cyrus' passing shot was like a bombshell. "There are other ways of accepting thanks. We wish to do business with you in the future. We can help each other. I have money to burn but you have fabulous bloodlines; together we can thrive. Young Sebastian, drop the 'sir' nonsense when we meet socially. You can call me 'sir' when you come to work for me. I need a good little jockey! We'll be in touch very soon!" With that, they entered their car and swept away, leaving everyone stunned into silence on the doorstep. I think, at long last, the miracle was happening...

★★★★

# CHAPTER 13.
# LEOPARDS & SPOTS

fter waving their guests off, our family just stood
motionless in the porch looking dumb-struck. As the
Ferozshahs' car sped away silently, all the months of
worry about the business and the rubies with their perceived curse,
disappeared with them. As if by magic, a weight lifted from their
shoulders as they closed the front door on their troubles. Numbly,
our shocked people drifted into the sitting room and sat bolt
upright looking at each other.

David spoke first. "Did I hear right? They want to join forces with
us in our breeding business?"

June answered, "Yes, I think that's what they implied…"

"Did he just offer me a job, my absolute dream job, riding his
horses?" Seb enquired in a faint, incredulous voice.

Jacs replied, "Yes, I do believe he did, Sebbi. Or it certainly sounded that way."

Eddie, ever the joker, broke the dazed spell by announcing, "Well, Rocking Rubies! I do believe our fortunes have just changed for the better. Good job we decided to give them back their jewels, eh!"

Everyone started to laugh at his newly coined expression, but June turned on him with a vengeance exclaiming, "WE? If I remember correctly, you were all for smashing them up and selling them off as rings and brooches! I felt like the villain of the piece for wanting to give them back!"

Eddie shrugged off her accusation with a flippant comment, "Only 'cause you couldn't find any 'tame' jewellers in the phone book! No, seriously, June, thank you for saving our skins. Well done to your exceptional moral compass!"

The tension had melted away and our people were breathing a huge sigh of relief. The future looked to be secure, but they all agreed they must tread carefully. They did not want to be sucked into a large breeding organisation and lose their own identity or the control of their hard-earned, successful bloodlines.

"We mustn't sell our souls, agreed?" David asked the others.

"Agreed!" they all concurred.

Of course, although we were delighted how things had turned out that afternoon, I was concerned about Charlotte's state of mind. After that bolt from the blue visit from her beloved wards, I feared old memories and regrets may have saddened her. I needn't have worried as the Duchess was in excellent spirits because, as she explained, her decision coupled with June's wise choice had resulted in both families benefiting. She looked at us kindly through her lovely new eyes and said wisely, "Letting go of things sometimes gives you far greater power than hanging on to them." A more mellowed Charlotte also told us softly that she was uncommonly fond of us three and her new family. "From now on," she said with genuine affection, "it's all about us and our home here. No more living in the past." She thanked us for helping her make her miracle happen and stated that her mind was at peace since she'd seen Tehmina and Cyrus happy, prosperous and going home with what was rightfully theirs. "I've finally moved on from those days. But don't they both look wonderful and haven't they done well for themselves?" she commented, glowing with maternal pride.

Fireworks purred in a velvety tone, "Well, I thought your Tehmi was the most astute and divine woman I've ever had the pleasure of sitting with. And I got a good close look at that orangey-yellow thread around her wrist. Was that the same as the one you and Pasha were given, if you don't mind me asking?"

To our surprise, the Duchess talked freely and without distress about the marriage ceremony held for her and her husband. She told us again about the thin, coloured strings placed around their ankles and lastly about the fine saffron-gold twisted strands of thread that Fu Ling Yoo had presented to them and the children, declaring it would keep them safe and together whatever befell them. She added cheerfully, "I thought that was a forlorn hope once I'd lost mine, but just maybe it only needs one recipient to work! After all, it's led my grown-up children back to me, hasn't it?" We thought it best not to mention what was going through all our minds...where in the world were Pasha and Pashmina now, and were they still wearing their saffron-coloured anklets?

Everybody slept like proverbial logs that night. For once it was not from physical exhaustion but through our people having restful minds. We four enjoyed the calmest night we'd had in weeks, grateful for each other's company. I knew I'd soon be off back to Airborne Lodge with Seb, Jacs and Eddie, and lovely as that was, I would sorely miss my companions. Fireworks was a godsend as a go-between; he could flit from house to house relating any essential news or just interesting gossip. He also took my eavesdropping information over to the others, when needed. We certainly had a good system worked out, but I knew I'd miss our heart-to-heart chats and Charlotte's 'tales of the unexpected'! Never mind, I felt sure I'd soon be back for a visit. Nowadays, for security reasons, I was always taken over to Wick House whenever the people were away on business and I had a feeling things were going to hot up in that direction.

Before I left to go back to my Lodge, two wonderful things happened the very next day. True to his word, Cyrus telephoned the partners as he was keen to put his carefully worked-out proposals to them. Everyone crowded around David who had taken the call, to listen to the conversation. He suggested that as our mares were not in foal that year, he would like to invite them to visit his Gwalior stud to meet new, suitable husbands so they could produce foals for us the following year. This would be part of the partners' promised reward, with an option that he could keep back one of the babies himself. It was a brilliant deal and would provide long term security for the future of Wick Stud. He said they must meet soon to discuss choices of sires. He also wished to gift them an illustrious brood mare that he could no longer use himself as she was too closely related to his own stock. He assured them he'd delved into her fabulous pedigree and thought she would be perfectly compatible to be bred to our stallion, Grey Refrain. The icing on the cake was when he then asked if Master Sebastian would be willing to come to Newmarket for a job interview. He added, "I could use him as a 'second string' jockey. He obviously won't be riding the cream of horses yet, but we have many that I think he'd enjoy partnering. He can learn and grow with us." If that wasn't enough amazing news, everyone was speechless when he mentioned that the brood mare he was sending them next week was due to have her baby in early January and its father was a Derby winner. "Of course, you are to have that foal as well," he added firmly.

When David eventually found his voice, he stuttered a strong objection, "No, no, this is far too much, we couldn't possibly accept all this! It's all a shock, and frankly, you really don't need to be so generous..."

Cyrus was rather stern and serious in his answer. "I don't think you quite realise what you've done and what it means to us," he explained. "You've acted with such integrity by returning something of immense value. Those rubies are priceless. Although worth more money than you can imagine, we will never sell them. We don't need money, but we need that connection to our beloved grandfather. All we desire is to keep them in our family to be handed down. Nothing we offer you can repay what you've done for us. Please don't insult my trying to thank you. Please accept this graciously." He then finished on a jovial note, saying with a chuckle in his voice, "Your bloodlines are almost as precious to us as those rubies, if only you knew! A direct line back to our beloved Mumtaz! So please, do NOT look a gift horse in 'the eyes'!" No one could argue with that!

After the phone call, the men went out with new enthusiasm to finish various jobs in preparation for the expected return of the horses. Mirabel appeared at the back door in time to receive the good news. She'd galloped into the house after her usual morning shift looking after the mares and foals at their temporary lodgings. She was dying to tell June and Jacs her own bit of interesting news, but before she could, she was asked to sit and listen to what the women had to say. They announced that they'd secured financial backing, which meant our wonderful stud was going to survive and hopefully flourish again, with new foals to look forward to and the imminent return of all our stock and resident stallion. They warned her that the workload would increase, and they'd better start looking for more staff again. Mirabel was thrilled. She adored her role as head stud groom and dearly wanted the horses back where they belonged.

"Oh, I nearly forgot MY bit of amazing information with all this exciting news of our recovery!" she exclaimed excitedly. "Well, you know the un-named chestnut baby, the one the stable owners are desperate to buy from you? I just don't understand what's going on BUT...she isn't a chestnut anymore! Her fluffy foal coat has come out in handfuls, which is normal around this time of year, but underneath that, she's a most peculiar colour!" Mirabel went on to explain that when the filly was a few weeks old, she'd noticed many dark smudges scattered all over her body. They'd looked like someone had dabbed her in engine oil! She'd tried washing them off but soon realised they were definitely pigmented, rather like birthmarks. Of course, with all the disasters going on she hadn't bothered to mention it to anyone. It had seemed too trivial. "But now," she said with wide eyes and a smile, "I honestly think she's going to be grey! But the strangest grey I've ever seen. The chestnut is turning iron grey and the big dark spots are getting whiter by the day. She looks like she'll be a weird splodgey sort of dapple! Not like the normal dapples we breed. What's going on there?"

Jacs and June looked at each other with huge, knowing grins of delight. "We just may have bred ourselves our first ever Chubari Spot," Jacs declared triumphantly. "It makes perfect sense because she goes back on both her parents' sides to The Tetrarch."

"A true throwback!" June added.

Mirabel looked fascinated as the women explained the genetic link to the famous horse nicknamed 'The Rocking Horse' and later in his career, 'The Spotted Wonder'. They told her that the foal's 'grease' marks were called 'Bend Or' spots (after the stallion of that name) and sometimes appeared on chestnuts, but as she was destined to be a grey, they'd changed dramatically. They rummaged about, sorting through their old racing books to show her pictures of the amazing Tetrarch with his superb, un-defeated racing record and some of his offspring with similar, rare colouring known as 'Chubari'. Mirabel was also shown photos of horses sporting the dark Bend Or marks she'd seen on the filly.

"Well, that settles it," June said adamantly, "our foal isn't going anywhere! We can afford to keep her now and even put her in training. We'll ask Cyrus if he'll take her when she's old enough to race. Mirabel, you'll have to tell them at the stables that she's definitely NOT for sale and give them notice that we're bringing everyone home as soon as possible."

Jacs felt tears of joy welling up. She'd always had a soft spot for the chestnut baby as she'd seen her come into the world, having assisted with her birth. "That foal is very special, like a butterfly who's emerging from her chrysalis," she whispered.

"We'd better name all three of those foals TODAY; we've waited long enough to do it," June declared happily as it was a job she relished.

The three women made coffee, and as they sat around the kitchen table, many choices were bandied about. The British Horseracing Board only allowed eighteen characters in total within a chosen name and it must it be absolutely original with no other horse registered the same. Also, ease of pronunciation had to be considered. They felt the word 'ruby' should be in the foal's name as a nod to those precious stones that had saved the stud and because the foal had begun life as a red chestnut colour. They thought the inclusion of the words 'spot' or 'leopard' would be an appropriate twist as the filly was changing her colour. Several suggestions were put forth; Ruby Grey, The Grey Ruby, Ruby Leopardess, Leopard Spot, Dappled Ruby, Spot the Ruby, Chubari Jewel and finally Chubari Ruby, which they liked best. Of course, it wasn't entirely up to them – everybody needed to be involved and offer their input. Then a vote could be taken to decide the most popular name, a system that had always worked well in the past.

We three rocking horses were basking in this wonderful new atmosphere in the house. It felt like a return to the old days with everyone throwing themselves gladly into their day's work with joyful energy and coming home full of happy chatter. Little Fireworks was totally content again, napping most of the day on one or another of our saddles. He'd played a big part in helping everything fall in to place in the last week or two and was feeling exhausted. He would never admit it, but I think he was feeling his age. Worrying is an exhausting pastime but when it's replaced with relief, it can leave you feeling quite drained.

When the men came home, they were greeted by two very effusive women bearing exciting news about the foal. The amazing transformation of the filly's colour was explained to them, and they agreed with slightly less enthusiasm that yes, it was a pleasant surprise. What really excited them was the idea of retaining her and racing her later. I could read Sebastian's mind so well; I noticed a small smile creep across his face and a faraway look in his eyes and I knew immediately. My lad was dreaming about his future job with Cyrus and maybe an opportunity to ride the little butterfly filly to success in all her races. Jacs and June pressed the men into naming her that evening. After they'd eaten and settled down with us in the sitting room, the process began. In the past, a lot of foals had been named after loved people or even after us! When Izzy's mother Grace, now sadly passed, had been re-united by chance with her childhood rocking horse Cobweb, the next dappled grey filly to be born had been named 'Cobweb's Grace'. Also, a racehorse colt had been called 'Blitziboy', after me. The lovely mare 'Graceful Charlotte' was named in honour of the arrival of the Duchess, and it was her foal that our people were now struggling to name.

Jacs said simply that she liked 'Chrysalis' and explained her emerging butterfly image. Seb was being madly creative by mixing the words and letters up to form something unpronounceable. His choices of Crubalys, Chrysarubi and Rubari Spot were unanimously thrown out as being too far-fetched. June suggested that Chubari Ruby was quirky and unusual, but the others thought it a mouthful, especially for a commentator to voice during a race.

Finally, after much discussion, Eddie said, "Why aren't we doing our usual thing of using the names of our lovely horses here?" He glanced at the Duchess and declared he'd found the only fair choice of name. "Any objections to us honouring this wonderful mare who saved our stud? We should call the foal... Charlotte's Rubies."

No one disagreed; they raised their wine glasses to toast the Duchess, shouting out, "Charlotte's Rubies!" You can imagine how touched she was, and I swear I saw a faint blush sweep across her elegant cheeks.

# CHAPTER 14.
# THE TROUBLE WITH
# WILD ROSES.

It wasn't long before I was back at Wick House again as I'd predicted. Two weeks after that life-changing phone call from Cyrus Ferozshah, the partners were preparing to head off to Newmarket for lengthy talks concerning future plans for their business. Seb was also going as he had his daunting job interview with the eminent trainer to decide his new role within the famous racing establishment. They were about to book a few nights at a local hostelry, but Cyrus had insisted they should be his guests at his residence, Rowley Heath Hall, where he, Tehmina and her husband lived. He told them it made good sense as they would be on the spot to have a guided tour of the whole Gwalior set up, the racing yard and connecting stud farm. Tehmi had told June it would be lovely to have a bit of company, and she wanted to introduce them all to her daughter and granddaughter, who were also visiting. June felt they would be imposing but Tehmi had laughed, saying they had eight bedrooms, domestic help and a huge dining hall that was rarely used. She looked forward to the house being full of life again as she adored entertaining. "I'll be in my element, I assure you. Life can be so dull here in the winter, no racing or social events…I do get rather fed-up and lonely," she added sadly.

Jacs and June decided they'd better pack some smart evening wear after hearing that! They really hadn't expected to be doing anything other than feeling awe-struck whilst being shown around Cyrus' successful empire and maybe having meetings in an office. They knew he owned an extensive training complex with equine swimming pool, miles of gallops and indoor schools. No wonder Seb had initially felt intimidated about approaching this man – he was extremely influential, someone who could make or break an aspiring jockey's career. There was also the stud with its own state of the art facilities, ultra-modern stables and manicured paddocks. Their little stud was dwarfed in comparison, but they knew it would be an education to see how this establishment operated. It had been decided that Sebastian would stay in the large, well-appointed 'lads' digs'. This was a lovely old converted stone barn offering individual rooms for the staff with a communal refectory-style canteen. Cyrus had suggested it would give Seb an opportunity to meet the other lads and see if he liked his future accommodation.

As the families prepared to leave on their adventure, Charlotte, Cobweb and I could sense their excitement. None of them ever thought that after such an awful year, they'd have such high hopes for the future. They felt as if they were going on holiday; everyone was buzzing about, checking nothing had been forgotten, and giving last minute instructions to Mirabel, who was staying as usual to keep the home fires burning. At last, car loaded and ready to go, they waved goodbye and Jacs shouted back to us, "Now then, you lovely lot, behave yourselves, no more plotting!" Well, I'm so glad that we had. Those rubies had turned their lives around.

Everything had gone back to normal in a rush over the last few weeks. All the horses were home in their own stables and paddocks; we had one new member of staff and another joining us soon. As the lodges weren't now needed for income as holiday lets, one had already been utilised to provide very pleasant staff accommodation. Our stallion, Grey Refrain, was happy to be back and his beautiful new future wife Varasha, who had been gifted to the partners by Cyrus, had arrived and was settling in nicely. Most of the old clients and owners had brought their mares back, either to have their foals or to be put in foal. Business had suddenly picked up and was booming with the prospect of healthy babies arriving within the next two months. Our own mares would soon be off to Cyrus's prestigious Gwalior Stud to have their pick of blue-blooded husbands. We really were back to life as usual!

It was a scary thought, knowing what could happen in a blink of an eye; how the stud's normal equilibrium had been destroyed earlier in the year by a single germ. Mirabel was particularly fussy nowadays. After that devastating virus, she was extra careful about biosecurity and all staff had this impressed upon them, with a new disinfecting regime in place. However, life was quiet and uneventful in the house without our families around and we were dying to know how they were getting on; not that we are nosy – we just like to take a healthy interest. Although we eavesdropped on phone calls every evening to try and glean what was happening in Newmarket, Mirabel's conversations were hard to decipher because all we heard were a series of 'Ohs', 'Ooohs' and 'Aahs'. It did sound like positive things had been decided, but we had to wait as usual to hear the full-blown account.

Three days later, our patience was rewarded. Our families were home, tired but full of news and enthusiasm for the stud's future plans. They arrived back that afternoon and Mirabel insisted she must hear everything in detail, even though they were weary. She ushered them into the sitting room, plied them with tea and crumpets, and sat looking at them expectantly. Jacs laughed and said resignedly that they weren't going to get any peace until she'd had an account of the whole trip.

June started with a description of Rowley Heath Hall, the gardens, the décor, their luxurious bedrooms and the hospitality they'd been shown. She continued with the events of the first evening which had been spent enjoying a sumptuous five-course feast with their hosts and meeting Tehmina's daughter Teresita and granddaughter, Nazrin. Both mother and daughter were extraordinarily beautiful: Teresita had her mother's elegance and sophistication; but she'd gathered Nazrin was very different, being young, arrogant and headstrong. She was about the same age as Sebastian but had enjoyed a very privileged upbringing, wanting for nothing. Everyone had expected the two of them to find common ground and get on well, but Seb had told his parents later that he'd found her obnoxious, opinionated and abrasive. Sheer good manners had prevented him from being rude to her.

Apparently, Nazrin had done exceptionally well in her studies but had deferred going to university; she'd decided she needed a free year in which to explore other opportunities. She was an extremely good horse woman, rode in point to points, and adored being around horses generally. Nazrin also had a passion for breeding racehorses. If she had her way, she'd said petulantly, she would be opting to join her great-uncle in his business. Her mother was opposed to her working with horses but had stopped arguing with her stubborn daughter and given in to the idea of a 'gap' year. Apparently, her father was out of the picture, having split from his family years earlier to return to his home country. It seemed her great-uncle was the only person who supported this young woman in any of her decisions or actions. Cyrus was the only person Nazrin had ever listened to.

Seb had sighed with relief when she and her mother departed the next morning, leaving them all free to enjoy the tour and to view bloodstock of breath-taking value. The meetings had been conducted back at Rowley Heath Hall in a resplendent library packed full of old racing record books which fascinated Sebastian. He had sat quietly and read while the partners and Cyrus decided which sires to use in their joint breeding plans. June and Jacs were pleasantly surprised by the respect he'd shown them for their knowledge and how carefully he'd listened to the suggestions they put forward. He was full of admiration for their small but successful breeding venture and complimented their astute judgement. It became clear to the partners that rather than bully them, he genuinely wished to join with them for their mutual benefit.

Their last evening at the Hall had been a more relaxed affair. After another delicious meal, they'd retired to a comfortable sitting room and ended up talking about how all this had come about. How Mumty had appeared in June's life and after years, in fact just when they were in danger of losing everything, the vial had turned up with life-changing results. It was uncanny. Once again Tehmi had touched her wrist and twiddled the saffron thread round and round as she often did. She'd said thoughtfully, "Perhaps it really has held us together, even after all these years…" Seeing the puzzled looks on her guests' faces, she explained its significance and began telling them all about her childhood memories of India with her beloved rocking horse.

David then butted in on June's account to Mirabel, saying that when Cyrus and he had risen to replenish everyone's drinks, the trainer had said quietly to him, "I haven't heard her talk about this for so long. This might really help her; she has the most awful nightmares over our mother's death, you know. It affected us both, but she has suffered secretly because she never speaks about it. I'm so happy she can talk again. Perhaps seeing Mumty after so long has done her good." At this point in the telling of the tale, Charlotte had a faraway, nostalgic look in her eyes. Cobweb and I glanced at one another knowingly. So, it wasn't just the Duchess who had suffered night-visions.

Jacs took over the story from there saying the evening then became rather emotional. It may have been due to consuming a bit too much after dinner brandy or perhaps it was the soulful way Tehmi had recounted her memories, but they had felt magically transported back to her mansion in India as they listened. She'd described her charmed childhood and how the whole family had avidly followed their own and the Aga Khan's racehorses back in England. Tehmi explained how they'd taken their precious rocking horse Mumty back and forth to India over the years, how she'd been named in honour of the Aga Khan's brilliant filly Mumtaz Mahal, who was never really theirs but had felt as if she was. Many years ago, that mare had been responsible for their successful breeding empire as their father had acquired many relations carrying her blood. Everything had then been lost since his death and the outbreak of the war.

Lastly, she'd told them about her grandfather's wonderful gift of a husband for Mumty, a Marwari stallion carved in the image of Rustom Pasha but with the famous hallmark ears. Later, they'd celebrated the arrival of the exquisite rocking foal (with lyre ears) to honour the birth of Mumtaz Mahal's real live daughter, Rustom Mahal, who was born in Ireland. The women were captivated with the whole story. David and Eddie vaguely recognised these illustrious equines from racing's hall of fame, but for June and Jacs, this wasn't just history. They felt a real connection to these names that were as familiar to them as their own relatives. They had spent years absorbing these legendary horses' genes into their modern bloodlines, and now it was as if Tehmi was bringing their heroes to life.

Tehmi had explained about the vivid coloured saffron thread, how Fu Ling Yoo had gifted one to her, her brother and each of the horses with his promise that it would always re-unite them. After the untimely death of their mother, she told how their desolate father had rushed to escape to England, almost leaving Mumty behind. She'd added dramatically, "If it hadn't been for my hysterical screaming fit, I'm sure Papa would have forgotten to bring her with us. I needed my Mumty, she was always my comfort. Never more so than after losing Mama. I refused to leave the house unless she came with us. Of course, the other two were left behind..."

Jacs had whispered incredulously, "Yet your Papa knew your mother had hidden the family treasure in her? That's very odd."

"Well, he was so distraught; I don't believe he could think straight or knew what he was doing. That's what grief can do to a person,'" she added with emotion.

Suddenly everyone had felt quite drained and decided it was time to retire as they planned to leave early the next day.

Jacs then told her audience how just before heading to her and Eddie's guest room, she'd turned round to her host and voiced what had been on her mind since hearing the end of the tale. "Tehmi, I suppose that beautiful little foal and Mumty's husband that you had to leave in India are now lost, gone for ever? Aren't you terribly sad at losing them?"

Tehmina had smiled sweetly and said in a most casual manner, "Oh no, my dear, they're here, up in the attic. Goodnight, Jacs."

Well, after hearing that, there was no way she'd sleep until she had let June know the exciting revelation that probably the most unique and beautifully carved horses they would ever come across were languishing in the attic above their heads! She'd softly knocked on the door of June and David's room and when her friend appeared, looking at her inquiringly, she'd said with stifled excitement, "You'll never guess what I've just been told…"

Well, we couldn't imagine how Charlotte might be feeling after hearing that her own little family was alive and well, and actually here, in Newmarket! We both gave her a covert, sideways glance, trying to gauge how she had taken this news. She certainly looked very odd, as if she was holding her breath with wide staring eyes and very still. We didn't dare interrupt her in her deep trance-like state.

This was all too much for Mirabel; her mouth had fallen open as she grappled with everything she'd heard and its wider implications. "What about Seb's job?" she enquired hesitantly.

Eddie then finished the saga, relating how the next morning before they departed, to Sebastian's absolute delight, Cyrus offered him a job as second jockey, to start at the beginning of the flat racing season in March. That gave him a few months to help at home with the predicted busy foaling time. He concluded that the farewell had been warm and genuine, each feeling they'd found true friendship in this new partnership. Nothing had been formalised on paper yet, but this in itself re-assured both David and Eddie that no surreptitious take-over was being planned. They hadn't been pressurised to sign their lives away. Perhaps they were being over-cautious, but early naivety had turned to cynicism over the years, having dealt with unscrupulous people on several occasions. Mirabel nodded wisely; she'd had a few concerns over how fast everything was moving, but hearing this allayed all her fears.

Mirabel turned to Sebastian, congratulated him warmly and added teasingly, "So, you weren't too impressed with your new boss's great-niece, then?"

Poor Seb pulled a face and retorted, "I tried my best to make conversation but she thinks she's right about everything. AND she told me she doesn't like rocking horses! WELL, I'm sorry, but that did it for me! I refused to speak to her again after that…and no, I don't like her. I don't like her one little bit."

The next few weeks had proved very busy and Seb's help in the yard had been invaluable. One Sunday, Jacs found time to tackle her beloved walled garden at Airborne Lodge. Her son wandered out to give her a hand as she was struggling with a huge overgrown rambling rose. She needed to prune back the tangled stems but was suffering from scratched and torn hands.

"Come on, Mum, let me do that," Seb said kindly, taking the secateurs from her.

Jacs stepped back gratefully and remarked, "The trouble with wild roses is that they're so pretty when they flower, you forgive them for ripping your hands open! They can be vigorous, headstrong and uncontrollable. Yes, they're hard to tame and they fight back – but I wouldn't be without them here. They make this patch perfect, full of cottage-garden charm. You either love' em or hate 'em!"

Seb had done a skilful job on the rambler and sitting down on the old stone bench beside his mother, he said thoughtfully, "Funny you spouting on about wild roses like that, you could've been describing Nazrin. When I was trying to be nice to her, I said she had a pretty name and she told me it was Persian and meant 'Wild Rose'. Huh, more 'wild' than 'rose' in her case. Anyway, you're right; you either love or hate them. I hate them." With that, he stalked off and left Jacs wondering about her son's strange comment. Nazrin had obviously been in his thoughts and on his mind. Good or bad, she's left an impression on him and that made Jacs smile fondly to herself. She went indoors thinking how contrary teenagers could be.

★★★★

# CHAPTER 15.
## A WILD AFFAIR

T hat Christmas of 1991 was a wonderful time. In December, I was happily ensconced with my family back at Airborne Lodge with Fireworks. Everything had slipped back into the old familiar contentment we had always enjoyed in our home before that year of the virus. Cobweb and Charlotte were also revelling in the atmosphere of newfound peace and security at Wick House. The four of us basked in the knowledge that we'd pulled off the biggest miracle in rocking horse history. The future looked bright.

Our people were now feeling confident about the viability of their blossoming business and decided to celebrate by treating all their friends to the party they'd been promised. A massive get together was planned which would run from Christmas Eve through till Boxing Day. There was an open invitation for Christmas Day itself for anyone who didn't have family commitments, and for those who did, they could attend on either of the other two days. As we still had one empty lodge on the estate, our people were able to invite everyone to whom we owed a debt of gratitude, as space wouldn't be an issue. The partners wanted to repay all their friends for the work and help they'd offered us so unselfishly through our 'dark days'. Having the lodge accommodation enabled anyone who had travelled far or had consumed alcohol, to be able to sleep over comfortably. The guests included Wick Stud staff old and new, the New Forest gypsies, Manfri and his sister Sinni, her son Roybin, grandson Joby and the two cousins, Oxo and Billybob. Although always referred to as cousins, no one had ever quite worked out whose cousins they actually were! Brenda was invited, as were the owners of the local stables who had kindly housed our horses after that devastating storm. Family would be there too: Eddie's mother Ethel, Grace's daughter Izzy, her husband Alec, Mirabel and her daughter Suki. Even June's elderly parents promised to attend for one of the evenings.

*'Those who joined you in battle should eat at the table of your victory party.'*

Jacs had been making plans for several weeks before the event. She had organised all the catering, arranged when the marquee would arrive and who would be available to help erect it. Having a marquee was David's brilliant idea – he didn't want to risk anyone getting cold and wet if the weather turned nasty. They decided to have a huge outdoor log fire and the fire pit would be utilised as a

BBQ option for some of the evening food. A massive buffet would run during the days, but a traditional lunch indoors was planned for Christmas Day itself. It was a big undertaking but as the guests were all good friends, everyone said they'd pitch in to help, so Jacs was very relaxed about it.

As she sat at the kitchen table, she went over her guest list checking that no one had been left out by mistake. Jacs knew that all those who had been invited had accepted with enthusiasm, but she could not rid herself of a nagging feeling that she'd forgotten someone. Then the horrible truth hit her. She shouted to June from the kitchen, "Quick, in here. We have a bit of a problem..."

June looked mystified as Jacs asked her the reason why they were holding the party. "To thank all our helpers, and they're all invited and all coming, so what's your problem?" her friend answered, looking perplexed.

"But who's helped us the most, above anybody else? Who actually got us out of our mess? Who's given us SO much?" Jacs asked, pressing her friend for an answer.

Suddenly the penny dropped and June said guardedly, "Oh no, oh no... you're not suggesting we should have invited the Ferozshahs! Seriously? You can't think they'd lower themselves to attend our crazy, rough and ready BBQ booze-up... They wouldn't want to come, they'd hate it. No! Bad idea."

But Jacs said she felt awful that she hadn't even thought to invite them; she said it was ungrateful, insensitive and downright rude. "What will they think if they hear through the grapevine that we're having a massive thank you party and haven't asked them? We're being inverted snobs thinking they'd hate it. I'm sure it wouldn't really be their 'thing' and they might not want to come, but we HAVE to ask them," Jacs said firmly.

"OK, go ahead then, but I hope they think up a good excuse not to. It'll be so difficult if they do, no one will be able to relax and have a laugh. It's bad enough that my parents are coming…" June added sullenly.

Impulsively, Jacs got straight on the phone to Tehmina while she had the courage, to tentatively ask if she and Cyrus would like to attend a small informal 'get together' around Christmas time. She gave the woman every opportunity to make her excuses, saying she knew it was a busy time with family commitments and other social engagements and she wouldn't be offended if they couldn't make it. To her dismay, quite the opposite answer came gushing down the phone.

"Oh my dear, how awfully sweet of you to think of us! I'll check with Cyrus but I know I'd simply love to come! It's dreadfully boring here and I would just adore seeing you all. And I can see Mumty again! Wonderful! Thank you so much, dear."

Jacs sat heavily on a kitchen chair, feeling deflated. "What have I done," she thought.

A few days before the big 'do', I was brought over to Wick House to make more room at Airborne Lodge. The place was being thoroughly cleaned and cleared of excess furniture, which was being temporarily stored in a shed. The spare bedrooms were made up ready for Manfri and Sinni. June had pointed out that the other younger ones could happily sleep anywhere, but these two deserved a bit of comfort. Although they looked and acted so much younger, they were actually in their eighties, as elderly as June's parents.

That evening in the sitting room with us all present, a rather sheepish Jacs made her admission that the Ferozshahs were now also invited.

"Oh well…it'll have to be silver service then," David said cheerfully.

"Oh no," Eddie cautioned with mock seriousness, "perhaps we should hire a butler."

"Oh hell's bells. My future boss is coming? I won't be able to swear, get drunk or have any fun. I'll have to be on best behaviour," groaned poor Sebastian.

June added hopefully, "They'll probably decline. It's really not something they'd enjoy, they'd be roughing it."

Then Jacs had to break it to them that it had been confirmed, Tehmi had phoned earlier to accept with pleasure. They had moved their engagements about so it was possible for them to attend on Christmas Eve day.

"Don't worry, dear, we won't impose for too long and we've booked ourselves in at the little B&B in your village to stay over, as it's a long drive back and we're not spring chickens anymore!" Tehmi had said so happily, with excitement in her voice.

Jacs was actually glad she'd invited them now and defended them fiercely. "We wouldn't even be here or having any sort of party – except perhaps a leaving do – if it wasn't for them, so don't be so ungrateful and mean!"

Seb answered sullenly, "Oh well, I suppose we do owe them. I promise I'll behave…just so long as they don't drag 'Wild' along with them…" He got up and headed outside to do a final check on the pregnant mares.

"Who or what, may I ask, is 'Wild'?" Seb's father enquired, amused and intrigued.

Chuckling, Jacs told Eddie that this was Seb's nickname for Cyrus' great-niece. She explained that 'Nazrin' meant 'wild rose' and Seb had concluded that she was more 'wild' than 'rose', hence the nickname.

"Oh, all this fuss about the girl he disliked intensely?" Eddie remarked, winking at Jacs.

"Yes, the girl he's only met once but keeps mentioning," she answered grinning widely.

"The lad doth protest too much, methinks!" Eddie declared with a knowing smirk. He despaired of his son's reluctance to find himself a girlfriend. Mirabel's daughter Suki had always adored Seb, and although he liked her as a friend, it had always been a case of unrequited love. When asked what the problem was, he'd answered that she didn't much care for horses, so she didn't interest him. Whereas Nazrin had ticked all his boxes concerning horses, but she'd killed any interest he may have had by declaring she disliked rocking horses. That was the end of that.

Well, after the huge drama of the past months and the emotional highs and lows of producing a miracle, it would be rather unfair to say that the four of us were now feeling a bit bored because that's too strong a word. Let's just say that we thoroughly enjoyed intrigue; it filled our days with something to talk about. We had all noticed Seb's strange behaviour and decided to watch closely. I dearly wanted my lad to be happy, so we all decided we'd not interfere, but we should try to help. The fact that Nazrin was not keen on rocking horses was a challenge in itself. Perhaps we could change her mind...

The big Christmas bash proved to be a resounding success, an amazing occasion that was fondly remembered by all the guests for years afterwards. Many people turned up on each of the three days. There was never a dull moment, groups of friends and family chatted animatedly with each other, seated on the many chairs arranged on the lawn outside or in the marquee. Delicious food appeared magically out of the Wick House kitchen in relays, and wonderful BBQ meats were periodically produced off the outdoor grill. Everybody took turns in cooking, serving and tackling the never-ending washing up. It was a great team effort with everybody still having time to sit and socialise and no one feeling they were unfairly burdened with work.

Christmas Eve day had started with a surprise. The working party of old friends had arrived the night before to help erect the marquee and set up everything ready for guests arriving at 11 o'clock. Brenda drove in first, followed by the local stable owners, and then Mirabel and the stud staff appeared once all the work had been done. At midday on the dot, an opulent Ferozshah vehicle glided up the drive and came to a halt. From its interior emerged the elegant brother and sister attired in the most surprisingly warm and practical clothing, but managing as always to look immaculately turned-out. Both June and Jacs had envisaged Tehmi appearing in a fashionable but flimsy haute couture outfit, dressed to impress but perhaps not suitably attired for an outdoor December 'do'. Instead, she sported expensive pure wool tweeds and buckskin leather knee-high boots with sensible heels. She was wrapped in a thick cashmere shawl and matching beret. Cyrus, as always, looked extremely dashing in a beautifully tailored suit with a three-quarter length camel overcoat on his shoulders. He touched his Homberg in a gesture towards Jacs and June who were ready to greet him, but then proceeded to open the rear passenger door to let out a third person. It seemed 'Wild' had come after all!

Seb was standing behind Jacs, ready to welcome his new boss, and she heard him let out a stifled groan as he spotted the vivacious, attractive teenager approach. As the adults greeted one another warmly, Jacs listened to the two youngsters who spoke through clenched teeth.

"Oh, hello. I didn't know YOU were coming," Seb said icily.

"Not by choice," she muttered back darkly.

"Oh dear, well we can't have everything our own way," he'd answered sarcastically.

Jacs was highly amused as none of the animosity between them was truly convincing and she noticed that as Nazrin stalked off to join the party, Seb's eyes followed her into the distance. Only a mother would notice these things, she thought to herself.

The Ferozshahs were a surprise all round. After explaining apologetically that they'd had to bring Nazrin as she was staying with them for a month to learn about stud management, they headed off to mingle. Within minutes they had melted seamlessly into the crowd, chatting happily to everyone. Tehmi was offered a chair sitting next to Manfri and his family. She conversed with the cousins, intrigued to learn of their skills in renovating the beautiful estate lodges, which she found charming. Then she and Manfri wandered over to Airborne Lodge, him telling her all about its history and how it had been christened after the Derby winner of the same name.

Later, they entered Wick House to view us horses and Charlotte was delighted to see her sweet Tehmi again. Quietly she approached her horse, her great childhood comfort, and stroked that elegant neck as she had done countless times during her youth. Then she produced something from her handbag and knelt down to deftly attach it around Charlotte's ankle. It was a bright saffron thread to replace the one her dear Mumty has lost many years ago. Manfri had witnessed the tender moment between them and wondered... Then the woman had spotted Fireworks, cooed how lovely it was to see the little chap, and the two had instantly cuddled up on one of the sofas. When Manfri saw the connection she had with her childhood horse and heard her story about Mumty, to our utter surprise, they began discussing their memories of when they'd been young and what we had meant to them. All three of us were touched to hear this. Manfri mentioned Grace's bleak childhood and how Cobweb had been her only friend and comfort. He told of his harsh days in the orphanage with his sister, and how I was by their side to help them through that awful time during the war. He mentioned how he and Sinni had rescued me from the dreadful fate of nearly being burned alive atop a bonfire. Tehmi was transfixed. Manfri was an excellent story-teller at the best of times, but now, with his receptive audience, he was in his element. The pair of them agreed that rocking horses were more important than most people realised. They weren't mere toys; they had provided friendship and comfort to countless children worldwide. Tehmi admitted that after losing her mother and then Mumty, she'd been unable to look at a rocking horse without feeling distress until recently. Seeing her precious horse again after all those years had somehow been cathartic and had helped her deal with past traumas that she'd buried. The woman told Manfri it had been her lucky day when Seb had phoned them, as meeting the family had changed her life. They must have talked for nearly an hour till Cyrus came looking for his sister. He and Sinni had been happily conversing but became curious about where the other two had gone. Now, standing together, they all marvelled at how similar the four of them were, being so bonded with their siblings. It was a rare and wonderful thing for a brother and sister to remain so close throughout their lives.

At 4 o'clock, as Mirabel and the staff headed back to tend to the horses, Eddie suggested the Ferozshahs should accompany them to the stables so they could have a look at Varasha and some of the other mares. Seb trailed behind the group, not wanting to be left out but hating to appear too keen in front of Nazrin. However, when Mirabel started showing off their animals, his passion took over and he came forward, telling the guests all about each mare, their race records and the previous foals they'd bred. When he started reciting their bloodlines going back several generations, Nazrin also forgot the cold war between them and joined in with enthusiasm, comparing the similarities of sires and connections to her own family's mares. They talked animatedly between themselves, unaware that the others had moved on.

"Hey, you just HAVE to come and see my most favourite of this year's foals," Seb declared with excitement as he led her to the weanling's loose-box, gazing over fondly at his pride and joy.

"Wow, that's an exceptionally well-grown filly with perfect conformation! I'd say she's probably the best I've seen this year," Nazrin added with genuine admiration. "Whatever colour do you think she'll turn out?"

Seb was happily relating how she'd unexpectedly changed her foal coat and as she was a direct throwback to The Tetrarch there was a good chance she'd inherit his rare 'chubari' colouring. He also explained that because of the way things had turned out, they could now keep and race her and so they'd decided to name her 'Charlotte's Rubies'.

All of a sudden, Nazrin's mood turned dark and she retorted, "What a silly name. Anyone would think those blessed rubies were the be-all and end-all of life. And who's Charlotte? Don't you mean Mumty? Anyway, I don't like rocking horses or boring rubies, so I hate that name. It's rubbish as a name for a racehorse…" With that, she ran to catch up with her family, leaving a shocked Seb feeling as if someone had slapped him with a wet flannel. He skulked back up to the house, resentful and confused.

*'Love and hate are nearly one.'*

My poor lad did not relish the idea of joining in the merriment outside. Light had now fallen and the log fire on the lawn was roaring, throwing out enough heat to keep everyone warm. Seb sneaked back into the dark, empty sitting room to sit with me as he often used to when he was younger. He would pour out his troubles and I would be a friendly ear, a comforting listener. This day, he slung his arm over my neck and told me his dilemma. He'd really tried hard to be pleasant, but that Nazrin girl was impossible – one minute they were getting on fine, the next she'd turned really nasty for no good reason. He also told me that she'd again mentioned she didn't like us rocking horses, which I thought very odd. Now, being a wise old rocking horse, I've found there is always a reason to explain strange behaviour; it's a matter of working it out, getting to the bottom of it. I also knew that Seb liked her more than he realised; she had got under his skin. As I was musing to myself, Seb said aloud, "There's got to be a reason why she's so moody and changeable. I'm going to treat her as a challenge and find out what goes on in that wild head of hers. I'll get her to meet you and change her mind," he rambled, adding with hint of a smile, "I really don't know why I give two hoots what she thinks of me…perhaps I do like her a tiny bit?" He looked at me and we quietly laughed. We always had been on the same wavelength.

Seb went back outside feeling calm and confident with his new strategy, a plan to handle Nazrin differently. A joyous sight greeted him: people had started to dance as Joby and the cousins played Irish jigs on the guitars they always brought to social gatherings. Sinni and Roybin were banging out rhythms on spoons and an old board. All the youngsters were up and jigging when suddenly Manfri approached Tehmi, took her hand and pulled her up to dance. It was heart-warming to watch so many people from different walks of life all enjoying each other's company and having such unadulterated fun. June and Jacs swirled each other around on the lawn, giddy with too much cider and thrilled with the success of their party. June's parents had come to join in the festivities, happily tucking into platefuls of food and engaged in conversation with Cyrus and David. Seb had joined Mirabel's daughter Suki and the others who were doing a crazy step dance with the yard staff, when he spotted Nazrin out of the corner of his eye. She was not having fun. She was sat by herself moodily gazing into the flames, her pretty face lit up by the fire, but etched in frowns. Nazrin looked thoroughly miserable. Seb was a kind lad and he just couldn't hold a grudge so he left the others and made his way over to her. He asked her casually if she wanted any food, as he was going to load up a plate for himself. "Go on then," she answered neutrally, "nothing too fattening though…" she shouted out after him. He laughed and retorted, "A lettuce leaf and a tomato, then!" The ice was broken.

They spent the rest of the evening happily talking 'horses', Seb steering away from topics he knew she was sensitive about. But after a while he just couldn't resist mentioning the rubies. He started by saying gently, "I know you think everyone's making a big deal over those rubies, but can I explain something? They are very important to us because if we hadn't found them and told your family, we would have lost all this! My home, all our precious horses, the lot."

She looked at him for a moment and said sourly, "Money, money, money, how I hate money. I hate having it, I hate people knowing who I am and being nice just because I'm rich and related to my great-uncle. And those rubies just prove my point. You lot are only being nice to us because of them…"

Seb frowned and answered, "You're so wrong. 'My lot' as you put it, never wanted or asked for a single penny from your family. It was Cyrus who was keen to do business with us because of our excellent bloodlines and yes, it's got us solvent again, but you should get your facts straight. And," he added firmly, "I never went begging for a job either. He wanted me because I'm good. Everything isn't always about YOU…" Seb trailed off at that point, feeling embarrassed and hoping he hadn't caused another rift between them. He got up and hurried indoors to do his stint on the washing up.

We, of course, were watching the whole proceedings of the party from our sitting room window, thoroughly enjoying the sheer delight of our families and friends celebrating their 'come-back'. However, the scene that we'd just witnessed left us with sinking hearts.

It was getting late and very soon after that conversation, Nazrin was summoned to leave with Cyrus and Tehmina so they could get to their B&B before it closed its doors. Jacs and June bid them farewell, saying they were welcome to join them for an informal roast turkey lunch the next day. Tehmi hugged the women and said they really had to be home by lunchtime, but she couldn't remember the last time she'd enjoyed herself so much; it had been a memorable day. Cyrus smiled warmly, Nazrin smiled wanly, thanking them meekly and hurrying into the back of the car, keen to escape. They promised to drop by in the morning for a coffee before setting off on the long drive back to Newmarket.

Hearing this, Seb felt it may offer him an opportunity to smooth things over with this girl whose behaviour he found unfathomable. So when they arrived at Wick House the next morning, he acted pleasantly and asked Nazrin if she'd like to see the historical plaque of a racing shoe which hung on the front door of his house and hear the story behind it. Surprisingly she agreed, so they headed off to Airborne Lodge to view the curiosity and then sat on the front doorstep to talk. Seb had cleverly held her attention by weaving his tale around the Derby winner Airborne's great day and his own family's involvement in the famous race. He told how his grandfather had gifted his father the actual shoe that the great horse had worn when he won the race. His dad had then made a replica of the plaque to be hung on the Lodge door to christen his parents' first home together, which had been an amazing wedding gift to them from June's parents. It was all a part of the history of his beloved home and Wick Stud, he'd explained with feeling. Nazrin had been so wrapped up in the fascinating account that she'd softened enough for Seb to try a new ploy to get through to her. He apologised for snapping at her the evening before and said he'd really be interested to know her side of the story and why she didn't care for her family's rubies and the huge wealth they had brought them.

She sat stock still for a moment as if making a decision, weighing up if perhaps she was being trapped in some way. Nazrin suddenly reminded Seb of a nervous filly he'd once dealt with, one that nobody could get near. He'd eventually won the horse over with patience, but he recognised that same look, the mind deciding whether to take flight or put up a fight. He held his breath and the moment passed.

"Have you ever heard of the paradox of values?" she asked rather condescendingly, deciding to give him a chance to understand how she felt. He admitted rather lamely that he hadn't, so she continued brusquely, "Imagine you're in a desert, dying of thirst but with your million pound ruby in your pocket. A stranger approaches you with a glass of water and offers it to you in exchange for something. All you have to give is the ruby worth a thousand reservoirs of water; water which compared to a rare, precious ruby is usually an everyday commodity. What would you do?" she asked triumphantly, feeling proud of the analogy she'd presented him with.

"I'd give him the ruby for the water to save my life, no question," he answered, intrigued.

"I rest my case," she continued, feeling she had the upper hand. "Now you see why I think the rubies are worthless. The paradox tale proves that value is only relative. They are only useful as currency for what's important. We'll never sell them so they're not worth actual money to us, they'll be hidden away because they're deemed so valuable. No-one would dare wear them in case they get damaged or lost, and although they're beautiful to look at, no-one will ever see them in case they get stolen. It's a useless waste of time having them. A curse in fact, because of the worry and stress they cause. They are nothing but trouble and that's why I hate them," she concluded defiantly.

## 'Better an honest enemy than a false friend'

Seb was thoughtful for a moment; he understood her sentiment but still wanted to make a point of his own. He knew he'd made a fatal error of judgement as soon as his words came out. "I do see your point – but you've missed MY point. To us, those rubies were exactly what you've described, they were our currency to save our business, can you not see that?"

Nazrin was furious and glowered at him; she felt he'd belittled her effort to explain her feelings. Who was he to tell her she was wrong? Her flashing hazel-yellow eyes had turned quite hostile as she said in a low but controlled tone, "I really don't care what your point is. I was simply answering your question. I don't give a fig what you think or do, and I don't appreciate being cornered and tricked into a conversation like this."

As she stormed off, Seb felt angry and annoyed with himself. She'd been eating out of his hand but he'd pushed her too far and his wild filly had bolted. Sadly, the disheartened lad decided that, although fascinating, Nazrin just wasn't worth the effort any more. 'Wild' was nothing but trouble.

# CHAPTER 16.
# NEW BEGINNINGS

The New Year of 1992 started with a wave of activity. January was always a busy month for studs as they aim for their babies to be born early in the year. A Thoroughbred foal's official birthday is always counted as January 1$^{st}$ and this determines in which age group it will race. Early foals have the advantage as they are bigger and stronger than others born later in the year. Wick Stud was lucky to have seven mares foal early in the month with Varasha being the first one to give birth. She had a big strong colt, the son of a Derby winner who now belonged to the partners as part of the Ferozshahs' reward. June telephoned Cyrus to give him the good news of the birth with heart-felt thanks, which he waived graciously. He then inquired how they were coping with the busy 'baby boom'. June answered wearily that they were managing but everyone was exhausted due to having worked through several nights with more long days expected. This was when the trainer asked if they could do with an extra pair of willing hands. Cyrus started in a persuasive tone, "I was wondering if you would consider taking on my great-niece for a couple of weeks' work experience. You would be doing me a huge favour; you see she just can't get any 'hands on' practice here. I suppose we're just too big, it's up to the stud manager and assistant vet to decide which of our trainee staff are allowed to help. Nazrin has no opportunity to get involved here. She's getting frustrated and fed up not being able to learn the practical side of things. I think she'll make a good stud manager one day, you know. She's dedicated and can recite pedigrees off by heart. And she's not afraid of hard work!" This put June in an awkward position; it was difficult to refuse his request. She said she'd confer with the others and ring him back.

During the elevenses coffee break the following morning with Seb, Mirabel and the partners present, June voiced Cyrus' request. "Whilst I've got you all here, what are your thoughts about an extra person to help us through foaling time? It's someone who wants to do work experience, apparently very diligent and willing to learn. Handy for the night shifts on 'mare-watch', perhaps?" June added hopefully.

"If he's willing to wade in doing 'mare-watch', I say a definite 'yes'! Anyone who wants to help out on that job can only be a blessing," Eddie said gratefully. Staying awake all night to ensure the mares were monitored whilst foaling was a necessary but exhausting task.

Mirabel enquired how much experience he had and Jacs added that it must be someone responsible with good references.

June then mumbled, "Tons of horse experience, comes highly recommended and it's actually a 'she'. It's Cyrus's niece, Nazrin."

Then June added apologetically that she felt they could hardly refuse as the trainer had requested this as a personal favour.

Everyone agreed they would have to give her a try and she may well turn out to be very useful. Everyone, that was – except Seb. He remarked disdainfully that actually she was Cyrus' GREAT-niece and probably not a barrel of laughs to work with. "As long as she keeps her distance from me and isn't going to live in our house, I suppose I'll have to tolerate her," he added begrudgingly. The partners assured him there was plenty of room in the staff's North Lodge for one more, to which he answered, "Thank goodness for that! Put her in the one furthest away from here."

By the way, all this information was related to me by Fireworks, who had eavesdropped at Wick House and rushed over to tell me the news. He'd said that although Seb sounded sulky, he had heard an undertone of excitement in the lad's voice. "It was thinly disguised, but I detected slight pleasure when he heard her name mentioned…you can't fool a cat," he finished triumphantly. As you can imagine, the four of us had been watching closely as the Seb and Nazrin saga had unfolded. We all hoped for a happy ending, but the way things were going, it could be a case of 'tears for souvenirs'.

Cyrus was delighted when June phoned to invite Nazrin to do a fortnight's stint at the stud. A week later, she was dropped off by her chauffeur and appeared at the front door with a designer leather hold-all over her shoulder, wearing an expensive bright pink, down-filled jacket and beautifully cut lime green cord trousers. Not many could have pulled off wearing that colour combination, but it worked beautifully for her, accentuating her large yellowy-hazel eyes, olive skin and dark, glossy shoulder-length hair. She was slim, petite and moved with natural grace. There was no doubting Nazrin was exceptionally pretty. David had hit the nail on the head earlier when he'd accurately remarked that the Ferozshah women would have even looked fabulous wearing hessian sacks!

As soon as Nazrin entered the kitchen, Seb mumbled a brusque greeting and marched straight out the door. Jacs apologised for her son's curt behaviour, but the girl was unfazed, saying boldly, "He doesn't much like me, does he? Well, that's fine because it's mutual and I'm here to work hard and learn – not to win a popularity contest. I'm really grateful to you for letting me come. I know you probably didn't have a choice because of my great-uncle, but I won't let you down."

Although June was taken aback by the girl's frank comments, she smiled sweetly and offered to show her to the lodge. "As soon as you've settled in, unpacked and changed into work clothes, make your way to the yard and meet everyone. You can get stuck in straight away," June informed her kindly.

"Thanks, I'd love to start as soon as I can, and...these ARE my work clothes," she commented casually.

Whatever else she may have been, Nazrin was the perfect student. She was eager and quick to learn, implementing everything she was taught in the practical management of the pregnant mares in her care. Stockmen are born, not made and this girl had natural intuition and an affinity with horses. She instinctively knew when a mare was ready to go into labour or if any were off-colour, and seemed able to predict a potential problem before any real signs appeared. Nazrin proved to be an asset, an invaluable help to the stud and everyone was impressed with her work ethic. On the other hand, the staff felt that, socially, she was stand-offish and outspoken almost to the point of sounding rude. They all agreed she seemed to have a chip on her shoulder and held everyone at arm's length. Sebastian had tried to keep his distance from her, but working night shifts had thrown them together. He couldn't help feeling drawn to Nazrin like a moth to a flame, but nowadays he was wary of getting scorched.

After a week of being around her, Seb came and sat by me for our usual catch-up. He just couldn't voice his emotions to his parents. "Blitziboy, what's going on with me?" he whispered. "Wild is so good with the horses, actually she's amazing! I really get on with her when we're working, we just gel so well and she's just as passionate about the mares as I am. But we clash dreadfully in other ways. She hates boys 'cause she thinks they only like her for her looks and her money. I really want to get to know her but she's such hard work," he'd finished sadly.

Things came to a head during Nazrin's last day at the stud. She and Seb were doing their final night shift together. The mare in question was due to foal that night, but at 2am, Nazrin had sensed a problem. She told Seb she thought the foal was positioned wrongly and the mare would have trouble delivering her baby. "I think you should wake Mirabel. Tell her to phone the vet, I'm sure something's not right," she'd pleaded.

When the vet arrived and checked the mare, he complimented Nazrin's good instincts and prompt action. Without his help, he added sombrely, they may have lost both mare and foal. They all worked together to bring a wonderful new life into the world, sound and healthy. Both youngsters were spell-bound by the miracle of birth and spontaneously hugged each other to celebrate the moment. Nazrin had then pulled away stiffly. When an awkward Seb thanked her for spotting that the mare needed a vet, she'd spat out, "It wasn't rocket science," and rushed off huffily. By now, Seb was fed up with her behaviour and felt he'd tolerated her mood swings for long enough. She was leaving soon anyway so he had nothing to lose and, for once, he decided to go after her. When he caught her up, he swung her round by her arm and demanded to know why she was treating him with such hostility. "I've only ever tried hard to get along with you. What have I done that's so terrible?" he demanded.

Nazrin was silent for a moment, then gazing down at her now filthy designer jeans and soiled boots, she said quietly, "I think it's because I quite like you really. And I don't want to like you. So leave me alone." With that she'd struggled free and hurried off back to the staff lodge to pack, ready for her departure later that day.

About an hour before Cyrus was due to pick Nazrin up to drive her back to Newmarket, Seb went looking for her. She was lying low at the lodge with her packed bag by her side, waiting to escape. The lad marched in and told her to follow him as he wanted her to meet a 'friend'. Seb strode off towards Airborne Lodge with Nazrin trailing reluctantly behind. He grabbed her hand and brought her in to our front room straight up to me and ordered her to sit. "I want your honest opinion about this horse," he said firmly. "What do you see?" he demanded.

"It's a blooming rocking horse!" she snapped. Seb told her to look closer, to really study me properly. She spent a full minute walking around me, studying every detail of my fine carving and taking in the beauty of my graceful galloping stance, admiring my flowing mane and peering into my shining eyes. "Where's your friend, then?" she asked, unable to wrench her gaze away from me.

"You're looking at him!" Seb said with a lopsided smile.

They both sat together on the sofa and Nazrin admitted that I was a work of art, beautifully and realistically carved and graced with an exquisite face. She said my eyes were almost alive, that I wasn't scary and crazy like most she'd seen. "I dislike the ones that have thick legs that are all wrong and wouldn't work in real life. This fellow could spring off that stand and gallop off into the sunset," she whispered appreciatively.

"Do you still hate rocking horses or have I changed your mind?" Seb asked.

She looked back at me and said kindly, "Let's say I'm warming to them and this one is the most amazing one I've ever seen, he reminds me of one..." Here she trailed off, never finishing her sentence, but the fight had left her and she turned and smiled at Seb with genuine warmth.

Seb told her I was his friend and confidante and he often spoke to me when he felt unable to talk to people. Nazrin looked almost envious in a wistful way and said quietly, "I wish I still had someone like that sometimes..."

At that moment, Jacs appeared at the door, telling the two of them to hurry over to Wick House for a de-briefing and that Nazrin should say her goodbyes to everyone before Cyrus arrived. Another stolen moment, Seb thought, but one he'd hold on to because he'd briefly glimpsed the real girl.

Later that morning, Cyrus had whisked Nazrin away after he'd received a glowing reference for his great-niece. The partners were full of praise and told him how she'd been responsible for averting a potential disaster for a mare and foal due to her quick thinking. Cyrus had swelled with pride and the girl had almost blushed, thanking everyone for her enjoyable and thrilling two weeks with them. As they were leaving, she turned to Seb and said softly, "See you, mate." Seb was quietly thrilled and took that as a sign of progress, a step forward in their tempestuous relationship.

Fireworks had witnessed Seb and Nazrin sitting and discussing me earlier when my lad had dragged her in to inspect me. He wasted no time in scampering back to Wick House to tell Charlotte and Cobweb what he'd seen and heard. They were delighted for Seb when the cat had added smugly, "Mark my words, there's a romance brewing there, my friends. It may be on the back burner for now – but I'll bet my stripes it'll happen!"

★★★★

# CHAPTER 17.
# REVELATIONS

B y the end of February, Wick Stud had only a few mares left to foal. They had experienced a wonderful two months with not one loss and a healthy crop of beautifully bred babies who were thriving along with their mothers. A new full-time member of staff had arrived to replace Nazrin as there was a very full and busy time ahead for everyone. Sebastian was about to leave and embark on his new and exciting career as second jockey to one of Newmarket's leading trainers.

Seb's mother Jacs adored her son and, with him being an only child, she knew she would feel his absence keenly. The two had always been close. She would miss him dreadfully and worry non-stop about his safety, knowing the profession he'd chosen was a rather dangerous one. She also knew she must allow him to spread his wings and make his own way in life. That meant him taking risks, learning from mistakes, choosing the right path and hopefully making good decisions, all without her interference. Jacs felt that she and Eddie had done their utmost to educate their son in a way that had given him a solid grounding and the best tools to navigate his way through life.

## 'Knowledge is valuable, insight is invaluable'

Before leaving for Newmarket, mother and son had a heart-to-heart talk. Seb thought he should disclose how he felt about Nazrin and was surprised that his mum seemed to know all about his turmoil of conflicting emotions. She'd said kindly, "I'm your mother so I knew you liked her very early on, maybe before you even realised." When Seb admitted he found the girl very complex and was struggling to unravel the workings of her mind, Jacs decided to let him in on the huge Ferozshah family secret. She thought it would help him understand Nazrin better. She proceeded to drop the rather surprising bombshell on her listening son.

"I'll tell you something, Sebbi, but strictly between us two, mind. I was told in confidence so don't let me down. When she was younger, the poor child lost her beloved brother who was everything to her, she had no other friends. The thing is...he was her twin and that's the problem with twins; they are so wrapped up in each other that they sometimes find it hard to let outsiders in. And then of course, when you lose a twin, it can hit you very hard and I suppose she's never got over it. It's coloured her whole life ever since."

Seb's jaw dropped open at this shattering revelation; he never knew she'd had a sibling, leave alone a twin. He was truly shocked, and as he processed this information, he began to see Nazrin in a new light. Jacs explained that Tehmi was so distressed about what had happened to her grandson that she never mentioned it, but Cyrus had told the partners the whole tragic story in confidence. He'd wanted them to understand why he'd taken her under his wing and was always fighting her corner and encouraging her to follow her passion for horses. Nazrin had proved to be a somewhat problematic child after losing her brother and had clearly become out of control. Her mother had almost given up until Cyrus stepped in and managed to get through to her. The two had always been close, bonded by their mutual love of racehorses. He had counselled her, offered her direction and guidance, and had supported her totally through the difficult years.

When Seb finally managed to speak, he uttered in a subdued voice, "Wow, that's a shock, I had absolutely no idea. However did her twin die?"

"Well, it was a horrible accident. Apparently he was born with epilepsy and occasionally had seizures. He was only nine. It's all terribly sad because he had a fall whilst fitting and suffered a fatal bang to the head," Jacs answered quietly.

"But where was he - when he fell?" Seb inquired, keen to know more about the tragedy.

His mother's answer was the missing piece of jigsaw he'd needed to understand this troubled girl. Everything now fell into place. "Oh, it was dreadful because it happened right in front of poor Nazrin, just imagine that. Apparently, he fitted and fell whilst he was riding his rocking horse."

### 'Kick on!' A jockey's advice for dealing with life.

Once Seb had left for Newmarket, life at home continued as usual, but I certainly missed my lad. The lodge felt so empty and quiet without his presence and our little chats. He had come to talk to me just before he went; pouring out the whole awful tale he'd heard from his mother. I'd listened, horrified at the image that came to me of a small girl witnessing her beloved brother dying in front of her. No wonder her childish mind had somehow pinned the blame on the rocking horse he had tumbled off. That prejudice and the painful memories had remained with her. I felt hugely sorry for what she'd been through; I had always known there had to be a reason for Nazrin's strange dislike of us. Poor old Seb would have his work cut out with this one; she may prove a lot harder to manage than his temperamental racehorse fillies, but I knew he had immense patience and a heart of gold. It may take a while, but I knew he would try his best to win her round.

Seb was similarly affected by what he'd heard from his mother. He went off to Newmarket excited to be starting a new dream job with a trainer he'd always admired, yet his thoughts kept drifting back to his boss' great-niece. She pervaded his thoughts no matter how hard he tried to clear his mind. His hopes of seeing Nazrin at Cyrus' house or yard were soon dashed when he realised she was not there. Of course she and her mother, Teresita, lived elsewhere. Funnily enough, Seb had no idea where that was or what the girl was up to nowadays, and it struck him he actually knew precious little about her. He decided to forget about Nazrin, keep his head down and put all his energy into riding to the best of his ability. All he wanted was to make a success of the wonderful opportunity he'd been given. When news came through the grapevine that she had gone abroad to stay with her estranged father for a few months, Seb felt relieved. Perhaps now with her many miles away, Nazrin would stop haunting him, her image would fade and he could get on with life.

It didn't take my lad long to re-establish himself as a natural, clever and talented jockey. Although Seb had taken a year out after being crowned leading apprentice, his many successes that summer put him back on the map. Everybody was ringing up Cyrus Ferozshah to ask if Sebastian Marland could ride their horses, but the shrewd trainer kept him busy on his stable's own quality inmates. Of course, his strength had always been in managing to tame the flighty or awkward female equines that other jockeys found difficult. Now he had forged a marvellous partnership with one such animal that no one else had been able to ride, a little filly with the strange name of 'Inscrutable' – and they were making the headlines. It seemed they won every race they entered, and the pair enjoyed many triumphs at the most prestigious meetings. It was a wonderful time for Seb, excelling in his profession and enjoying the life he'd dreamed about.

He regularly phoned home to chat excitedly to his parents, often talking proudly about his famous filly. Of course, I always listened in. Jacs had hoped her son had managed to put Nazrin to the back of his mind, but a casual comment made her think otherwise. Laughing affectionately, Seb told her he'd nicknamed his star filly 'Wild', as she was so wayward and difficult. He'd added, "But she's a diamond really, we just click and she'll do anything I want as long as I don't boss her. I have to ask her nicely! Huh, she's definitely sweeter than the real Wild, that's for sure!"

"Have you seen Nazrin lately?" Jacs asked innocently, not wanting to appear intrusive.

His answer was short and sharp: "Nope – she seems to have disappeared off the face of the Earth. And that suits me fine."

Jacs had detected a twinge of regret in his voice; she knew her son too well.

By the end of that 1992 season, Sebastian and the champion filly Inscrutable had won six consecutive valuable races. They had become a household name and the press had had a field day, referring to them as the 'dynamic duo'. Young Marland was a popular choice for interviews, being articulate, modest yet informative. His genuine love of the sport and passion for his little 'wild' filly shone through. Great things were expected of the pair for the following season and Seb was flying high, excited at their prospects.

Then some news reached the Ferozshah stables that shattered everyone's hopes and dreams for the future. Their star filly would not be racing next year. Her owner had decided to retire her to the breeding paddocks in case she suffered an injury; Inscrutable was now far too valuable as a potential brood mare to be allowed to race any more. This was a blow to my poor lad, who felt her owner was being unsporting and extremely unfair. The filly was young and sound and had a lot more talent to show. The man was depriving them both of doing what they lived to do and what they did best: winning races. It was a decision driven by finance and Seb couldn't help but hear Nazrin's words ringing in his ears. Her 'paradox of values' idea was at work here, in a twisted sort of way. It seemed ridiculous to him that a racehorse was valuable because it won races. But if it was excellent at its job, it became a liability, deemed too valuable to be allowed to race again. The ultimate racehorse became a horse not worth the risk of racing. Just like the rubies, too valuable to be worn, enjoyed or seen. Nazrin had a valid point, he thought bitterly.

Seb was devastated. Not only would he dearly miss the little mare he'd come to love, but she also represented his hard-earned ticket to success. No one else had even managed to coax her to race, leave alone bring out the very best in her. These talented horses only came along once in a while during a jockey's career and now their partnership was being cut short in its prime. Seb was due to return home for the winter and was glad to be having a break from his dream job that had turned rather sour. He felt let down, angry and strangely empty. Cyrus noticed how miserable Seb had become and invited him to his office for a 'chat'.

Once seated in front of his trainer, his bitterness overflowed and he began to voice his opinion on the situation, giving his version of the paradox of values. Cyrus laughed and looked fondly at him uttering, "Hah, you sound so much like young Nazrin…well, let me explain to you what I've told her in the past. It's actually all down to economics. Supply and demand. There is a constant and plentiful supply of potentially good horses coming in to prove their worth. But, there is a much bigger demand for the very few horses who have actually proved their worth, making them more valuable as breeding stock. It's simple economics, son. But I will do my best to buy the filly back for us to race next year, you have my word."

Seb then said something he regretted afterwards. It just slipped out before he could stop and think. "I really miss her…" he whispered.

The trainer instantly knew who he was referring to. He looked hard at the dejected lad and simply answered, "So do I, son."

As he walked back to his lodgings to pack for his departure, Seb cursed himself. Oh, why did he always make a fool of himself in front of this man? Why was he always saying the most idiotic things?

Back in the office, the trainer sat for a long while thinking about his grand-niece and also appreciating that his talented little jockey really was a lovely lad. He found Seb to be kind and genuine and thought Nazrin would be very lucky to have the lad's support. Only good could come of a friendship between the two of them. He also decided to try very hard to secure Inscrutable and return her to his yard. But even the greatly respected Cyrus Ferozshah could do nothing to persuade the owner to sell the stable's star performer to him. Despite all his wealth, the trainer was powerless. Money meant nothing to this owner and the esteem he placed on his animal could not be bought.

# CHAPTER 18.
# REUNIONS

I was excited that my boy was coming home once again. I'd missed him. Whilst eavesdropping on his parents' conversations, I'd swelled with pride at the wonderful successes my Seb had notched up all summer. From the first time he'd sat on me as a tiny toddler, I just knew he would be a talented rider. But my pleasure was short-lived at the news of the loss of his partnership with Inscrutable. It was up to me to offer a comforting ear when he returned and would undoubtedly approach me for a chat. Seb was learning that life in general, and racing in particular, was peppered with triumphs and failures, the heights of euphoria and the depths of depression. It was all a part of life's rich tapestry. The trick, I had learned over the years, was to dust oneself down and look forward to better times on the horizon.

### 'Today is merely yesterday's tomorrow'

About a week after his homecoming, Seb began to settle happily into his old routine back at the stud. He adored this work and dearly loved the old brood mares and their offspring who offered hope for the future. It didn't take him long to recover; in fact, he bounced back. On his first day home, he'd hurried out to the paddock to see his favourite baby, Charlotte's Rubies. The lovely-natured filly had recognised his voice and had whinnied a welcome as she'd charged over to greet him. Seb had hugged and stroked her, running his hands all over her shapely body. She had matured into a stunningly beautiful equine with an unusual and eye-catching coat colour. He just couldn't believe how she'd changed and grown through the summer.

Mirabel and the other staff surprised him with a cautionary tale and a warning to be careful around her. They described her behaviour as rather erratic and unpredictable. Although a kind, sweet creature who meant no harm, she was easily spooked and quick to jump and bolt at any sudden loud noise or movement. Her reactive behaviour had already caused several accidents in the yard. One poor soul had been knocked to the ground and dragged along whilst leading the filly. Another young lad who had recently joined the stud had been squashed against the stable door when she'd suddenly rushed out. Oh dear, his special foal had turned into a highly-strung, potentially dangerous teenager. Seb had to laugh to himself; his life seemed full of temperamental females, and he remembered his mother once saying how wayward and trying her thorny ramblers could be – "...but I wouldn't be without them," she'd said, "you either love 'em or you hate 'em." He equated those beautiful wild roses to the 'fillies' who surrounded him now and, like his mother, he knew he wouldn't want to be without them.

Early in November the partners, Seb and Mirabel were summoned by June to a surprise meeting. It began by discussing a solid plan for the future of Charlotte's Rubies, but ended with her making an astonishing announcement. The gathering was to be held at Wick House and Fireworks got wind of the news through Cobweb, allowing him to make sure he was present to be able to report every detail back to me. It was at times like this that I wished we rocking horses all lived under one roof. Perhaps I am guilty of being somewhat nosy, but I really hated not being present at important events like this. I also missed the company of my friends, but then I suppose when we did meet up, it was all the more pleasurable.

At the meeting, it was agreed that Roobs (everyone called her that due to her lengthy full name) could be quite highly-strung and would need treating carefully if she was to reach her full potential. Sensitive horses can easily be ruined through rough handling by uncaring people. It was unanimously agreed that although she didn't have a bad bone in her body, she must be treated with respect. Seb was to have full control of her care and give her quiet, consistent and gentle education. He would teach her how to accept a rider on her back and to comply calmly with stable rules. She needed a rider she could trust completely – only then would the filly be able to face the rigorous preparation needed to become a racehorse. Next spring, under the guidance of Cyrus and Seb, she would enter the world of racing. Everyone was hoping Charlotte's Rubies would be Wick Stud's greatest star yet. The anticipation was palpable; she had a lot resting on those pretty spotted shoulders.

It was just the exciting challenge Seb needed. The project filled him with delight. Both he and Jacs had doted on the 'butterfly foal' once she'd returned home again after the storm and their dream of keeping her had come true. Earlier, Roobs had undergone a thorough vetting and was pronounced perfectly healthy despite her difficult start and unsettled year. However, the vet did notice she possessed what he termed politely as a 'heightened awareness'. "She's just a bit of a nut-case," Seb had jested, "I'll take her over completely. Don't worry; I'm used to her sort, it's what I do best and that type are my bread and butter."

After all other stud business had been concluded and people were getting ready to leave, June stood up and declared she needed everybody's attention as she'd made a life-changing decision. Everyone plonked down again looking quizzically at June's serious expression, but noticing her shining, excited eyes. Even David was in the dark about this surprise announcement.

"As you know," she started after clearing her throat, "I've loved being hands-on with the stud, but my forte has always primarily been seeing to the estate paperwork, stud business, insurance, bills and the like...and I'll still continue with that side of things but, I am taking a step back from the horses. I've decided, after months of thought and planning, to follow my dream. My big passion in life!" She looked round the room expectantly with a happy grin, but no one reacted.

"What are you going on about, June. I haven't the foggiest what you're trying to tell us," groaned a confused Jacs.

Then David piped up with "Yes, love, please explain. What passion?"

"Rocking horses, of course!" she almost screamed. "I'm going to do what I've wanted to do for years. Restore rocking horses. Buy, rescue and collect beautiful rocking horses till they come out of my ears!" June then sat down meekly after the outburst that had surprised even her.

*'Passion gives us energy and purpose,
which is the very essence of passion'*

After a shocked silence, Seb started giggling and declared that his aunt June had 'lost it, big time' as he put it, but that he was delighted for her. The others looked unconvinced, but Jacs leapt to her friend's defence: "No, why ever not? That's a wonderful idea and you deserve to do absolutely whatever you fancy. We're only here once and we should follow our dreams. Good for you, June!"

Any sceptical comments about finance were quickly quashed. June reassured everyone that she was planning to use her own savings to set her plan into action. Eddie mentioned that as all the stables were in use, where was June thinking of setting up some workshop space?

"Ah," she replied mysteriously, "that's all in hand, I've more big news for you…" June then went on to explain that her parents had recently made a big decision; they wanted to go and live in their holiday villa in Tuscany. They had told her that while they were still of sound mind and in good health, they intended to enjoy a few years eating delicious food in warmer climes. That left their own house, Holmwood Hall, free for June to use however she pleased.

The Holmwood Wick estate had been built in the 19<sup>th</sup> century and consisted of the large Hall, the smaller Wick House, built for the original owner's son and the three lodge cottages which had been home to various staff who had manned the coaching stables, grounds and gardens. It was a magnificent place and we all felt privileged to live there. But it was expensive to maintain, and the success of the stud business was integral to the estate's viability. June had given her new venture a lot of thought and had done her sums carefully. She did not intend to put the estate at risk, but felt confident that she could build up a business of her own within a couple of years. After speaking to Brenda, she realised that she'd never make enough money from just restoring her rocking horses. Restoration was skilled and labour-intensive work with small returns. It would be a learning-curve and a labour of love that she'd have to support by finding other lucrative avenues. She already had many exciting ideas.

When this news had sunk in, David fetched a decent bottle of wine and poured everyone a glass to raise a toast to his clever and ingenious wife. "I'm proud of you, love," he crooned, "I'll support you all the way and I know you'll make a roaring success of it, you always do!"

June was swept away with passion for her vision and proceeded to tell them of her bigger plans. "Yes, it'll be all change round here, but fear not, you won't be losing your homes. David and I may move into the Hall to look after it. I can use my parents' garage and outhouses as workshops and eventually…I want to open a rocking horse museum!"

As the wine flowed, so did the ideas. Everyone was full of enthusiasm and endless possibilities were mentioned.

"I've made arrangements to go down to Dorset for a few months to do a course in restoration with Brenda – but I'll be back every weekend," she admitted.

"Oh, so Brenda's in on this? Have you two been scheming in secret?" David asked with mock hurt.

June told them she'd mentioned it a long time ago and when the rubies had bought them security, Brenda had encouraged her to re-visit the idea. "If people are worried that you'll never sell any of your rocking horses, you don't have to. Sell some but keep the ones you fall in love with and start a collection. You could open to the public and charge people to visit," Brenda had said convincingly.

June grew excited at the thought – she'd envisaged giving a home to many lost souls, rocking horses that may have rotted to death or been burned on bonfires if she'd not have rescued them. "I think I'll place an advert in antique and country home magazines asking for all old and forgotten horses to be brought to me for restoration to then be placed in my museum!"' June rambled on, flushed with emotion.

"Hey," Sebastian interrupted, "I've just thought of a cracking idea! Why don't you also make your own horses? You could offer to make our owners a bespoke rocking horse in the image of their big winners. That way, they have a family heirloom for them and their children for ever. A bit like Mumty was for the Ferozshsahs! And you could carve foals! A rocking foal of their favourite baby, to stay a youngster in perpetuity. Oh, the possibilities are endless."

June was taken aback by the suggestion – it sounded marvellous but she knew she didn't have that sort of skill. The others encouraged her and Eddie added, "You'll learn; look how good you were at furniture restoration and French polishing."

But June was doubtful until Seb was struck with another clever thought and said mysteriously, "Well I know a man who can. A man who could probably do it and teach you. Perhaps he could branch out and go into business with you?"

"Who?" everyone shouted, intrigued that Seb should know such a person.

"Joby," the lad declared triumphantly, "the best carpenter and carver of the most beautiful animals I've yet to see. He's sick of his present job and has been making and selling his chain-saw log sculptures in his spare time. I'm sure he'd jump at the chance to hone his skills as a rocking horse maker. He knows horses inside out."

Finally, Mirabel enquired what would happen to June and David's lovely home, Wick House, if they moved into the Hall.

"I've considered that too," the woman mused; "this will still be our stud's headquarters and my office. We can still convene here for our daily coffee breaks and meetings. This can be where we entertain important clients and owners, the bedrooms can be for guests or as an overflow for staff accommodation. But one day, you never know, Seb may want a place of his own. He could live upstairs, a sort of self-contained flat within the house but sharing this kitchen. What do you think, Seb?"

"Oh my goodness, June! How absolutely fantastic of you. I love the idea; it's a wonderful, generous offer, and yes, yes, I'd love that... one day!" He glanced at his mother who smiled approvingly at him and nodded a silent thanks to her best friend.

June's final announcement was to remind everyone that they would again be hosting a Christmas party this year, but this time, a slightly smaller affair. Then she declared the meeting was over and added she knew it was a lot for everybody to take in, they should all sleep on it and discuss finer details on the morrow.

As they all parted for the night, each was absorbed in their own private thoughts on how June's major news-flash might affect their lives. It would be an upheaval, big changes lay ahead, but the future looked full of positive and exciting prospects. Fireworks had trotted home to our lodge behind Eddie, Jacs and Seb, and came into the front room to report to me once they had retired to bed. I was so keen to hear every detail but the little cat was exhausted and would only give me a brief precis of events. His mumbled words sent my head spinning. "Seb's going to tame the crazy filly, June's going to Brenda's to learn how to restore you lot and then buy hundreds and put them in a museum, and Joby's coming to make more of your lot with a chainsaw and June's parents are emigrating so her and David are moving into the big house and Seb might live upstairs at Wick

House and we're having another Christmas bash, and – oh I'm too tired to remember the rest. I'll explain more in the morning..." He promptly fell asleep curled up on my saddle while I was left to try and make some sort of sense of these garbled statements. I felt strangely excited at what I knew had been June's long-held rocking horse dream, coming to fruition. Hadn't I always said that idea was a winner?

Although life continued as usual, there was a buzz in the air. Everyone seemed filled with renewed energy and purpose. Seb had already started working on Roobs' education in earnest. He spent every waking hour with her, leading her all over the estate to familiarise her with different stimuli. He'd introduced her to saddle and bridle, and with a bit in her mouth, he taught her how to obey various orders, the ground work before riding her. June had decided to start her course with Brenda in the New Year, so got to grips tackling the paperwork to bring everything up to date. She promised to keep up to speed with the office work when she returned at weekends. Her parents packed up and left in mid-December for their adventure in the sun. The Christmas party was efficiently organised as usual by Jacs, who had already sent out invites and had some guest rooms prepared in readiness. Their dearest and oldest friends from the New Forest were coming and of course the Ferozshahs were invited again... Seb didn't want to ask if Nazrin might be coming with them. He dearly hoped she would – he missed her more than he dared admit to himself.

*'Absence makes the heart grow fonder.'*

Time just flew by and Christmas was upon us in a flash. A few days before the party, I was whizzed over to Wick House in the back of the pickup truck to be reunited with my much-missed friends. We hadn't seen each other for months and had a lot to catch up on. Charlotte told us she'd felt unsettled after that meeting, mainly due to overhearing the mention of rocking foals. She wondered if she'd ever see her husband, Pasha, and little Pashmina ever again. The second evening I was back, we all heard it clearly – June and Jacs were talking in hushed tones in the kitchen and definitely mentioned Charlotte's family. After they'd discussed the last-minute party food arrangements, they started whispering about how they planned 'to bring up the subject' in front of Tehmina.

"If we tell her all about my plan to open a museum and how I'm going to trawl all the country houses around here to find hidden attic horses, surely she'll take the hint and offer Charlotte's hubby and baby to us?" June had said hopefully.

Jacs replied that she couldn't understand why she hadn't already; she obviously found it too upsetting to have the two on show in her own house. Tehmina had told her they were in the attic, a magnificent Marwari rocking horse stallion and a foal just wasting away out of sight.

"Perhaps we'll just grab the bull by the horns and ask her outright if we can give them a loving home?" suggested Jacs, adding fondly, "Wouldn't it be lovely to be able to reunite The Duchess with her old family from India?"

Cobweb and I looked over at Charlotte with concern, but this statement from Jacs seemed to have transported her to a faraway place. Now deep in thought, fond memories had her gently swaying with a new warm glow in her claret eyes.

The day of the party dawned bright and mild. Everything had been planned and prepared beautifully by Jacs so that now, she felt she could relax and enjoy the highlight of the year. With great anticipation, she waited to greet her precious old friends again, particularly Manfri and the rest of his extended New Forest clan. The Ferozshahs were due to arrive and Seb was on tenterhooks, hoping beyond hope that Nazrin would come along too. At midday on Christmas Eve, the partners grouped outside Wick House ready to welcome their guests. Seb hung back, almost hiding behind everyone, sick with anticipation. As the Ferozshahs' sleek car pulled into their drive, the lad could hardly bear to watch as brother and sister alighted. After what seemed an age, Cyrus swung round to the rear door and let his great-niece out of the vehicle. Seb's stomach did a double somersault as he watched her approach and hug June and Jacs. She was more beautiful than he remembered; with a healthy glowing tan and looking fit and lean, she moved with an almost feline grace. Something about her countenance had also changed; she'd matured into a stunning young woman with a new air of calmness about her. Very soon her eyes searched for Seb and when their gaze met, a small smile was born on both their lips. Jacs watched with a singing heart as the two quietly strolled off together without words or fuss. It had been a sweet, gentle reunion, a natural meeting of kindred souls. Cyrus and Jacs exchanged delighted glances and he whispered in her ear, "Just what I was hoping for…your son will be the saving of that girl. She badly needs a friend like him."

She replied happily, "He's smitten! They'll do each other the world of good."

The nerves Seb had felt earlier just melted away; he was totally as ease in Nazrin's company. She too was relaxed and there was no awkwardness, both were just brimming with eagerness to tell each other their news.

"Cyrus hasn't stopped going on and on about you and Inscrutable and I'm so sorry you've lost the ride on her," she added with sympathy. "And he said you rambled on about the paradox of values, sounding just like me!"

Seb teased, "Oh, it's 'Cyrus' now, is it? Yes, it took me a while to see your point of view about the rubies...but I get it now."

Nazrin gave him a warm, grateful smile. "I'm too old to keep calling him grand-uncle now," she retorted and added graciously, "It took me ages to see the point you were trying to make, but I've had time to think and I get it, too. Lately, I've found out all about losing things you love. I can understand how those rubies helped you all to save what's precious to you. I've had the most wonderful adventure with my father and I've been helping him preserve something he loves passionately. It's been an emotional summer. I never knew about those hard struggles people have to go through... that's what comes of being a complete brat with everything handed to you on a plate since you were born! I've learned so much since being away."

"Oh, I want to hear ALL about everything you've been up to. I've missed you..." Seb blurted out, feeling instantly stupid.

But Nazrin was kind and answered steadily, "I've never missed a single person in all my life, since I was a kid, anyway... but I did keep wanting to tell you all about the mad, exciting things as they were happening, so in a strange way perhaps I did miss you, a bit."

Relief flooded through Seb as he replied, "Same here. I wanted to tell you every amazing detail about last season. I knew you'd understand all of it."

They decided to have a long catch-up later, but for now, they agreed they really should get back to the party and be sociable. Both felt strangely peaceful and content as they split up to go their own way, chatting and mingling among the newly arriving guests and joining in with the merriment. Their relationship seemed on solid ground now. They had all the time in the world.

★★★★

# CHAPTER 19.
# FLAMINGOS AND
# FESTIVALS

The Christmas party was in full swing. Manfri came to see me as soon as he'd greeted his old friends and could slip away. We sat in companionable silence for a while but I knew something was on his mind. Eventually he spoke softly, "Youz is lookin' a picture as always, forever young. Not like me, time's marchin' on for me, Bokky (he always used the Romany name meaning Lucky that he'd given me years ago). Don't know how many more times we'll be able to see each other like this. I'ze is gittin' old and tired now. Youz is the best liddle friend a young 'un could have had all them years ago an' I'm that fond o' you...but don't worry, when I'm long gone, you'll be teachin' Seb's kids an' grankids ta ride, for sure!" With that, and a long, warm stroke down my neck, he rose slowly and strode out. It was never mentioned again but his strange conversation left me feeling unsettled. Cobweb and Charlotte both gave me a pitying look, but I soon shrugged the incident off. I didn't want to think it meant anything and put it firmly to the back of my mind, but it did remind me that people get old so quickly compared to us rocking horses. I knew at some time in the distant future I must prepare myself for losing loved ones; much as I couldn't bear the thought, it was all a part of the cycle of life.

Soon after Manfri's visit and while everyone else was busy laughing and joking outside, we rocking horses had more company. Seb and Nazrin sneaked into the quiet sitting room and sat near us, glad to have escaped the party activity. They were keen to talk and discover what each had done during almost a year's absence. With Fireworks perched on my saddle, we all listened intently to an exciting story that unfolded.

"So, where have you been all these months and what was your adventure all about?" Seb inquired earnestly.

Nazrin gazed into the distance as if transported back there as she spoke. "I've been staying with my father down in the south of France. It's the most beautiful, wild, windswept area of sea, marshes and ancient horses…"

Nazrin then explained that her father was a Gallic cattle herdsman and a protector of the very special breed of semi-wild horses indigenous to that area. He was one of a tough band of men who lovingly devoted their whole lives to preserving and managing the free-roaming herds that flourished there. These men were guardians of the Camargue horses and were known locally as 'gardiens'.

We were held entranced as Nazrin described the landscape, one of river deltas, lakes and flat wetlands filled with saltpans and rice fields. A world of fierce Mistral winds blowing over marshy bogs, home to pink flamingos and bands of robust mares and stallions galloping in the sea spray along the beaches till they merged to become one with the foaming white crests of the waves. She told Seb they were the most inspiring horses she'd ever seen.

"They're a world away from our cosseted racehorses. These are tough and feral and can survive on meagre rations. They are so well adapted to their homeland that they can thrive on a diet of marsh grasses, reeds and samphire. Oh, they're truly magnificent creatures! Not 'pretty', more noble and ruggedly handsome – not unlike those statues and friezes of ancient war horses hewn out of marble. There are many legends about them, how they were born in the sea spray and came on to land thousands of years ago. I bet they're one of the oldest breeds in the world!"

Seb was swept along by her passionate, evocative descriptions. Nazrin explained that Camargue horses were among one of the rarest breeds alive today and were now protected. Each and every foal born had to be formally identified to be entered in the stud book. But there were conditions and strict rules to be adhered to. Any that were born away from their homeland may be registered but were labelled 'hors berceau', but foals born within their region were the most coveted. They were known as 'sous berceau'. Registration was only allowed if the foal was born outdoors in the area of its natural habitat and was seen to be suckling from its purebred Camargue mother. These horses were never contained in stables but lived out in the elements all year round. It was such a tough existence, only the hardiest, most vigorous foals survived the harsh lifestyle and frugal diet. Her father had a small registered herd of his own, consisting of ten mares and an ageing stallion. He also had three purebred riding horses. The very best stock were left alone to breed but checked daily, along with his small band of Camargue bulls, farmed free-range for their meat.

Nazrin told Seb how she'd joined her father on his small ranch-like property consisting of corrals, a dilapidated barn, a grain store and his tiny medieval stone dwelling-house, which had only two rooms downstairs and a make-shift bedroom up in the loft. There was no real bathroom, she'd said and laughed, remembering the culture shock she'd suffered until she'd acclimatised to the twice daily cold bucket wash.

"It was pretty primitive living — but I absolutely loved every minute of it. Anyway, we were hardly ever at home, we were out riding practically all day long. These Camargues are the best horses for the job of rounding up the cattle; hardy, stocky little black bulls and their harem of wives. The horses know where to find them better than any of the men; they handle the terrain and know where the dangerous bogs are because they were born on the land and they have amazing stamina to keep going all day."

We were totally enthralled by now, but Nazrin proceeded to tell us another exciting piece of her French adventure. She continued, "Near the end of May, an amazing and ancient festival is held at the nearby town of Saintes-Maries-de-la-Mer. This event is to honour three revered saints, one of whom is Saint Sara or Black Sara, the patron saint of all nations of gypsies. It is a major Roma pilgrimage and many thousands of Gypsy travellers from all over Europe journey to the area to meet up with relatives, celebrating with dance and music. They pray and even baptise their children whilst there."

At this point, Seb butted in, apologising to Nazrin and asking if he may go and find Manfri. He wondered if she would be willing to tell her story to their lovely old Romany friend as he knew the man would be fascinated to learn of this marvellous festival. After all, it was a part of his heritage. The girl hesitated as she considered his request. For an instant Seb saw a glimpse of the old Nazrin – she looked like a filly about to bolt in panic. But the moment passed, and she said cautiously, "Only if you make him come alone and promise not to breathe a word to anyone else. My family aren't keen on my dad and I don't want them knowing what I've been up to…"

Seb grinned happily and retorted, "Don't worry, secrets are Manfri's 'stock-in-trade'!" and galloped off to find the old man.

While he was gone, a very surprising and touching thing happened that left us horses quite speechless. Nazrin rose from the sofa, approached quietly and looked upon us with the most radiant, gentle smile. She never touched us but gazed down and whispered, "Hope you're enjoying my tale? I don't know why I thought I hated rocking horses. You three are so beautiful, you actually remind me of my beloved sea horses prancing through the surf. I hope you forgive my awful behaviour in the past and we can we now be mates? Seb's right, you lot are really special. I was blind before – but I see you clearly now… And as for you, Mumty, we really should be friends. After all, you knew my grandma and great-uncle as children and they adored you." She then calmly sat herself down again and waited for the other two to return. That rare and wonderful smile she'd bestowed upon us had been like a halo of sunshine and we felt strangely blessed.

Manfri had been intrigued by Seb's insistence that he should come quickly and quietly back to the sitting room with him. Once out of earshot, the lad explained all about Nazrin's Camargue adventure and invited the old man to listen to the rest of her story which he felt would be of great interest to him. So, with a new addition to our audience, the young woman started her tale of the festival from the beginning.

Nazrin told us about the crazy, colourful event with its electric atmosphere and the fervour and excitement of the gypsies who had journeyed through many countries to attend their Mecca. We were spell-bound and actually felt transported to those narrow bustling streets of that medieval town. She described how a huge procession of gypsies followed the traditionally dressed gardiens on their sturdy white Camargue steeds as they led the teaming throng of people down to the sea front. Behind the horses came a select few men who carried the ancient statue of their beloved Saint Sara, held up high in all her glory, bedecked with many brightly coloured garments and adorned with jewellery. Once they had walked right into the lapping waves, the Bishop gave a blessing to Black Sara and the other two saints, and then, he also blessed the sea. This was an annual religious ceremony steeped in history.

The young woman's face was flushed from reliving her experience. She had been lucky enough to be one of the riders, mounted on her father's favourite Camargue mare, who had led the massive, reverent crowd down to the sea. She laughed as she remembered how her father had made her tuck her hair up into a borrowed Stetson so she would resemble a youth. He advised her not to utter a word as female gardiens were frowned upon. Nazrin had also managed to get a glimpse of the holy Saint Sara inside the tiny church. She painted a picture of that sacred interior, the intense heat and flickering light given off by hundreds of tall white candles that lit up Black Sara's dusky face looking down on her worshippers as they gazed at her in awe. Many chanting voices, prayers and reverent salutations echoed within, mingled with the peel of the church bells above. Outside, beautiful local Arlesian and gypsy girls wearing traditional dress, danced to many street musicians playing flamenco guitars, violins and accordions.

Also, a celebration was held to honour the area's local heroes, the gardiens. How splendid they looked, mounted upon their best horses, dressed in traditional garb of leather trousers, colourful floral shirts and wide-brimmed Stetson hats, as they proudly paraded through the streets, holding aloft their trademark three-pronged trident sticks. During the week, this small peaceful provincial town was transformed. All gypsies were warmly welcomed. There was no trouble or hostility. Celebrations went on for days with food, drink, dance, family reunions, parties and non-stop music everywhere you ventured. At the end of the week, everybody disbanded to hit the dusty road, leaving the little town to return to its sleepy, quiet self until the following year. Nazrin finished her story by saying it was one of the most fascinating and moving experiences of her life.

Her rendition of the festival had left Manfri strangely quiet. His handsome, weather-beaten old face had a new glow and his dark, tired eyes now twinkled with excitement. All his life he'd travelled with family from one fair to another around the country. It was an age-old tradition to meet up with other members of the clan and celebrate at these reunions with music, dancing and feasts. As time rolled on, these old ways had all but died out and he'd sorely missed this nomadic way of life. Nazrin's tale had awakened a deep yearning within his soul. After thinking for a minute, he leaned forward and looked keenly at the two of them. Then he grabbed their hands and in an intense whisper said simply, "Take me there!"

Much to our surprise, we listened on as a secret plan was hatched between the three of them and a solemn pact was made. Oh, how we loved a bit of intrigue! Somehow, they promised, they would get Manfri to the festival next May. They would both take time off from whatever they were doing to take the old man on a pilgrimage which would be the biggest adventure of his life. Nazrin was certain Cyrus would agree and persuade her mother Teresita and Tehmi to allow this trip for the sake of the old man whom they held in high regard. This could be the perfect excuse for her to make a return journey. She reluctantly explained that both her grandmother and mother didn't care for her father since he'd deserted them when she was about nine years old. She just said he'd missed his home, his horses and his way of life so terribly, he'd felt unable to stay, and the marriage had broken down.

Nazrin told us that she'd actually been born in France and originally they had lived at her father's ranch, but when she reached the age of four, her mother just couldn't put up with the harsh lifestyle anymore and had forced the family to come home to England. Her father loved them dearly and stayed for five years, but then, she said sadly, "things went wrong and he just couldn't stay any longer". We knew the tragic truth, but Nazrin didn't mention anything about having a twin brother or his fatal accident. One day she might confide in Seb, but till then, her secret was safe with us.

She continued her story, explaining that when she was in her early teens, she had demanded to see her father, but was refused. After running away from home several times in defiance, Cyrus had come to her rescue and talked Teresita into agreeing to a short visit. He took her to France himself, where they'd stayed in a small local hostelry and had visited the gardien daily. Cyrus had formed a great bond with Nazrin's father, Gabriel. He'd developed a deep respect for the man who felt as passionate as himself about keeping and breeding the horses he adored.

The covert meeting was then disbanded and each melted away to mingle with the guests and socialise with their old friends, but their inner thoughts were elsewhere. Nazrin's description of the Camargue's magic had left a lasting impression upon us all.

# CHAPTER 20.
# KID GLOVES &
# KINDNESS

O ver those few days of Christmas celebrations, three important topics were discussed and decisions were made. Four, of course, if you count Manfri's secret future trip! They occurred as both our families and the Ferozshahs sat down to enjoy a superb lunch prepared by June on Christmas Day. Manfri, his family and the Wick staff were dining over at one of the lodges. At the Wick House gathering the conversation drifted to Nazrin's summer in France. She was quite vague and her description of her stay was so different to the passionate version we'd heard the day before. With a pleasant smile, she listed all the things she expected her audience would want to hear, leaving out any details of her father or her adventures at the festival. Nazrin told them how she'd brushed up on her French; how it had all come flooding back to her and how, within a week, she'd been able to converse fluently with the locals. She said she now had experience helping mares to foal in sometimes challenging circumstances and had gained valuable knowledge about the management of a semi-feral herd. Lastly, she felt she'd learned a lot about local Camargue culture and history, she'd even visited a local church. It had all been a marvellous education, she confirmed. Everyone seemed satisfied that it had been time well-spent, but her grandmother insisted that now, having had more than a year off, she should think about her future and make decisions about universities and which subjects she wished to pursue.

A horrible hush descended over the room. After an awkward minute, in a cool, calm and clear voice, Nazrin declared that she would definitely not be attending any university as she had made her own decision about her future. She would enter the world of horse breeding and stud management. It was a clever ploy – nobody wanted to have a family dispute around the table of kind hosts on Christmas Day. Tehmina's impeccable manners prevailed, and she graciously stated that perhaps they could continue the discussion at a more appropriate time. Seb had caught Cyrus's eye and the pair had dropped their faces to hide the shadow of a smile that had hovered on their lips.

Luckily, June leapt to Nazrin's rescue with her enthusiastic reaction, "That's wonderful news! We all think you have natural talent and an instinct for this business. You'll do so well! What's your next move?"

"Well," Nazrin deliberated, "I need a lot more hands-on experience and I intend to get a qualification in stud management and business studies. I want to do both simultaneously, perhaps a correspondence course? It will mean a lot of hard work and long hours, but I'm determined."

June glanced at Jacs; both knew what the other was thinking so she decided to forge ahead with a bold statement. "OK, Nazrin, I have a plan. Depending on what all us partners and your family say, we are willing to offer you a placement here. It will be a proper job, board and lodgings included, but the wages won't be much. We'll give you time and space to study and attend tutorials or whatever, but you'll be hands-on here, learning all aspects of stud work. You can help me with the books at weekends to learn the ropes of running a business. Interested?"

Well, Nazrin was not the sort of girl to gush or show emotion lightly, but now she declared with open enthusiasm that it was the most perfect offer that she could have dreamed possible. Reactions around the table were varied – Cyrus and Seb both grinned with approval, and the partners regarded the proposition as a positive move with benefits for all concerned. Tehmina, however, looked resigned but not unhappy with the idea. After the many dramas and difficult years they'd had with their wayward ward, her grandmother had to concede that time at Wick Stud could be the balanced environment Nazrin needed. She'd be well looked after and would receive education and guidance from people whom she trusted.

After her cleverly stage-managed conversation, the young woman felt pleased she may have secured herself a future at Wick Stud and of course it left an opening for June to announce *her* future plans, and that led to the second momentous decision, reached by Tehmi. June explained that she was going to be away during weekdays for the next few months, hence the stud's need for a new member of staff. She would be at Brenda's, attending instruction in rocking horse restoration. Her dream was to start buying, learning to restore and then collecting antique horses. June outlined her plans to create a place to house her future collection which eventually could be opened to the public as a sort of rocking horse museum.

She declared with enthusiasm, "I will visit auctions and search the attics of country houses and put out 'wanted' adverts everywhere to find old horses that need help or a safe home for life..." This statement was thrown out carelessly to no one in particular but subtly aimed at Tehmina.

Everyone was busy congratulating June on her determination to follow her long-held dream and the initiative for the museum idea, when Tehmi spoke up. "Oh, it's perfect, June! Now I can rest in peace over where to place my two lovely wasted creatures. The two my grandfather had carved for us back in India. I can be the first to help you on your way!" She added that it would give her great pleasure to donate the Marwari stallion, Pasha, and the little rocking foal, Pashmina, to June. She couldn't bear to see them on show in her own house, but she'd love them to bring pleasure to others.

Of course, we three and Fireworks had been eavesdropping in our usual manner from the sitting room so you can imagine how our hearts sung at this statement. This was the news Cobweb and I had been waiting for, not only for Charlotte's happiness, but for our own selfish reasons of being able to meet these fascinating characters we'd heard so much about. The Duchess was strangely still but her eyes shone brightly with joy at the thought of a long-held dream of the family reunion she had waited for so patiently during the last fifty years.

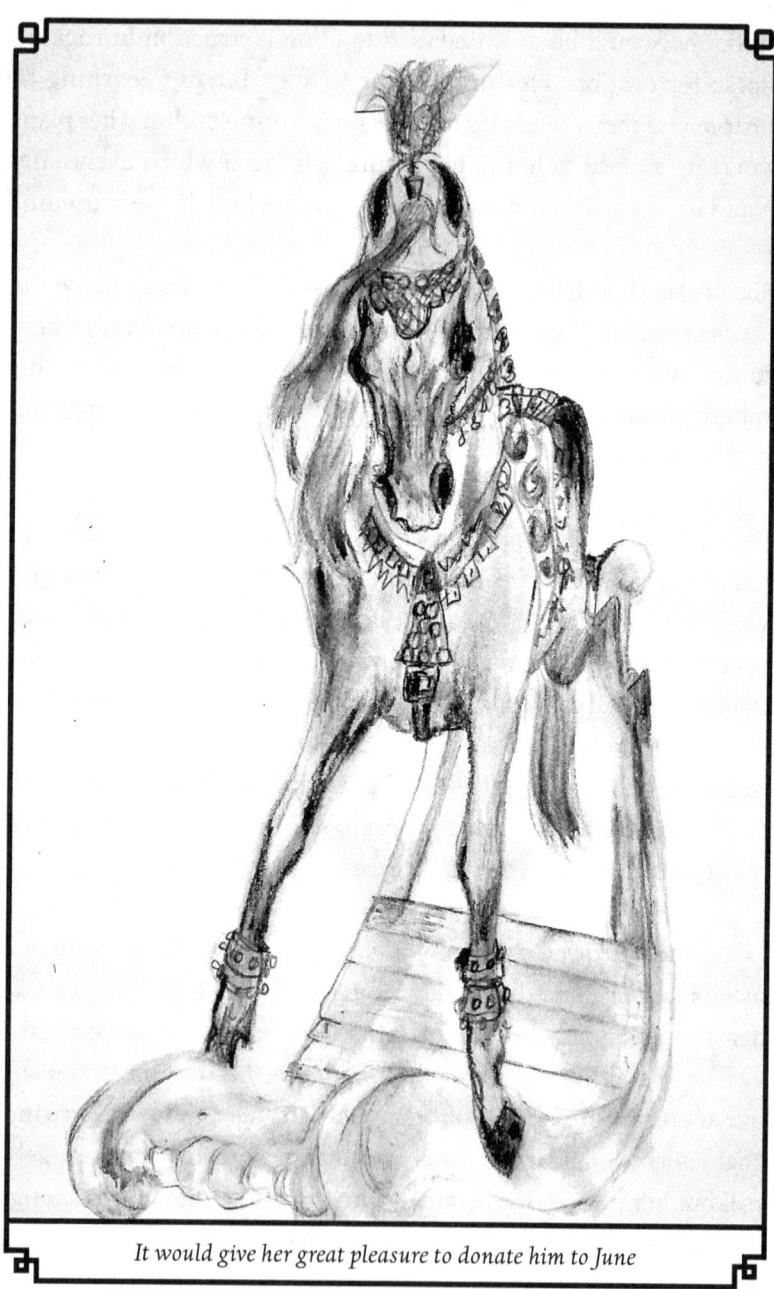

*It would give her great pleasure to donate him to June*

The third conclusion of that day was reached whilst the partners and their guests were enjoying port and cheese near the end of their wonderful meal. Everyone was basking in the glow of feeling replete and relaxed and enjoying pleasant company. Jacs tactfully brought up the subject close to Sebastian's heart, the future of their beautiful but temperamental filly, Roobs. The partners had not yet broached the subject with Cyrus, the idea of sending her to be trained by the great man himself. It was widely known that there was a waiting list for horses to be accepted by the Gwalior establishment to start their careers. Owners of youngsters were queuing up to have their horses in training with Mr Ferozshah, like parents hoping to enrol their offspring at the most prestigious of schools.

Cyrus listened kindly as Seb made a passionate case for his filly. The trainer told the lad that once he had ridden and tried her out at home, if Seb still believed she had raw talent, he would be willing to give her a chance. He added with confidence, "You say she's quirky? Some of the most brilliant performers are and I wouldn't hold that against her. You know the old maxim when dealing with fillies: treat them with kid gloves and kindness. You've proved you are more than capable of doing that. And I trust your judgement. So yes, I'll train her if you give me the thumbs up."

Cyrus was secretly relieved that his budding champion had regained his spirit and had recovered from the blow of losing Inscrutable. Seb was putting his energies into this new project and that made the trainer happy. But now the pressure was on, the filly would have to show her mettle and prove her talent to have any chance of joining the successful Ferozshah string of young contenders. The lad had a huge task ahead of him.

Before the traditional Christmas get-together was wrapped up on Boxing Day, June had approached Joby with an offer to work with her on her new rocking horse idea in the future. He was very enthusiastic and said it would give him great pleasure to be involved as he badly needed a change of direction in his life. Everyone was in agreement that Nazrin should join the staff at Wick Stud and it was decided that she would commence her new job on the 1st of January, while Sebastian would return to his Newmarket position at the start of the new flat racing season near the end of March. This gave him three months to work on Roobs; a tricky job he knew would be hard to achieve without some careful assistance. He could think of no one better suited for the task than Nazrin. He needed to put the proposition to her with a plea for help. She also had a big favour to ask of Seb. She hadn't yet told him of a huge drama that had unfolded during her time with her father and the dilemma it had presented. A situation she had left behind in France as unfinished business.

On the morning of the Ferozshahs' departure, she had led Sebastian into the deserted sitting room, saying she had to talk to him urgently. They plonked down on the sofa with all four of us listening on. Nazrin started in earnest, "I haven't told you half of what really went on at the ranch, it's complicated but I really need to tell you now, before I get dragged away..."

We were all ears.

"Go on then, you have my full attention," Seb said encouragingly.

"Well, it's to do with a very special foal I helped. He very nearly died but I pulled him through and now the authorities won't register him and there's a big debate going on. My father is heart-broken as he is the jewel in the crown of his breeding project and I'm the only one who was there when the mare foaled; I've somehow got to go back and fight Father's corner. You see, I ended up in hospital with suspected pneumonia and time ran out and I lost track of my only witness and…"

"STOP!" Seb hissed at her. "You're not making any sense. Start slowly from the beginning. Take a breath," he ordered.

So Nazrin took a deep gulp of air and started her incredible tale of woe.

"It was a normal day in July and we were out rounding up the last of the pregnant mares to check on them. Most had foaled but a couple were late that year. Suddenly, the sky was ominously dark and the weather turned nasty very quickly, as it can in that region. I was riding a wise old mare, Segolene, and she sensed something was amiss. It wasn't the awful storm that had whipped up in minutes. She was unfazed by these freak winds they call 'Mistral Noirs' – she'd lived through plenty of them. No, she sensed there was a mare nearby in deep trouble. I shouted to my father and the others, but they rode on, heads bowed, trying to get home as quickly as possible. But I just couldn't leave – so I gave Segolene her head and she took me to a clearing in the marsh only fifty yards off.

"There was a sight I'll not forget in a hurry. My father's favourite, beloved mare Fabulosa, bleeding from a deep leg wound, an artery nearly severed and heavily in labour. She was standing, swaying about, half in shock but knowing she had a job to do. I removed my leather belt and fastened it tightly above the cut as a tourniquet to stem the flow of blood—and it worked! For a long time I worked in that fierce storm to bring a new life into this world. Amazingly, I had help. Segolene had galloped off and was caught by a fisherman's son who brought her back to the clearing and actually saw the foal born. He helped me birth him from his exhausted mother and rub him down with reeds to revive him. He was a beautiful, rather small but strong, dark-coloured colt. We knew he must suckle soon to get the important 'first milk', essential for any foal's survival in that tough place. His mother had collapsed and was too weak to move, but between us we dragged the foal to Fabulosa's flank and helped him to draw milk from her. After an age of helping the two, I felt very unwell. I was freezing cold and soaked to the skin, so the young boy, who said his name was Milou, leaped onto Segolene and rode off to fetch help.

"Next thing I remember was my father picking me up from the hospital in Arles. Apparently, Milou had told the men at our ranch what had happened. They had hitched up a trailer to the Land Rover and driven to where the boy said we'd be. The storm had blown over, but I was collapsed in a heap when they found me at the clearing. Both mare and foal were alive, so they put me in the front, loaded them up and dropped them back home to continue on to the hospital. I was there for two days till the fever broke, then they allowed me to go home. Strong as an ox, me!" Nazrin concluded, stopping to take a breath and laughing at Seb's face which was a picture of shocked disbelief and worry.

"Wow, you don't do things by halves, do you?" Seb exclaimed. "But why was there a problem about registering him? And I can see why you couldn't tell your folks what happened… you'd never be allowed back to the French Wild West ever again!"

Nazrin's face was etched in sadness as she explained that Fabulosa had died the next day, leaving the orphaned foal to be hand-reared. When she came home from the hospital, she tended to that little colt, bottle feeding him up until the day she had to return to England. Her father was full of admiration for his young daughter's bravery in rescuing the foal and trying to save Fabulosa's life. He announced he would gift the colt to her and register him in her name. Nazrin decided to call him 'Mistral Noir' after the fierce windstorm that had nearly cost him his life.

The problem came later in October when the breed representative came to the ranch on his yearly visit to inspect the beasts of Gabriel's manade (herd) for 'marquage' or branding. The ranch's own individual brand had to be placed on the hind quarters of all his purebred Camargue horses in order for them to be registered in the stud book. The breed inspector was not happy and said there was a problem with Mistral. Where was his mother? Why was he not suckling from his dam? Why had he been brought down to the ranch? He should be living free on the marshes, he'd said with concern. The offered explanation of the outside birth occurring during a violent storm, the subsequent death of his mother and the fact he needed to be hand-reared seemed to make no impression on the hard-eyed official who refused to register him. The man stated he needed proof, witnesses, dates and details. He declared there would be a grand assembly of the Breeders Association and Stud Book Commission, and Gabriel must attend the meeting for a case to be heard in front of registration officials. Only then, if they were completely satisfied, could 'Mistral Noir' be deemed as a purebred Camargue with the title 'sous berceau' which would denote he'd been born in the land of his breed's birthplace.

Nazrin explained that this colt's registration was very important to her father. His small herd relied on a good stallion of the best lines to maintain quality. With the death of Fabulosa and his present stallion in his dotage, it was up to Mistral to continue the precious blood of Gabriel's life's work. She compared his passion for breeding his Camargues to that of Cyrus and his racehorses, and added thoughtfully, "I never knew how much these things meant to people. There are problems that can't always be solved by throwing money at them. I'm the only person who can save my father's herd. I have to go to that meeting and convince the authorities to register Mistral. But first, I have to find my key witness who has vanished into thin air, a small ten-year-old boy called Milou…"

Seb was stunned by the whole affair and asked what he could do to help. Just as Nazrin was about to outline her plan, Jacs appeared at the doorway, telling the pair that everyone was waiting to leave and they must say their goodbyes quickly, adding, "You'll be back here soon, young lady, you'll have time to chat then, now GO!"

As they headed to the waiting car, Seb whispered, "I'll help you to get to that meeting in France if YOU help me get my filly ready to be a racehorse!"

Nazrin gave him one of her warm, beaming smiles and answered, "Deal!"

★★★★

# CHAPTER 21.
# FACING A CHALLENGE

1993 proved an exciting year with projects coming to fruition and interesting friends appearing in our lives. Cobweb and I had become extremely fond of Nazrin; she seemed to have cast a sort of charming spell over us and I'm sure Seb felt exactly the same. Charlotte was more reserved, saying the girl possessed a heart bigger than she allowed the world to see and had potential, but still needed to prove her true worth as a Ferozshah. Fireworks remarked she was a complicated human, and he was too old to bother unravelling her female mind, but, he added, she did have an amazing grandmother. He was besotted with Tehmi and never stopped harping on about her.

In January Nazrin became a full-time member of the Wick Stud staff, just in time to assist with the usual rush of foals arriving. Life for her and Sebastian proved busy and rewarding as they helped with the most common miracle of all, birth. It was a miracle that no one ever got tired of seeing; it never lost its magic. Whenever they could spare a few hours, they would take Roobs into the paddock to continue her education. Her 'home training' was tackled in earnest; she was a wonderfully responsive filly to ride, being eager to please, possessing a soft mouth and perfect manners... most of the time. The trouble was her tendency to overreact to any sudden noise or movement which often caused her to bolt, a dangerous and difficult problem that needed careful management. She was also proving rather claustrophobic, which could be the biggest set-back to her career. Roobs needed to learn how to enter the large imposing 'starting stalls' without fear. Youngsters had to begin their races from these metal 'boxes' and they needed to be relaxed yet alert enough to sprint out with the other horses for a fair chance of reaching the winning post first! If she was to ever to be successful, Roobs must learn to conquer her fears.

*'True endeavour will always be memorable, no matter the end result.'*

The two of them worked tirelessly to prepare Seb's little filly for her future as a racehorse. They would often come and sit next to me at the Lodge as they drank their mid-morning coffee and discussed their strategies. I admit I loved being in Nazrin's company, she had an electric energy about her and it was good just to be near her. I felt like this when I was with my lovely Jacs. Some people have that quality and we rocking horses are sensitive souls. As I stood by and saw a very special bond develop between these two, I secretly hoped they'd build a future together. So, I fondly watched on as they plotted and planned and worked extremely hard to 'tame' the strangely coloured youngster.

Roobs was walked daily through the practice stalls with a special rug placed over her flanks to lessen the impact of the cold metal against her skin and to dull the noise of rattling ironwork. Soon, she became adept at this task and could be led or ridden through calmly. Next, the pair progressed to asking her to stand still within the structure, at first for a few seconds, later for minutes on end. Seb decided they had won a small victory when the filly stood within the practice stalls in a relaxed manner with both doors shut, happily munching on a carrot. Nazrin suggested they should 'up the ante' and raise the bar on Roobs' acceptance of stalls. She stated, quite rightly, that it was fine doing everything quietly at home, but at the racecourse the atmosphere would be frenetic, with heightened levels of noise and activity. Seb was grateful for Nazrin's help, which was proving invaluable. Her drive and ambition were similar to his; between them they made a strong team, working together in complete harmony. The young woman's imaginative ideas and novel ways of solving problems made the whole project exciting and enjoyable fun.

I was alone at Airborne Lodge and watched through the bay window one morning as the two of them put their latest plan into action. They were in the paddock at the bottom of our little orchard, so I had a good clear view. Seb was holding Roobs within the stalls whilst Nazrin was driving the stud's tractor in sweeping arcs around the pair. As the filly snacked on delicious apples, she was un-fazed by the noisy machine which drew nearer and nearer in ever-decreasing circles until it came to idle quite close by. Nazrin dismounted from her high seat with a huge grin and gave Seb a delighted 'high-five' hand slap. Many other innovative exercises were mastered under different circumstances until Roobs was as steady as a proverbial police horse.

I don't wish to bore you with details of how much hard work and dedication went into that little horse's education, but suffice to say that within three months they had taught her everything needed and expected of a youngster about to enter a training yard. During this time together, Seb and Nazrin had also discussed her own worrying problem. A deal was a deal – and he'd promised to help her resolve her dilemma. They thrashed out many ideas about how she should return to France to be able to locate her crucial witness and attend the all-important meeting to fight for Mistral's right to be registered. At first they had disagreed because the girl wanted to go in secret, but Seb had strongly advised that she should explain everything to Cyrus and allow him to help. Without his assistance, the plan could backfire badly.

A week before Sebastian was due to return to Newmarket, the trainer came down to visit and assess 'Charlotte's Rubies'. He was delighted with the filly's physical and educational progress. Cyrus agreed to accept her and said Seb could travel up to Newmarket with her in a horsebox to join the Gwalior yard. Whilst the two were alone with him, they asked him back to our Lodge for an important private chat. Intrigued, he followed them into our front room and accepted the offer of tea. Seb prompted Nazrin to tell Cyrus the whole story of Mistral's birth as it had unfolded (but wisely leaving out her episode in hospital) and the problem it had presented with the registration official. She ended her tale by saying she was only confiding in her great-uncle because Seb had insisted.

She knew he would understand the huge importance of the colt's acceptance and what it would mean to her father. Cyrus felt touched that the youngsters were asking for his help and relieved that Seb's level-headed-thinking had curbed Nazrin's impetuous nature. He knew that without the lad's influence, she'd be halfway to France without telling a soul. He resolved not to let them down; he must devise a solution, a way to get the job done. As the trainer drove back to Newmarket, he felt satisfaction in knowing his great-niece was flourishing and that she had found such a stalwart companion in Sebastian.

Within the week, a plan was hatched: Cyrus would take them both on a trip to France on the pretext of assessing a new brood mare. Once the date of the registration meeting was confirmed, they would head over a few days earlier to try to find Milou, and convince him to give crucial evidence as a witness to Mistral's birth during the storm. Gabriel was informed of the covert plan and tasked with making inquiries into the whereabouts of the fisherman's son. After all, the small boy was quite a hero among the gardiens of the region; he'd saved several lives that dreadful day. Surely someone recognised him and knew where he lived?

Good news arrived back from France quite soon. The hearing was scheduled for April 17th and Milou had been found. One of the gardiens remembered a fisherman, Monsieur Moreau, who had a young son of the same name. But it hadn't been an easy situation. The boy had been too scared to tell his father what had happened that day as he'd ventured out during that awful storm without permission. When the riders came to see his father, he'd hidden in the barn, too shy to admit his role in helping Nazrin during the mistral. It took a clever idea to convince him to speak up; Gabriel explained how vital it was for the colt to be awarded his papers and if Milou came forward and told the truth, he promised him he would gift the boy one of Mistral's future foals. Little Milou's eyes had opened wide with excitement as his childhood dream had been to one day own a magnificent Camargue horse. He'd always been so envious of the gardiens astride their dancing white steeds, so he'd stepped boldly from the barn and blurted out the whole tale in front of his father and the others. His audience had laughed heartily and told him, "That'll do nicely. Just tell them that at the meeting!"

March turned into April and Seb had taken Roobs back to Newmarket with him. Nazrin felt the strange emotion of missing her constant companion whose company she'd taken for granted over the last few months. She'd never felt quite like this before, but consoled herself that they'd soon be together again, sharing an adventure in France. Then, the partners received a phone call from Cyrus, requesting if he could 'borrow' Nazrin for a few days. He explained that a surprise trip concerning 'stud business' had come up and he thought it would be educational for her to accompany him. No lies were told; everyone was quite satisfied and gave their consent happily, adding that she'd worked so hard through the busy foaling months, she deserved a short break. Seb was expecting the three of them to travel by car and ferry, but of course time was valuable to Cyrus – he couldn't afford to waste hours on the road. Instead, he whisked them to the airport and they flew to the south of France and taxied down to meet Gabriel at his homestead.

With me stuck at Airborne Lodge and the others at Wick House, you can imagine what a busy time poor old Fireworks had relaying all this exciting information. From what I heard here at home and conversations gleaned from telephone calls at Wick House, between us we managed to piece together the general plot. It was going to be a frustrating waiting game as usual, but in the meantime, two things happened to take our minds off the French affair. One of these things was quite extraordinary and changed my life for ever.

# CHAPTER 22.
# A CHALLENGING FACE

T he first wonderful surprise came just after Nazrin's departure, in the shape of a delivery van. The driver was adamant he couldn't off-load the valuable cargo until he was in the presence of a woman called June who owned the property. Apparently, she would be the only person able to advise him how to proceed with the delicate unloading operation. Luckily for all concerned, June was home from Brenda's farm, having completed her arduous course. She grabbed the delivery note and read the sender's name with great excitement. Instructions were from a Tehmina Ferozshah, stating that the items should only be signed for after careful examination had revealed no damage had occurred during transit.

"Two wooden 'orses, Madam. One big 'un and a little 'un, very delicate by all accounts. Any chance of an 'and off the lorry with 'em?" the harassed man inquired.

June managed to find David and between them they gingerly brought out the precious cargo and carried them tentatively into the sitting room where Charlotte and Cobweb looked on in shock.

"Blimey, you've got a stable full 'ere," the driver declared in genuine surprise, "you could open an 'orse moosium!"

Huh, and that was without me being there! I was completely miffed that I'd missed this huge event...thank goodness for Fireworks' account of the whole proceedings.

The delivery man stood by the door waiting apprehensively for confirmation that the valuable consignment was intact, so he might continue on his way. Slowly and carefully the swathes of bubble wrap were removed from the equine forms. Beneath the mountain of padding stood a magnificent, powerful and proud rocking horse stallion in full war regalia, and next to him, the sweetest, prettiest little foal of exquisite proportions. Even the lorry driver let out a soft whistle of appreciation at this splendid sight. "Cor, they's an eyeful! I can see what all the fuss was about now. But if you're 'appy with 'em, I'll be on me way..." He obtained the all-important signature and slipped away gratefully.

David and June couldn't summon any words at first, but walked round and round the pair in awe. Eventually David came out with a massive understatement: "Nice start for your collection, love."

June was fingering the elaborate trappings on Pasha's head and body in disbelief. Every bead, tassel and silver bell was intact and gleaming. "I can't believe how well-cared for these two have been," she uttered in a disbelieving whisper. "They're perfect, their condition is amazing and all the colours of the materials are as vivid as the day they were made. Oh look, they're both still wearing those pretty orangey threads on their front leg, just above the hoof, just like Tehmi's one around her wrist! And there was I thinking they'd been abandoned in some damp and mouldy loft..."

June should have realised that Tehmi had made provisions for her childhood treasures. She had indeed kept the pair in the 'loft', a temperature-controlled storage space rigged-up with an atmosphere monitor designed to befit the family's valuable antique rosewood furniture and other items brought back from their Indian mansion house.

She continued, "We'll leave them here for now. How lovely that the Duchess and her family are finally re-united, bless them. Where to put everyone eventually is going to be a big question for later... but I must phone Tehmi straight away and thank her a thousand times for this amazing pair!"

You may be wondering how Charlotte reacted to the massive shock of seeing her beloved husband and foal again. It takes a knowing and clever person to see the subtle show of emotion in a 'mere' wooden rocking horse. A perceptive eye will notice the slightest of tremors and an extra brightness to the glass eyes of a horse feeling excitement. A happy or grateful reaction may cause it to gently sway and the eyes will be soft and dewy. Suffice to say that Charlotte was overwhelmed with joyous emotion and all of the above signs were displayed in succession! Cobweb said later that he'd felt quite embarrassed and had turned his gaze away to allow the little family some privacy during their long-awaited reunion. We both couldn't have been happier for them. It seemed that the magical promise of those saffron threads was finally being upheld.

The very next day the second surprise occurred. It was mid-morning and Fireworks had just finished telling me all about Pasha and Pashmina's arrival when we heard a commotion outside on the Wick House driveway. Fireworks leapt on the windowsill and spied June standing by the open back doors of her van. Everyone had crowded around the vehicle, clamouring to get a glimpse of June's new acquisition which from a distance vaguely resembled a rocking horse.

"Looks like she's bought another one of you lot! I'm off to have a good look. Report back soon!" Fireworks declared as he dashed off to investigate. Apparently, the little cat told me later, it was quite a shocking reveal. As this latest purchase was quite small, June had carefully lifted the poor unfortunate thing out of the van single-handedly and placed it in front of everybody. To say they recoiled at the little horse's appearance may be too strong a word, but certainly their excitement dissipated in a flash. No-one stepped forward with appreciative comments; they just stood there taken aback, dismayed. For a start, this creature was not the attractive dappled grey colour they had come to expect, but a sort of lurid orange. Although it may have once been bright and fresh, now the scuffed, scratched and dulled tangerine paintwork was covered in a film of filth.

"Eeew, it's practically bald and bashed to pieces," said Mirabel; "in fact, to be honest it looks quite ugly and downright vicious." It didn't help that both ears were totally absent, giving it the appearance of a horse that had laid its ears flat back in temper. The bared teeth were yellowed and chipped and looked ready to take a chunk out of anyone who ventured near enough. Orange paint had spilled over on to the glass eyes, causing the horse to wear a livid expression.

David remarked quietly, "It's not one of your best buys, love..."

*Not one of your best buys, love.*

"You've got your work cut out there. It'll scare the living daylights out of most kids, looking like that!" announced one of the stud workers. He was referring to the little horse's face, which was hideously decorated with garish crimson and black paint. It resembled the face of a child who had played around with some theatrical make-up.

Eddie joked, "Hope you've had a rabies jab, Juney!"

"Good grief, I feel sorry for the poor little thing," Jacs had blurted out with feeling. "It's suffered a lot of abuse, June. I'm glad you rescued it. You can only help it now and thank goodness it's here."

June was a bit peeved by everyone's reaction to her first ever project and defended her purchase strongly. "Well, say what you will but this was cheap and in need of my help. There's a nice horse lurking under all that paint. It's something to start me off and at least I can't make it look any worse! It'll be good practice for me, and I hope you all eat your words when it looks gorgeous…"

"Good luck with THAT!" she'd heard someone mutter as the crowd had wandered off in disdain.

But Jacs was full of empathy and consoled her dear friend. "Let's take the little mite back to mine and sort something out from there. You'll have to ring Joby quick smart and get him on the case. Then ring Brenda and she'll have to guide you through the best course of action."

So, the two oldest of friends carried that shabby and damaged wooden apology of a rocking horse straight back to Airborne Lodge and straight into my heart, changing my life for ever.

It's strange, isn't it? That one's perception of something can be the total opposite to another's. As soon as they brought her in to our front room (yes, she was obviously female. Well, you just know, don't you) and placed her near me, I was overcome with a feeling of warmth. I didn't see the things Fireworks said the others had seen. I saw through colour, condition, scary external expression and all the damage that had been inflicted on her over many years. I just saw – or rather felt – a shy, sweet, scared and misunderstood character crying out for a friend but who had lost all hope of finding one. I also saw that rare thing, quality. It shone out of her like a beacon. She possessed the sought-after combination that was coveted in all stock: quality with substance. Whoever had carved her had given her refinement coupled with strength. To have survived what she'd been through she'd had to have been strong and soundly made from the best timber available. There she stood, battered but still standing, de-faced but still beautiful – in my eyes, anyway. The only thing wrong with her was her broken spirit and damaged soul. I felt it keenly. I wanted to take that pain away from her heart. There and then I felt great affection for her and swore I'd help her come back to life. If only she realised, she could have a good life in a safe home, surrounded by kind people.

We stood together for three long, silent days. Not a word did she utter. I just hoped my calm, steady presence would comfort her in some way. I didn't try to converse, just stood close, quietly and patiently. Fireworks came storming into the Lodge on the fourth day with news that Nazrin was due home on the morrow. To be honest, with so much going on here, I'd almost forgotten about the on-going drama in France. Anyway, we would never know what had happened until Seb returned. The partners were in the dark about the real reason for the trip, and I doubted we'd see Nazrin as she stayed at North Lodge, the furthest away from our home. I was too taken up with this strange little horse whom I'd decided to take under my wing. The cat lowered his purr and gently enquired if there'd been any progress. I whispered back, "Nothing at all. She's sort of shut down."

"Perhaps she just can't speak. I bet a lot of you don't. They're not all like you three," he stated, trying to sound reasonable.

"No," I hissed back, "she's JUST like us but she's very hurt and quite terrified. I think she's scared of people…or doesn't much like them – at best."

We both glanced at her, but those orange-rimmed eyes were dead, not a flicker or spark of life showed within their depths. With no news of an improvement, Fireworks was quickly losing interest. "Oh well, you'll have to do as Seb does and work your magic on her. Actually, if you don't look at the face, she's got a rather attractive shape to her," he remarked casually as he stalked out.

June and Jacs had been back and forth to discuss their new project and their conversations had been very revealing. While drinking coffee, they'd stared hard at her and Jacs had asked her friend if she'd gleaned anything of the horse's history.

"Not much," June had answered, quite perplexed. "It's all very odd. Most people love their old rocking horses. Not this family. It seems they couldn't wait to be rid of it; in fact, the mother told me that her kids had hated it. Apparently, her eldest son had terrified the younger two by telling them the horse was a witch's 'familiar', you know—like a black cat! He told them the witch came and rode it each night and if they ever got on it, it would take them back to her cottage and they'd be eaten alive. Can you imagine, Jacs? I'd have punished him severely. The mother also told me that they'd never wanted the thing in the first place, but its original owners were getting divorced, moving away and were throwing it out. A neighbour had thought her kids would like it and appeared on their doorstep with it! Their dad had painted it orange because he'd had a chestnut pony when he was young. The little boy rode it a lot at first and that had caused so many rows because he wouldn't let the younger ones ride. Then, her daughter was sitting on it and somehow fell off and broke her arm. They stopped anyone riding after that but there were still rows because the little ones cried constantly, saying their brother was being 'mean' to the horse. So 'Witchy-Poo', as the son called it, was thrown in the garden shed, where it stayed for years. When she saw my advert, she thought I'd be interested as she'd been told the horse was a valuable antique. She wanted far more than I gave her, but eventually said I was welcome to it as it was unlucky and cursed. Her parting words were 'Good riddance'!"

My lovely Jacs had welled-up at this horrible tale and told June it was the most vile, cruel and heartless story she'd ever heard concerning a rocking horse. I too felt sickened and almost tearful. Why are some people so heartless? June then suggested they take it out into the garden to try and clean it up a bit before the arrival of Joby and Brenda. She had realised this may be too big a job for her first attempt at a restoration, so Brenda had agreed to come and stay for a while to help her learn on the job.

"Come on, let's relieve poor Blitzyboy of having to look at it!" joked June.

Jacs was quick to retort, "No, Blitz really likes her. Can't you see?"

June smiled fondly at her friend and said, "No, sorry, I can't. You are funny! How do you know? I love rocking horses, but I really don't understand these strange communications you seem to have with them. Whatever makes you think it's a 'her' and why do you think he likes her?"

Her friend answered simply, "I just feel she is and I know from his eyes and the way he's moved himself closer to her."

June shrugged and admitted the finer nuances of it all were completely lost on her.

No one quite knew what to call the small, broken toy. Jacs refused point blank to use that awful Witchy-Poo appellation and June agreed, saying there would be time to decide a name later but now, they really must get the little mare outside and cleaned up before tomorrow.

"That's it," Jacs declared with satisfaction, "we'll call her 'Little Mare', until we think of something better!"

They carried Little Mare outside, and as I watched through the window I saw a tiny transformation as some of the dirt and grime was lifted from her graceful body. They had to take great care handling her. Her joints were unstable and many lines and gaps were showing through the peeling paint. Loose flakes revealed areas of bare wood where even the gesso was long gone, but hidden under other patches were definite signs of faint dappling. Her face was gradually relieved of large rolls of old orange paint that curled up willingly to expose a pale grey colour. June delicately scraped and picked at the thickened tangerine drips that had enveloped the glass eyes and surrounds. It was a small triumph and her start to a new identity. After an hour's labour they brought Little Mare back indoors and Jacs made sure to place her very near to my body. She whispered in my ear as she left, "Tell her she's safe here, Blitz. Tell her we love her, too."

As they left the room, I stole a glance at her. She was beautiful. I may be mistaken but just then, I think there was a sign of life... I think I heard the tiniest hint of a soft sigh.

★★★★

# CHAPTER 23.
# FULFILLING PROMISES

The trip to France had been a complete success. In fact, the battle they'd been dreading had proved an easy victory for Gabriel and his daughter. Registration had been accepted and issued without any fight or fuss. It had been a simple procedure once all the evidence was presented to the officials. Milou had been a splendid witness, bravely giving his account of the events as they'd happened. He'd drawn courage on the back of a promise that one day he'd receive one of Mistral's foals. It was a huge reward to bestow upon the youngster, but one Gabriel would honour gladly in the future. He would be eternally grateful to the lad. Milou may well have saved his daughter's life by riding for help that day.

Nazrin had returned to Wick Stud glowing with happiness and feeling triumphant, but of course she couldn't confide in anyone or explain why. The partners remarked the break had obviously done her a power of good – although Jacs was secretly convinced her contentment was due to having spent time with Sebastian. It hadn't escaped her 'mother's eye' that the pair had become very close. Before leaving Newmarket, Nazrin and Seb had discussed another promise which had to be upheld, their pledge to take Manfri to the gypsy festival at Saintes-Maries-de-la-Mer. There wasn't long to organise the trip and they hadn't yet approached the people whose consent they badly needed. However, both of them had already broached the subject with Nazrin's great uncle as he was proving to be a wonderful ally. They explained how much it would mean to Manfri, how his eyes had lit up at the description of the ceremony. Cyrus would always go the extra mile for his great niece – she meant the world to him – and he felt honoured that the youngsters trusted him with their secret plans. He'd sighed heavily at the request to persuade Teresita and his sister to allow a visit to the festival, but agreed it certainly would be a trip of a lifetime for Manfri.

So Cyrus talked to his sister and niece, outlining the youngsters' plan to escort their friend to Saintes-Maries-de-la-Mer. Both he and Tehmi had developed a great respect and affection for the wise old man. They also understood his desire to explore his roots and Romany heritage. It was so important to embrace one's history, to understand about the blood that ran through one's veins. As the years had rolled by, Cyrus himself had felt a keen need to return to India one last time. He'd heard it was a common desire, especially for those estranged from their homeland or a way of life they'd once cherished. He also felt strongly that Nazrin should not be denied her right to explore her relationship with her father and the world she'd originally been born into. After hearing Cyrus' eloquent speech outlining these thoughts, Tehmi and her daughter relented and agreed that Nazrin could accompany Manfri to the gypsy gathering. Teresita knew this meant her daughter would be seeing Gabriel again, but realised she must not begrudge the young woman time with her father, despite her misgivings. If she was not allowed to spread her wings, they both risked losing her forever.

Near the end of May, Manfri arrived at our lodge a day in advance of the biggest adventure of his life. Joby had driven his great uncle up from the Forest, both of them filled with excitement as they approached Airborne Lodge. Manfri was slightly apprehensive at the thought of flying, but the lad was extremely envious, because he would have loved the experience. I was delighted when my old friend came to sit by me as usual and his reaction to Little Mare was all I could have hoped it would be. He saw her in her true light. "Who's yer little friend?" he enquired softly with a kindly smile spreading across his weathered, nut-brown face. "She's a rinkni rakli (pretty girl) but..." he stopped mid-sentence and gazed deeply into her clouded eyes, "she's troubled, Bokky. Her heart is heavy, poor gel. I c'n see ya loves her so you look after her good. Could be the best thing wots ever 'appened to ya, Bokky!"

His comments and that wide grin he gave me bucked me up no end. I still hadn't got very far with the little creature and almost felt she was a lost cause. I was relieved to notice that Manfri appeared rejuvenated by his forthcoming trip. He seemed vigorous and strong again, almost as though the thought of travelling had awakened his soul. He and Nazrin left early the next morning to meet up with Seb at the airport. It was the start of a magnificent adventure where wonderful memories would be made. The journey was the result of a rashly given Christmas promise, now being fulfilled.

## 'Explore the past before discovering the future.'

Although happy that everyone else's lives seemed to be swinging along nicely, I was feeling distinctly sorry for myself. In truth, I was missing my friends over at Wick House. I lamented that I'd not yet even met the two new arrivals and it hurt to imagine them as one big happy family, conversing and sharing things without me. My present situation seemed hopeless, and although I felt quite miserable, I refused to give up on Little Mare. Unrequited love is a lonely emotion and despite giving her my warm support and all the kindness that was in my heart, she gave me nothing in return. Apart from the odd little sigh which served as indication that she was actually alive, there was no reaction from her. I had started chatting to her, but I may as well have talked to the wall as it made no difference, she just didn't appear to hear. I even wondered if it was because she had no carved wooden ears, but I knew she didn't need to hear actual words. We could communicate with thought alone. I'd ramble on about my previous life or tell her about our home here, anything to pass the boring hours of solitude. Then one quiet afternoon whilst everyone was busy working elsewhere, it happened. A breakthrough!

"Don't speak to me, I don't deserve it. I'm wicked." A small hesitant voice had come floating over to me from where she stood close by.

I was so shocked that I checked the room to make sure no one had walked in un-noticed. But I knew it was her. She had actually finally spoken, maybe her first words in many, many years. As calmly as I could and controlling my trembling thoughts, I tried to find a suitable answer. "No, you certainly aren't wicked. You are sweet and lovely and whoever told you that, deserves to be punished." June's story about the boy who'd last owned her had angered me greatly. It had touched a raw nerve because long ago, I'd also experienced the vile behaviour of a cruel child. Now I tried to soothe Little Mare – the last thing I wanted was for her to clam up again. Gently, I tried to probe for more information. "Whatever makes you say that? I think you're beautiful, good and kind. I can feel it and I'm never wrong."

This time the voice was a shade stronger and quite determined. "You ARE wrong; I'm wicked because I hate children, I hurt children. I'm cursed because I'm a witch."

Oh dear, this was worse than I'd thought. Whatever horrors her past held, it had badly affected her. It seemed she'd been brain-washed, believing all the nasty accusations that had been levelled at her. Thinking quickly, I answered with quiet authority, "You are definitely NOT cursed. I am an expert on curses. I've lived with gypsies and my dearest friend, whom you met the other day, is a Romany. He would have known straight away if you had been. And who told you witches are bad? Some are wonderfully clever and helpful people. But you're not one anyway, trust me."

Just at this crucial point, we were interrupted as June and Joby came into our front room, gathered Little Mare up in their arms, took her out and loaded her onto the pick-up truck. To my utter surprise, I was also carried out and put next to her. We were driven a couple of hundred yards away to the Holmbury Hall garages, one of which had been adapted into a new workshop for June's restorations. Here stood Brenda, awaiting our arrival. She seemed surprised to see me and asked if I also needed some remedial work done. June explained that I was fine but Jacs had insisted that I should go with their new project to give her 'moral support', as she'd put it. Good old Jacs, she knew us rocking horses so well! She knew Little Mare needed me to help her heal inside whilst the restorers worked on her outside. Both women smiled with affection at Jacs' strange request and June said apologetically, "She's a strange one, our Jacs!"

But Brenda replied generously, "I think she's lucky to have that connection with these horses. If she feels Blitz should be here with this little one, then so be it. I'm envious of her gift and grateful for her insight."

I'm happy to report that Brenda seemed quite taken with Little Mare. She saw the quality that I'd spotted and the fine, pretty features that Manfri had commented on. Overall, Brenda reckoned it wouldn't be too hard a job to strip her of that awful orange paint, fix her wobbly joints, re-gesso the bald areas, and enhance her original paintwork. June would attempt the work under Brenda's beady eye. Joby was tasked with making her some new ears, a job he'd find enjoyable and easy as he was a talented woodworker. He felt confident he could even repair the original old stand she had once stood on. "There's more good news," Brenda declared happily. "Her eyes are actually the old Victorian glass ones she was given when she was originally made. The only thing is… they're horribly dull and misted over. We'll have to clean them up somehow, find something to brighten them."

June replied that she had a secret recipe somewhere, given to her by an old antique dealer she'd worked for. It was fantastic for getting Waterford crystal to gleam again when age and wear had dulled its lustre. "If I can dig it out, I'm sure that'll brighten them up to perfection!"

Unfortunately, a new mane and tail would be needed. It looked like someone had ripped handfuls out of both and the top of her mane was frazzled and singed to the roots.

"I wonder what could have happened there," June remarked thoughtfully as they packed up for the night and left.

*'Folk gather round when there's goods for the taking. But friends gather round when your heart is breaking'*

In that darkened workshop, a small sad voice piped up again. "HE did that to my mane. He singed it purposely with a sparkler on Guy Fawkes Night. I was awfully scared..." she trailed off resignedly. I was again lost for words. Relieved that she had willingly started up a conversation, I just listened, giving her an occasional encouraging prompt. "My heart is frozen," she said flatly.

"But it's still beating," I answered quietly.

"My spirit and body are broken."

"But you're still standing," I retaliated.

"My soul is sick; how can I get better?" she asked plaintively.

"By talking to me," I assured her.

This did the trick. It was as if the floodgates had opened. Her emotional stories just poured out. Little Mare told me how that vile boy had scared his siblings with horrible stories about her, how when he'd caught his sister on her back, he'd pulled her tail so vigorously that she'd jerked up and backwards causing the little girl to tumble off and break her arm.

"I'll never forget those screams of pain and their mother's fury at me. She called me dangerous and a damned menace. That horrid boy told me then that I was cursed and I was going to prison." Little Mare finished with a pitiful gulping sob that I found quite heartrending. "That's when the fog of hate descended on me and he said I can't ever be free of it, not until I rot away in the shed..." This last statement sent shivers across the dapples on my back – we all knew that being locked away in a damp shed spelled a slow death for a rocking horse. I felt out of my depth and wasn't sure if I would ever be able to convince her that she was safe now. Little Mare's outburst seemed to have exhausted her so we both fell into an uneasy silence.

I must have dozed off for a few hours until the most pitiful wailing shriek emitted from deep within her belly, piercing the pitch-black night and waking me instantly. It literally caused the hairs of my mane to rise like a dog's hackles. I supposed she'd had a night-vision and I knew all about those, so I tried my hardest to calm her quaking little body with soothing thoughts. When I'd spent time in an orphanage many years ago, I'd heard the Matron talk about a dreadful, screeching wail that was uttered by destitute folk who were inmates of the poorhouse. It was known as the 'Workhouse Howl', it told of an agony and desperation beyond all words. She'd said, "Once heard, never forgotten." I think I'd just heard it for myself.

So, all through that first night in the workshop I kept close to Little Mare and kept telling her that none of what had happened was her fault and she must keep talking about it to rid herself of the poison that had filled her heart. I also made her a fool-hardy promise that I would make sure she was healed very soon. She asked again how she could ever be free of the fog that had frozen her heart. I had no answers, so I sidled even closer and hoped that the warmth of my own heart may help to thaw hers.

*'Love will always triumph over hate.'*

May turned into June and during those long weeks of Little Mare's restoration I felt I was making good progress too. She'd certainly come a long way on her road to recovery. We'd explored her term 'the fog of hate' and what it actually meant. She said that when it descended upon her, she'd lost all memory of a previous life. Slowly, odd recollections came back, but some memories were too painful for her to express. It seemed that trouble had plagued her even before her last abusive home.

Two strange things happened at this time. The first occurred when June found something deep inside her hollow body. She'd shouted to Brenda to come and see what she'd discovered. The two had used narrow forceps through her pommel hole to carefully extract something soft and light and apparently very meaningful. Don't ask me what it was; I was too far away to actually see what they were excitedly examining before popping it into an envelope for safe-keeping. Brenda had always found pommel-hole discoveries fascinating and now June was experiencing that thrill. However, I did hear Brenda admit she would have just thrown this 'find' away as she'd had no clue of its significance. June had grinned proudly and answered, "Good job I recognised them then, eh!"

Oh, how frustrating all this was! I quizzed Little Mare, but although she tried really hard to activate her foggy mind, the answer eluded her. "I vaguely remember – she was very sad and cross and dropped something into me but I can't tell you what..."

I was intrigued. "Who? Do you remember who 'she' was? Was it the little girl who broke her arm?" I asked.

"No," she answered sadly, "it was my lovely girl, and I caused her so much pain..."

I had hurriedly changed the subject because her eyes were clouding over dreadfully and I didn't want her to shut down again. This is what it was like; every now and then glimpses of her past life would peek out from behind grey clouds and they were not always pleasant. It was exhausting treading on eggshells—but oh, so worth it. I had grown uncommonly fond of this strange little character. There was this inexplicable connection...

The second strange incident was my own revelation about something in my past. During our nightly talks, I'd teased another memory out of Little Mare. Whilst reminiscing about my own beginnings in a Victorian workshop in London, she suddenly had a flash recollection and uttered words that had me reeling in shock. She spoke apologetically and whispered, "I disobeyed what I was told to do. I didn't mean to, but I hurt children and the man who carved me told me to be kind to all the children who rode me."

My mind was racing with excitement and disbelief... surely it couldn't be a coincidence? Those words were so familiar because they were my very own mantra in life! When I was lovingly chiselled to life by my maker, a carpenter called Wilf, he'd talked to me all the way through the process. At the end, when I was ready to leave the shop to go into the wide world, he'd come to see me off and had whispered words of advice into my young ears. He'd said the VERY same words. "Be kind to all the children who ride you." And then, another revelation hit me... I'd actually seen Little Mare, albeit very briefly, many years ago. Could this explain my feelings of attachment towards her?

I'll try to explain when and where I saw her. A long time ago when Jacs was a little girl, she and I met at a fairground where I was being used as a carousel horse, and fell for each other immediately. She'd returned for a secret ride on me, and I dreamed that I'd taken her back in time to gallop through my previous life, visiting places in my past. Our first destination had been the workshop in London owned by Mr Leach, where I was created. I remember gazing through the shop-front window to see Wilf busy chiselling away making another little horse, very like me. I'd wanted to stop and tell him I was fine after all those years, but we had to keep going, to visit other places. However, the image of that little horse I'd spotted through the window was burned into my memory, and now I'm convinced – it was Little Mare. Sounds far-fetched? Well yes, it certainly is. To this day I don't know myself if the whole thing really happened or was just a fantastic dream. I now realised that the little horse standing next to me seemed familiar because she was almost a replica of me, but smaller and more feminine! I guessed Little Mare and I shared the same pedigree, we were both Leach rocking horses and perhaps even carved by the same maker, my lovely Wilf.

# CHAPTER 24.
# COMING BACK TO LIFE

After all those weeks in isolation away from the outside world, I fear I may have gone a little batty. I know one thing for sure. I had fallen hook, line and sinker for Little Mare. Whenever she was taken just out of sight to have a 'procedure' done on her increasingly beautiful body, I felt stupidly bereft. When she was carried back in, I experienced that weird sensation of butterflies in my belly. It was as if some had flown in through my pommel hole and were then blundering around to find an escape route. It seemed I was only content when she was near. Oh, I was besotted! Even her little voice had become sweeter; her dulcet tones were like honey. Yes, I knew all about honey. One of the beloved children I'd known in my past life, a small toddler named Annie, would often be given a hunk of freshly baked bread smothered in this golden delight. She would waddle up to my lowered face and offer me the delicious morsel on her outstretched hand until the liquid gold touched my muzzle. I'll never forget the taste and smell of that flowery-fragranced treat. The sticky nectar smeared onto my lips and tongue and remained there for me to savour until Annie's mother roughly sponged away the tacky mess, admonishing the small child for trying to feed a wooden toy! To me, Little Mare's voice had begun to sound just as sweet as the taste of that honey.

Then one day, after being worked on for an hour outside, she was brought back indoors to stand proudly in the centre of the workshop. I can't tell you how lovely she now looked with a flowing silvery mane and tail finally attached to her neat little body. Her whole countenance had changed. She'd slowly been emerging from her 'fog' but now the transformation was more than remarkable, it was tremendous. Over the weeks of her restoration, with each stage of physical progress, her mental anguish diminished. As the bricks of her prison crumbled, the fog slowly lifted, revealing a kind but timid soul. When the clown-like paint came off her face her expression softened, the fluted nostrils no longer bore that snarl they'd assumed before. Joby's delicately fashioned ears now lent an air of poised intelligence to her head. Her carefully preserved dapples were as subtle and natural as morning sun filtering through a leafy glade. If Brenda was proud of June's meticulous work, I was prouder. Those elegant limbs were now strong and supported a shapely body with finely chiselled neck and gracefully turned head. I couldn't tear my gaze away from my sweet companion. I suppose the only one thing I lamented over were those eyes. They were generous, well-placed, beautifully edged with the finest sweeping and feminine eye-lashes…but they were still veiled and lacklustre.

After we had all gazed at her in awe for several minutes, Joby went to fetch the tatty and broken old swing stand she'd arrived on. It was unrecognisable, having been skilfully repaired and polished to perfection. He and June had toiled hard to bring it back to its best, befitting a horse now brought back to life. "I know Blitz worships the ground she stands on, but let's get her back on her pedestal for him!" joked Joby, as he took her away to fix her to the stand.

*I couldn't tear my gaze away.*

That's when Brenda came out with a statement that confirmed my earlier theory. "I have to say, she's one of the prettiest little Leaches I've seen in ages and that stand is totally original with its lovely wavy rails. It's a marriage made in heaven!" Now I knew for sure that Little Mare and I shared the same Leach pedigree, I understood why I'd felt that attraction, that strong bond. We were cut from the same cloth.

Our long confinement was drawing to an end. Plans were made for us to return the following day and I hoped fervently we would be joining my old friends. That night I was restless and just couldn't think straight. The excitement of catching up with Charlotte and Cobweb and meeting the new members of our little clan was getting the better of me. Sleep seemed impossible.

"I'm very nervous about tomorrow..." admitted the tiny, timid voice of my companion.

"They'll absolutely love you," I assured her; "you don't need to be shy, and remember, I've never met the other two either but I can't wait!"

"Do you think they've heard the horrid stories about me?" she inquired tentatively. I explained that Fireworks had told everybody all about her and her cruel last home and they were completely on her side.

That cat had indeed been a godsend all through our exile – his visits were probably the only reason I'd kept a piece of my sanity. He'd popped in regularly to gather news on Little Mare's lengthy recovery and skipped back to keep the others updated. Apparently, he and Pasha had struck up a great rapport. Fireworks was in awe of this stallion's calm and caring nature. He was also a master of one-liners and carefully considered quotes. His conversations were liberally scattered with these gems of wisdom which absolutely delighted the cat. Of course, being in love with words himself, he felt he'd found a true soulmate in Pasha.

On each visit, Fireworks related some of Pasha's wise comments to us. When he'd first heard what Little Mare's family had said about her, he'd regarded everyone solemnly and declared, "Every war-story has three sides. You can guarantee history will always be written by the victors." The cat admitted it had taken him a while to fathom that one out, but guessed it meant that Little Mare was the loser and so her version of events would never be heard. He'd asked what the third side of a story was and was told, "The truth". When Pasha had seen people's unfavourable reactions to the sad and broken mare's arrival, he'd remarked, "You only get one chance at a first impression, but nothing is ever written in stone. Try to be a witness rather than a judge." Oh, it was all a bit much for my simple love-addled brain at the time; it seemed to me he was talking in riddles. However, Fireworks was in raptures over his wise words, much in the same way as he appreciated Charlotte's use of flowery language.

As Joby loaded us carefully on to the back of the truck, we waved goodbye to that strange time exiled at the workshop. We were returning to my old life, and I couldn't wait to introduce everyone to this beautiful, sweet mare. Still not quite sure where we were heading, my heart leapt with joy when I heard June tell Joby to drop us at Wick House. Apparently, in my absence David and June had moved up to the Hall to keep an eye on the place for her parents. My heart sang at the news that Wick House would now be used to house all us horses. It would be our own rocking horse headquarters. How absolutely perfect was that!

What a reception we received. The occupants of the now rather bare sitting room were veritably fizzing with excitement at our arrival. I swear Cobweb whickered at me, Charlotte swayed with glistening eyes and Pasha performed a majestic low nod of welcome. The cute little foal cavorted on her bows looking curious and delighted. No one noticed this rocking horse activity as they were too busy moving us in and were deep in conversation. We were placed facing our friends and soon left to ourselves as June had an important unveiling ceremony to organise. Little Mare's restoration had been done under a shroud of secrecy. No one had been allowed near the workshop and frankly nobody had appeared to care. They had written off the small toy horse as an ugly curiosity, a stooge only suitable for June to practise upon, where mistakes wouldn't matter or even be noticed…first impressions and all that. No matter, all the better the impact would be when they saw her now, re-born in all her glory. June couldn't wait to hear their humble apologies and the praise they would undoubtedly shower upon her.

All that day we talked, gossiping late into the night. There was so much news to catch up on. I tried to keep Little Mare close under my withers so she wouldn't feel overwhelmed, but she seemed content to just listen, pleased she wasn't the centre of attention. I noticed that everyone included her in the conversations without pressing her to speak. That was just what she needed and my lovely friends understood perfectly, bless them. I was keen to discover what had happened at the registration meeting in France, but no one seemed to know. Nazrin had said nothing so we wouldn't learn anything until Seb came back from Newmarket. However, they had been privy to the conversations about Manfri's trip to the Camargue. It had been a wondrous experience by all accounts. The gypsy had been overwhelmed with emotion at meeting so many of his own people and had even discovered distant relatives there. Manfri had communicated easily with them as the Romany tongue is basically universal. He and Gabriel had bonded immediately, and despite language barriers, had formed a true friendship. He'd come home a contented soul. I was thrilled for my oldest, most treasured friend and I couldn't wait for him to visit again and see the change in Little Mare.

Another piece of riveting gossip had come to light. Fireworks' diligent eavesdropping gleaned from myriad phone calls had revealed news from Newmarket. It appeared that Charlotte's Rubies' career had got off to a shaky start with serious trials and tribulations. Although she'd settled in well and had shown astounding speed in her preparatory gallops at home, it was never going to be plain sailing with a temperament like hers! Her first juvenile attempt on a racecourse had ended in disaster. Nerves had got the better of her and she'd burst out of the dreaded starting stalls before the gates had opened, causing delay for the other runners and disqualification for herself. Seb was devastated as he knew she'd have to undergo an official 'stalls test' before being allowed to race again. Guilt flooded through him. Had he been over-zealous in assessing her talent and let emotion cloud his judgement? Had he selfishly taken up a coveted place in the Ferozshah yard with an un-trainable filly? He feared news of her erratic behaviour may reflect adversely on the family's Dapple Stud. They certainly didn't need any bad publicity during their recovery. Poor Sebastian badly needed Nazrin's support – but they were miles apart. They spent hours talking on the phone, Seb seeking comfort and advice, she supplying him with calm and sensible solutions. "We knew this might happen, we know she's quirky, we expected this and solved it at home," she soothed, "so we can solve it again. Go back to square one with her. Take her through the practice stalls every day after morning exercise. Then ask Cyrus if you can take her to the races several times and try her in their stalls at the end of the day. It'll do her the world of good and get her used to the hustle and bustle. It'll become a normal thing for her. Then she'll fly through her test and be able to compete. It's a lot of hassle, but worth it. Cyrus told me last week that she's the fastest youngster he's trained since Inscrutable! Promise you, it'll work and she'll make you proud!"

Fireworks believes Nazrin's encouragement and those pep-talks worked miracles because the next succession of phone calls recorded improving results. The crafty old cat would rush to the hall whenever Nazrin was summoned to answer a call from Seb. Here he would alight upon her lap, placing him perfectly to hear both sides of the conversation. Even though separated in distance, those two were still a winning team. It appeared their plan had worked. Roobs passed her stalls test and won her very next race with ease. She was subsequently stepped up in class to compete against the very best youngsters racing that year, and by late June, she'd won two more prestigious races. It was decided that Roobs should have a quiet couple of months off to allow her to grow and flourish. Then she would be re-charged and ready for her final race of the year. Cyrus always gave his young horses plenty of time, but this filly was special. She had already hit the headlines, being dubbed 'The Jewel of Newmarket'. The press had declared, "Another Inscrutable success for young Marland" and the reporters had nicknamed her 'The Spotted Speedster'. Her eye-catching iron grey colour with those weird white splashes had turned heads and won her a place in the public's affections. Yes, Cyrus intended to nurture this particular rising star with utmost care. Happily, the short break in Roobs' career allowed Sebastian to grab a few precious days' holiday and head home for a flying visit. I was excited to learn that my boy was due back the very next day! Oh, we had lots to talk about, so much to catch up on. More than anything, I wanted him to meet the new filly in MY life.

★★★★

# CHAPTER 25.
# DOUBLE-EDGED SWORD

June was planning her unveiling ceremony to coincide with a small welcoming-home party that Jacs had arranged for Seb to celebrate his recent racing successes. It was to be held on July 3$^{rd}$, two days after us coming back to Wick House and a day after my lad's return. It just so happened that this was also Seb's birthday, but he would never have agreed to the fuss of a birthday party so it was tactfully disguised as a celebration for his success with Charlotte's Rubies. The door to our rocking horse headquarters had been firmly locked and remained so while June and Jacs prepared food and drink for the evening 'do'. Everyone who worked at Wick Stud was invited. Roobs' career had taken off with a bang, bringing plenty of new business to their door. The stud was thriving, and the partners wanted all the staff to be present to congratulate Sebastian and enjoy their moment of glory together, as a team.

June didn't want to steal the lad's thunder but felt it would be a nice opportunity to showcase her recent labours by revealing Little Mare to a captive audience; the very people who had mocked her first-ever project. It was also Brenda's last evening with them and June wanted to show her huge appreciation for her friend's patience over-seeing her work. Since arriving home, I hadn't actually seen Sebastian as we rocking horses were being kept 'under wraps' and as soon as he'd arrived, he and Nazrin had wandered off to enjoy the few precious days they had together. The following afternoon they'd visited his beloved mares and then strolled over to inspect the latest batch of this year's foals. These were now termed 'weanlings' and they were enjoying their new-found independence since leaving their mothers' sides. They leaned over the far paddock gate and gazed at the youngsters playing mischievously with one another, full of joy and innocence. The pair felt at peace with the world and grateful to be back in each other's company. Nazrin thoughtfully began reciting a poem, her face a picture of serenity,

"What is this life if, full of care, we have no time to stand and stare…"

"Oh my goodness," exclaimed Seb, "that's my favouritest poem ever! That's 'Leisure' by W H Davies…"

Nazrin burst out laughing and remarked, "And that's the worst ever English I've heard! I thought you wos well-hedjucated!" she jested.

He then continued where she'd left off, in a bid to demonstrate that he really did remember the poem he'd claimed to love.

"No time to stand beneath the bows, and stare as long as sheep and cows…" He then skipped a verse and continued:

"No time to wait till her mouth can, enrich that smile her eyes began..."

Seb then looked straight at Nazrin and told her that it was her wonderful smile that had first drawn him to her. This was all too much for the young woman, who'd always avoided any show of emotion. She swung round and strode away saying, "If you're going to go all soppy on me, I'm off. We may as well help bring the mares in now, seeing as we're here. Or is that too much to ask of a top jockey?" She made light of the moment and not wanting to hurt his feelings, waited for him to catch up and affectionately linked her arm in his. "Come on, we've still got to get ready for your hero's welcome," she teased. "You can't be late at your own party, you're the guest of honour!"

"I think June's more excited about showing us how that poor little horse turned out—she's got it under lock and key!" Seb replied fondly. "She's really proud and pleased with herself; apparently it was in a right state, almost beyond saving. They all thought she was crazy buying it, but this restoration stuff's made her so happy. I take my hat off to her."

Nazrin promised to give June plenty of credit for her efforts, but in her mind, Seb was the real champion and it should be HIS night.

At 7 that evening, people started to walk up to Wick House. The yard work had been finished quickly to allow the staff time to smarten up for the 'do'. They arrived at the celebration anticipating a delicious spread, free flowing drink and an atmosphere of good camaraderie. Sebastian was a popular lad. The staff loved him as they would a brother, and June and David treated him as an adopted son. Wick House was soon filled with happy chatter and a buzz of excitement as the guests awaited Seb and Nazrin's grand entrance. Brenda, who had been staying in the guest room upstairs, was on hand to assist Jacs in serving up some rather luxurious bottles of champagne that were on ice, ready to be poured and shared with their hero.

The young couple soon appeared arm in arm, Nazrin looking radiant and Seb rather embarrassed at all the fuss. Right on cue, corks popped among cheers and congratulatory back-slapping. The evening was in full swing with high spirits flowing through the house. Back in the sitting room, we waited excitedly for Little Mare to have her own moment of glory. After her many years of abuse and unhappiness, I felt her turn had come to emerge into the spotlight and show the world her true beauty. She deserved to know what it is to be loved and treasured by a family. Although apprehensive, she seemed quietly confident about facing the crowd, knowing we were right by her side. I felt quite proud that we'd come so far and my hard work had paid off. When most of the food and drink had been consumed and there was a relaxed lull in conversation, June took her opportunity and announced that she had something to show everyone.

She'd picked her moment well. Her audience stood attentively as she explained what she was about to reveal. "You know I bought a broken, rather scary-looking wreck of a toy horse a few months ago," she addressed them with a half-smile, "and you all said it was beyond help?"

"Yes," answered one of the stud lads, "it was hideous and completely unsuitable for any child. It was rotten and ugly. Sorry, June, but we all thought you'd bought a lemon, or rather an orange!" He looked round with a grin, proud of his quip and pleased to see many nods of agreement.

June was unfazed. "Well, I thought you may all want to see what I managed to do with her. She is the first horse I've worked on properly and I have to say, I'm pleased with the end result!" she finished triumphantly. Leading them into the hall, she proceeded to unlock our room, flinging the door open with a flourish.

There was a hush as many pairs of eyes scanned over the stunning collection of six beautiful rocking horses, searching frantically for the pathetic, small creature they remembered. "But – where is it then?" asked the first lad.

June proudly pointed at Little Mare, enjoying the drama of the whole thing immensely.

"You're kidding me? That's never it!" declared another disbelieving voice. Once they had all absorbed the horse's incredible transformation, there were many comments ranging from 'Wow' and 'Incredible!' to 'Totally amazing!' Genuine and heart-felt praise was heaped upon June who actually felt quite humbled by everybody's reactions.

No one except Seb had noticed, but Nazrin had reacted very differently. I also think I was the only one to be aware of Little Mare's quaking body which, it seemed, had become awash with fear at the sight of the beautiful girl on Seb's arm. It was imperceptible to the naked eye, but her whole aura had changed. She was in utter turmoil. Nazrin was similarly distressed, so much so that Seb had to support her wilting body or she surely would have collapsed as she stared disbelievingly –straight at Little Mare. The lad quickly took hold of her as she shook, and guided her out of the room, through the front door and out into the balmy evening air, hoping it may revive her. Here she sat hunched on the step, hugging her knees and swaying back and forth. Seb was concerned; it was as if she'd been plunged into a state of shock.

All at once, she leapt to her feet. "I need to go back home NOW. I need to think. Just leave me alone." She refused his offer to walk her back to her lodge, running off like a scalded cat.

Sebastian returned to the party feeling extremely confused. He hurriedly invented an excuse about Nazrin consuming too much champagne when questioned about his partner's absence. In truth he had no idea what had occurred, only that the sight of the rocking horse had caused her an emotional melt-down.

The party had eventually drawn to a close, the sitting room door had again been shut once the room had emptied and the guests had gone home. We were also left totally confused about Little Mare's fearful reaction on having spotted Nazrin across the room. All I could presume was that they'd met each other in the past, but I was unable to extract anything from the frightened mare. It was as if she'd been struck dumb.

Pasha told me quietly to leave her be. "She's teetering on top of a cliff; if you push to help, you may push her over the edge. Be there for her but let her come to you," he advised kindly.

Back at her Lodge, Nazrin had locked herself in her bedroom and refused entry to anyone. Seb returned to Wick House the next morning as the partners were having their mid-morning break. Because Nazrin had failed to turn up for her yard duties, they'd presumed she was still unwell and asked how she was now feeling. Sheepishly, Seb had to report that she'd not let him in to her room and wouldn't even talk to him. The partners were just about to summon a doctor to visit when he felt obliged to tell them she was not actually ill, more distraught for some unfathomable reason. He explained she'd had a peculiar reaction on seeing June's restored horse. There had to be a logical explanation for her suffering such an emotional shock, but despite racking his brains all night, the reason eluded him.

That was when the penny dropped for June. She exclaimed she may have a clue to the answer and it could be connected to something she'd found, something of significance which she needed to show them all. Rushing off excitedly, she returned moments later clutching the envelope containing her earlier pommel-hole find. Slowly and carefully, June tipped the items on to the table, spreading them out to form two individual thin saffron-gold coloured bracelets made of finely twisted thread.

Jacs bent down and looked closely at them whispering, "Oh my goodness, where have we seen THEM before?"

"Well, take your pick!" exclaimed Seb. "Tehmi wears one around her wrist and her two childhood horses have them around their feet right now...she told us they were made from some sort of sacred thread, they're supposed to be a lucky amulet that was meant to keep the family together or something. I think she said Charlotte, sorry Mumty, also had one years ago."

Suddenly the truth was staring them in the face. They had never forgotten Cyrus' explanation for his great-niece's unruly behaviour since the tragic death of her twin brother.

June began, "And I found these inside Little Mare…"

Seb finished saying what everyone was thinking, "…so she must have once belonged to the Ferozshahs OR, more likely, to Teresita's family. OH LORE…your little horse may well have been Nazrin's own rocking horse, both of theirs, hers and her brother's."

There was a painful silence as everybody tried to imagine how poor Nazrin must have felt recognising her childhood toy, the little horse her brother was riding when he'd died. And now, the rocking horse she'd blamed and hated all those years ago had suddenly reappeared to remind her of the most traumatic event of her life.

"Look, this may all be pure conjecture. I mean to say, what are the chances? We're probably putting two and two together and making five," announced David full of optimism, trying his best to alleviate the gloom that had settled on the room.

He rose cheerfully to make everyone tea, the cure-all for most disasters, but Eddie was not convinced and remarked thoughtfully, "Unfortunately, it does makes perfect sense. Our theory fits every angle of this conundrum, and I don't want to be the voice of doom but what other explanation is there?"

David, still trying to be practical, decided some detective work might help confirm the theory one way or the other. He asked his wife where she'd acquired the wrecked horse and had she been told anything of its past history?

June turned to rummage through her dresser drawer until she located a crumpled hand-written receipt given to her by the harassed mother. The scrawled address was given as Kells Dyke, Suffolk. "Oh yes, I remember driving there; it was much further than I'd anticipated. Another twenty minutes and I'd have been in Newmarket. Oh dear, that's quite near the Ferozshahs' place. Gabriel and Teresita may well have lived close by. And the woman did say their neighbour had rescued the horse from a family who were throwing it out because they were getting divorced and moving...oh no, it all seems to fit..." she finished lamely.

It was another nail in the coffin. It confirmed their worst fears and they sat in numbed silence, completely stumped as to what to do next.

After some thought, Eddie turned to his son and said gently, "I suggest you go back to Nazrin and tell her you've guessed what's upset her. Say you understand her distress, but she needs to talk to you about it. Tell her you can help her but only if she tells you the whole story."

Seb groaned and said with desperation, "But she doesn't know I've been told about her brother. She's never once mentioned it. It'll seem like we've all been discussing her behind her back...".

Jacs advised him to encourage her to explain why the sight of the rocking horse had upset her. "Try and get HER to tell you." The poor lad headed off to tackle this difficult task, fearing it may break her fragile bond of trust which had been so hard to win.

Back in the sitting room, we'd heard nothing of this conversation, yet I was wrestling with a similar problem. I'd taken Pasha's advice and left Little Mare to herself. After a long and worrying night, the next day she broke her silence. Her sweet, honeyed voice came as a surprise as it drifted up from where she stood by my side and I was thrilled to hear her words. "Blitz, may we please talk? I need your help, I don't want the fog to come back…" Oh, this was music to my ears and in my calmest voice I replied that I'd be very happy to listen and I'd be there for her, always. However, what I heard next shocked me to the core.

"I've remembered everything now – it was HER. I saw her last night. She is my lovely girl, the one I hurt so much. But she hates me and I'm scared because she doesn't want me here, she may send me away again. I once belonged to her and her brother and they both adored me, and I loved them too. But then, I let him fall from my saddle – and he died. She screamed and shouted at me and told me she wanted me gone, far, far away."

My mind whirred as I put all the puzzling pieces of her past life into place. Why had I not worked all this out before now? Why hadn't I seen what now seemed obvious? I felt a stabbing pain of sorrow for this poor lovely horse who had suffered for years, fearing she'd done something terrible. Life had dealt both her and Nazrin a cruel blow, and I had no idea how the dilemma could be resolved.

Fireworks came to the rescue. He sprung from his usual position sitting on Pasha's ornate saddle to land directly facing the noble warrior horse. He gazed up at that wise old face with knowing eyes and lyre-shaped ears and asked him what should be done. Pasha dipped his long nose down to nuzzle the cat, swung his gaze towards Little Mare and me, and after a considered pause he spoke solemnly. "To fight a battle, draw your sword, but to fight darkness, light a candle."

"Oh, oh, oh, dearest Pasha, we don't have time to work out what you mean. Please explain!" pleaded the poor cat, who usually loved the task of making sense of those riddles.

Despite not knowing him for very long, I think my assessment of the great stallion had been accurate. Although carved in the image of the greatest breed of courageous war horse to ever go into battle, he was a true Marwari. He was fair, brave and kind. He would avoid bloodshed if possible and was always on the side of peace. I felt I understood what he was saying and tried to convey it to the others. Charlotte had nodded quietly, gazing at her husband with a deep respect. She understood perfectly.

"I think Pasha is saying we must tackle this 'darkness' without aggression but shine some gentle light on the problem and solve it with kindness."

"Precisely, Blitz," Pasha continued, "your charming companion and that troubled young woman have fallen on a double-edged sword. They must now move forward to heal old wounds. Together they must face the past and forgive each other. They both stumbled and fell into the trap of hate and blame many years ago. Now whoever rises first must help the other up. Then they will move forward and both will be redeemed."

## 'Redemption: to be saved from error, sin or evil.'

"Well it all sounds marvellous in theory," Fireworks moaned, "but who's going to rise first and how will we ever get them in the same room together to thrash this out?"

"There will be no thrashing," the stallion said with calm certainty. "It will happen as naturally as the sun rising in the morning. The stars have aligned; they will be brought together in forgiveness and harmony. Soon, we will all be brought together in peace. That is why we all wear our saffron thread."

Of course, we still didn't know that June had found those strange bracelets or quite what it all meant, but Pasha's soothing and convincing prophesy had lulled us into a relaxed state. We decided to wait patiently and let things take their course. Sleep overtook us and early the next morning as dawn broke, the door to our sitting room headquarters gently opened. There stood Nazrin with my lad right behind her, whispering encouragingly in her ear as he nudged her forward. She entered hesitantly on her own and Seb shut the door quietly behind her.

We were frozen as still as statues, even little Pashmina stood motionless, looking up with huge, startled eyes. All we could do was watch with trepidation as Nazrin, looking red-eyed and drawn, made her way towards Little Mare. What happened next was quite lovely. Kneeling down next to her once adored rocking horse and looking into those sad and clouded eyes, she apologised. She blurted out how sorry she was for being so cruel and sending her away, for blaming her unfairly, for all the grief within her that had turned to hate and for all the misery she'd caused them both over many years.

It struck me then that although Nazrin had befriended us, talked to us and bestowed her lovely smile upon us in the past, she'd never once laid a hand on our bodies. She'd never touched us in all the time we'd known her.

Now, Nazrin gingerly bent forward and with an outstretched hand she caressed the mare's neck. It was a warm and loving touch, but its effect was electric. All the guilt, pain and animosity travelled from that touch through both their bodies and out of Little Mare in the form of a huge sigh of relief. Now, forgiveness and empathy flowed between them. The sitting room slowly lit up as pale rays of the early morning sun flooded in through the French windows. Nazrin shifted to sit cross-legged on the floor and turned to address us.

"Everyone, I'd like you to meet my very beautiful and much loved childhood rocking horse, Lina. Actually, her name is Basculina, Lina for short. My father bought her for me and my brother, Gabe. Sadly, Gabe was ill and he died, but it was no one's fault. I was so upset that I became angry. I've since learned that it's a destructive feeling and nearly ruined my life. I now have a gift for Lina, something I robbed her of years ago." She then produced the two saffron-coloured thread bracelets from her pocket. One she tied carefully around Lina's foot and the other she donned herself. "I was so heart-broken and angry when Gabe died, so I ripped both of our lucky threads off and put them inside Lina. I made Maman send her away, I didn't want the bracelets to keep us together." She paused, looking sadly at her little horse. "I felt so guilty. I hope she can forgive me. I missed her horribly when she'd gone and I hated myself…I swore I'd never love or even touch a rocking horse ever again."

Feeling spent and exhausted, Nazrin rose, gently hugged her horse and took her leave. We saw her fall into Sebastian's arms as she left the room and heard her sobbing quietly against him. I think they were sobs of sheer relief. She had found redemption at last, and we were all touched by her brave speech.

Now here's the funny thing. I turned to my beautiful Lina (oh I loved that name, so fine and feminine) and I realised that Nazrin had done her more good in those few intense minutes than I'd managed over many weeks. How did I know? I knew because one fundamental thing had changed and it was a very important thing. Her eyes. They were no longer clouded over with that veil of sadness. To describe them as bright and shiny would be an understatement, as they weren't just shining – they were positively glittering!

# CHAPTER 26.
# MANY FACES OF LOVE

S o much had happened during Sebastian's short visit and all too soon he was due to return to his demanding Newmarket post. However, he found time to pay me a flying visit to catch up on all that had happened since our last proper meeting. He entered our room, coming to sit by me in his usual fashion with his arm slung affectionately over my saddle. Fireworks, desperate to spend time with his beloved Seb, grabbed his opportunity and folded himself up comfortably on the lad's lap, totally content. "We've both had our work cut out with our flighty fillies, Blitz, but I think we've both done bloomin' well," he confided. "And by the way, she's absolutely gorgeous, your Lina."

I swelled with pride at this comment. It thrilled me to hear him refer to her as 'mine'. Wow, I must be completely besotted because I had also noticed my heart melted every time she uttered my name! Sebastian and I were sharing similar thoughts because he added softly, "I love my filly too, Blitz. I've never felt this way... I want to ask her something, but I daren't, not quite yet. Maybe at the end of the season; I'll take it slow and test the water first..." I knew exactly what was on his mind and could see why he'd have to tread carefully. Like Roobs, Nazrin was still quite capable of bolting...

Seb filled us in on the meeting in France and said how proud he'd felt when Nazrin had stood up and fought for her colt's heritage. He'd felt moved to see Gabriel's eyes filled with so much paternal love, as only a father can love a daughter. Cyrus, too, was full of admiration and love for Nazrin and he wondered if she knew how much they cared. Had she guessed the depth of his own feelings towards her? He marvelled at how she'd changed since the night he'd tackled her in her room as she'd struggled through her darkest hour. Eventually he'd persuaded her to go back to Wick House and talk everything over with the partners, a meeting which had culminated in June handing her those symbolic saffron bracelets. He told me it had taken every ounce of her strength to face her horse and, most importantly, to forgive herself. That dawn meeting had been her deliverance, a weight off her shoulders, a banishing of all that guilt. Now she was carefree and light-hearted.

"I've got to go back soon, but I really don't want to leave her," he lamented, "but I'm excited about riding Roobs – although, I'd never have got her to this point without Naz. She's amazing," he sighed, then glanced at me and we both laughed. Yes, we were both as ridiculously in love as each other. As he rose to leave, Seb gave me an affectionate rub under my forelock, he then turned to Basculina and gently placed a kindly little kiss on her muzzle, saying, "Look after my best mate, Lina!" She must have been quietly listening to our whole conversation because now those clear, bright eyes were alive with laughter and I'm sure I saw a hint of a smile on her sweet lips. The deliverance had also worked for her – she, too, was free.

Summer turned to autumn, life had returned to its comfortable old routine, and we were living in a happy household, content to be in the company of dear friends. It's all we rocking horses ever really crave, a settled, caring home surrounded by those we love. The added bonus for me was I'd found a perfect and delightful companion with whom I could share my future, knowing I'd never lose her. This had been a worry when Lina had turned out to be such a beauty, quite rare and obviously valuable. I thought June may be put under pressure to sell her 'asset' as she was starting up a new business. I shouldn't have worried though; I overheard her being quizzed in the kitchen not long after the grand unveiling. Several people had assumed Lina would be sold for a healthy profit but when asked, June had replied without hesitation, "Oh NO, I would never sell her!" On seeing the sceptical faces of those who believed she was being unbusiness-like or harbouring sentimental thoughts, she'd added hurriedly, "I'm keeping that one as an example of my work. In any case, she's not really mine to sell. Nazrin would be most upset if I let her go." This had pacified her critics for the time being and allowed me a huge sigh of relief. Lina was a 'keeper'.

Although peace and stability reigned over Wick House, don't for one minute think that life here was boring. Life was never quiet on a busy stud farm or, for that matter, on a busy rocking horse 'rest and recuperation' farm, a place where needy candidates could come for help. We were always hoping for more horses to arrive as June's adverts bore fruit. A few had come and had been glimpsed briefly before being transferred to the workshop for assessment. In August, a month after Seb's return to Newmarket, an unfamiliar van rolled into our drive. Fireworks had rushed in announcing, "Another one of you lot arriving, I shouldn't wonder!" We couldn't wait to see who would emerge from the van's interior. Not one but three new faces were spotted by the rather tall Duchess, who could peer out of the window for a clear view of everything happening directly outside the house. The stud lads had been called to assist with transferring these new acquisitions from the back of the delivery van onto the yard's pick-up truck to be transported up to the Hall's garages. It was always an exciting pastime, imagining who the interesting painted wooden faces belonged to. Who were these newly-arrived characters and would we ever get to meet them? That was a question that only time would tell, but it gave us endless hours of speculation and amusement, especially if the Duchess had managed to glean more than a cursory look at them. She would faithfully record details of their make and shape, their colour, if manes and tails were in situ, and even what expressions their faces bore. Charlotte would have made an exemplary police witness as she could reel off every detail she'd captured and retained in that photographic memory of hers!

This last delivery of rocking horses was most unusual as we'd never before known three to arrive all at once. We clamoured for information and pressed Charlotte for more detail.

"Two look to be very underwhelming, pinioned upon stands of no merit with ornamentation that is mundane and rather un-flourished…" On feeling our disappointment at this boring news, she continued her appraisal of the last horse with a tantalising description, "But the third looks to be an extraordinarily well-bred fellow with unparalleled bearing and structure. It would appear he was, in a former life, extremely handsome and I imagine he possesses an illustrious and ancient pedigree. Once dapper and beautifully groomed, he seems to have regrettably fallen upon hard times and now finds himself indisposed, in a state of pauperism and shrouded in shoddy apparel. Hopefully, this impecunious gentleman will henceforth be re-instated to his former glory by the indomitable June."

Fireworks beamed with delight on hearing Charlotte's magnificent rendition. He did a quick translation for us three as Pasha and their little foal were very familiar with the Duchess's turn of phrase. "Wow, apparently he's a REALLY good one but in a right state! Probably old as well – and the Duchess should know!" the cat enthused. "Perhaps when June's nursed him back to health, he'll come to live with us?"

We all fell to day-dreaming about this intriguing chap, wondering if perhaps we'd soon be welcoming a new friend into our midst. We decided to send the cat off on a mission. He must innocently trot up to June's workshop and hang about to catch any gossip concerning this new arrival. Being equally as nosy as Cobweb and I, Fireworks was up for the challenge and sped off to put the plan into action. Imagine our delight when he returned within the hour feeling extremely pleased with himself and bursting with news.

"I slipped in un-noticed just as she and Joby were triaging the three of them. The plain, boring ones are going to be titivated and offered for sale to some kids. Parents have been asking if June had any 'cheapies' for sale so Joby's got to strengthen the stands and mend a few bits on them before they go; but never mind those... guess what?!" the cat asked smugly, knowing full well we were on tenterhooks. He then proceeded to wash his face which was an annoying habit he employed whenever he knew he had us over a barrel. Patience was the only answer, and a bit of flattery. I told him we were so lucky to have him as our most trusted gatherer of information, without him our lives would be quite dull. This had the desired effect and he leapt aboard Pasha's comfortable saddle, ready to divulge his news. He glanced affectionately at the Duchess saying, "Of course, our dear Charlotte was quite correct because June thinks he IS rather special. In fact she rang Brenda to explain exactly what he looked like: all those details about shape, legs, head position, eyes, ears, teeth, tongues and how you lot are attached to your rocking bits, etc. etc...anyway, Brenda seemed excited too. June explained that he still had some paint on him but all his leather and material bits were rotten and tattered and he had some sort of crack on him. SO...she's going to take him with her down to Brenda's to do another course to learn all about making harness! They're going to work on him together. But here's the good bit. She doesn't have time to go till Wednesday and today is only Monday!"

"What's good about that?" I enquired, puzzled.

"'I'll tell you what's good about that, my wooden-headed friend! Joby needs lots of space to repair those other two in the workshop, so... they're bringing the ole boy down here to stay with us for a couple of days, before he's taken to Brenda's! We will soon have a new house guest!"

Yes, this was exciting news. Pashmina frolicked joyfully around Charlotte, who was happy that her assessment had proved accurate and the mighty stallion looked as pleased as a wise and solemn horse could. He came out with one of his famous sayings:

"Strangers do not come into our lives by chance. They cross our paths for a reason..."

Well, this mysterious statement made us all the more curious. We didn't have long to wait – an hour later June and Jacs came into our headquarters to clear a bit of floor space for the new boy.

"He'll only just fit in here...I know he's a big, tall horse but his bows seem oversized. They don't suit him somehow. They just look wrong..." June remarked idly.

Jacs answered that she couldn't wait to see him, he sounded magnificent. They were waiting for the poor stud lads to finish work so they could bring him all the way back down to the house again.

The door swung open and in staggered the two boys, groaning under the strain of the imposing, elegant horse. They lowered him carefully to stand by the far wall but facing in our direction.

"Blimey, he's built like a racehorse!" the smallest lad muttered, glancing at his well-spaced limbs in awe. "Look at the stride on that!"

"Please don't make us move him again, unless there's three of us!" pleaded the second lad.

June absentmindedly thanked them as they hurried off. She was holding a sheet of paper with the receipt note that had come attached to the horse from the sales room. "Well, what do you think of my latest auction buy, then?" June demanded, wanting an answer from her awe-struck friend.

"WOW…he's upstanding, he's…almost regal, quite breath-taking," Jacs said eventually, unable to wrench her gaze away.

Brandishing the top sheet, June read the small print below a rather spectacular photograph that had initially attracted her to the horse and proceeded to introduce her latest buy to all of us as we watched on. "Attention all! I would like to present to you…" She squinted again at the name on the tattered bill. "…erm, 'Aubrey Devere', my latest restoration purchase, who will soon return to delight you when he's finished! That's a funny old name for a rocking horse, Jacs. Anyway, I think I'm turning as barmy as you, introducing him to the others! Come on, let's go and have a celebratory drink on him, I think he's going to be a big winner!"

But Jacs was reluctant to leave, drinking in every detail of his skilfully-fashioned body. She asked if there was any information about him and June answered, "Not a lot. Only that he came from a great aristocratic family in Leicestershire. Apparently, they were related to the royal family, only very distant cousins or something, but still! And he's been with them the whole time. But he's had some sort of accident, there's a massive split along his right side. Oh, and they owned a castle! Obviously he's been in storage for eons judging by the state of his tack. Anyway, you'll make Blitz jealous, keep admiring him like that!" she jested.

My lovely Jacs threw an adoring look in my direction and smiled. "Not a chance. Blitz knows he's my one and only, he's my heart-horse!"

As they departed, all our eyes landed on the new boy. He cleared his throat and spoke. "Actually, chaps, there's been a misunderstanding…my name is NOT Aubrey Devere, that was the name of my grand master. I'm called Kingcraft, after the illustrious racehorse who won the Derby in the year of my making, 1870. I just wanted to put you all straight."

Well, as we got chatting, we all felt he was a fine, easy going, honest and straight-forward character and we instantly took a liking to him. After establishing his real identity, no one was quite sure how to address him. He felt 'Kingcraft' was a mouthful and a bit too grand for use among friends. It would also be pretentious to adopt his master's name, as the esteemed Aubrey Cecil Devere was from a long line of Earls of Oxford. We were quietly impressed. Fireworks remarked that he'd better get used to that name, now that June had it lodged in her head. How would they be able to convince her she'd made a clerical blunder? "You're stuck with it, old son. Perhaps we should go for middle ground and just call you 'Aubs', a sort of friendly shortening of what you're going to be saddled with anyway!" We all had a chuckle at that solution and the pleasant fellow agreed to it quite happily. So started a long and wonderful friendship with Aubs, one of the nicest horses I've had the pleasure to meet. Oh, and Pasha was correct…there was a reason for our paths to have crossed.

★★★★

# CHAPTER 27.
# DECISIONS

The start of October 1993 proved an exciting time. Sebastian reported that Charlotte's Rubies was beating her stable mates with ease during practice gallops at home and was entered to run in one of the most valuable sprint races of the year, the Queen Charlotte Stakes. Despite the usual niggling worries about the filly's nerves on the day, there was quiet confidence of success – as long as everything went to plan. Of course, the Duchess was adamant we'd have a big winner because she thought a race named after her had to be a good omen.

When news of Roobs' win reached our eager ears, we were cock-a-hoop, delighted for everyone involved and so proud of Seb. We now had a rather surprising new source of information; this was our lovely Nazrin herself. Since the emotional reunion with her childhood rocking horse, the girl visited us at our Wick House sitting room almost daily. She had entered coyly at first but with growing confidence as she'd spent more time in our company. Soon she was skipping happily into our domain with her remarkable smile, a smile that showered us all with warmth as tangible as the midday sun. Our resident philosopher, Pasha, had rightly commented that anyone with such a powerful and radiant smile had to be someone full of kindness and goodwill.

Nazrin would sit with us, happily chatting away, giving us all the news she'd received through her many conversations with Seb. But the main reason she came was to ride Basculina. This posed no threat to her elegant yet sturdily built horse as the girl was so lithe and slender. Mounting her fluently with the ease of someone completely at home in the saddle, the pair rocked together effortlessly in total unison. It seemed that their years of separation had only strengthened the deep bond between them. I looked on, quite moved; watching them reminded me of myself and Jacs, when she'd ridden me as a young child at the fairground all those years ago. Of course, you can love your rocking horse from the ground – but I don't care what anyone else thinks, I believe something magical happens when you actually mount and become one with your horse. As with the real animal, when you are astride, there is a fusing of body, mind and spirit.

As Nazrin and Lina swayed together, strands of silvery mane dancing and flowing about them, it struck me that she resembled a nymph riding a sea horse in the wild and swirling surf of the Camargue tide. Then a strange premonition hit me. I had a deep, uneasy feeling that the girl sitting upon her pretty dappled mare, longed to return to the land of her birth. Nazrin was born in that wild, tempestuous place; her early life had been woven into the fabric of her father's ranch, those rustic horses and the pink flamingos she'd so eloquently described. Nazrin reminded me of one of those graceful birds, standing free and proud in the untamed seascape of her Camargue. I had an overwhelming image of that bird launching itself upward into the endless sky. The moment passed and I gave it no more thought.

*As Lina and Nazrin swayed together...*
*a strange premonition hit me.*

June had returned from Brenda's Dorset farm each weekend and we'd heard snippets of conversation between her and Jacs as they'd discussed how work was progressing on the magnificent Kingcraft, who had been wrongly lumbered with his old owner's name, Aubrey Devere, but who had been re-named by us as 'Aubs'. Although we'd only known him for a couple of days, he'd made a big impression on us, more especially on Lina. She had drawn such comfort from hearing his story and it had helped her to grow in self-confidence. Over those couple of days he was with us, we'd all talked about our chequered pasts. Even when stuck in a room, one can experience the greatest of adventures just by engaging in simple conversation. Between us we'd had hundreds of years' worth of experiences under our saddles!

Cobweb had asked Aubs how he'd acquired the massive crack that ran along the length of his right side. His answer was honest and straightforward: "Oh, the blame lies entirely with me. You see, I have a vice – I'm what they call a 'rearer'. Whenever I was ridden, unless the child was an exceptionally well-balanced, experienced rider, I tended to rock back violently and go up, up, and very nearly over. I was quite dangerous. I never meant to, I just couldn't help myself and I'm not proud of it. I loved my three children, but unfortunately the younger two were not allowed to sit on me after they'd both slipped off backwards when I'd reared and were injured. Luckily, my master bought them a smaller rocking pony each and they seemed quite content. My boy, Hubert, was a very skilled little rider and could balance me perfectly but I was never a novice ride. Several of his school friends got hurt riding me and one day a cocky schoolboy pal of his decided to 'teach me a lesson'. I honestly think he was just copying his father's actions because he seemed to have a plan. He mounted me and as I rocked back rather too high, he sprung off me to land on the floor, and then with all the strength he could muster – he pushed me clean over. As I lay there on my side, split open and damaged, I heard him boasting to Hubert that his father always employed that trick with a horse that reared. Needless to say, my boy punched him on the nose and there was a lot of trouble over the incident. But that, my friends, was how I was injured."

I remember clearly that Lina had gasped loudly in horror; the story had upset her terribly. She had asked incredulously how he'd coped with the guilt of hurting children and if all the family had despised and banished him. Had he been made to feel evil or as if he deserved to be broken? With genuine surprise and concern for my poor distressed Lina, he answered her with kindness. "Why no, my dear Lina, why ever would you assume such a horrible thing? My whole family loved me very much and was very upset by my injury. They knew it wasn't my fault and I would never wish them harm. We are only wooden toy horses; we are not born evil, as no child is born to act badly. Bad children have only followed a bad example from their elders. Accidents happen; a toy horse can never be blamed. In fact, my master valued me greatly as a learning aid and a wonderful schoolmaster. Hugo was learning the art of riding thoroughbred racehorses, so I was made by the estate's carpenter to exact specifications to fit that bill. No, I have no doubt that I was a much-loved family member."

I saw a new light of understanding in Lina's eyes. She surprised us all by opening up to Aubs, telling him first about her young boy, Gabe, how he fell and died and the guilt that had haunted her. Then she told of her torturous life with her last family, how she'd felt responsible for hurting the children who had then convinced her she was cursed. Our lovely new friend explained to her gently that she should never have shouldered any blame and that her last family was very wrong and obviously quite cruel. Lina had given me an adoring look (which melted my heart) and answered, "That's exactly what Blitz told me and I realise he was right. He has helped me out of darkness and I truly love him for it." She then added, "And now, I have the love of my girl back. I never dreamt it was possible to feel so happy."

Aubs' kind eyes smiled at her and he whispered, "All that rocking horses need to know in life is how to give love and how to accept it in return. That is the recipe for our happiness." This speech had a profound effect on my sweet Lina, it had reinforced everything I'd tried to teach her. Now she fully believed.

At the end of October, Seb and Roobs returned home for the winter. The illustrious filly was now the stud's biggest star and was welcomed back for her well-earned winter break. A small 'end of season' celebration was planned, and the usual treasured friends would attend. I remember Seb visiting me as soon as he was back and moaning because I was no longer residing at Airborne Lodge with him nowadays. "I really miss you, not being there, Blitz, and I know Mum hates it too." The saying 'be careful what you wish for' had sprung to mind more than a few times when I'd missed the cosiness of our own home and having Jacs around all the time. But hadn't I often said how I wished us rocking horses could all live under one roof....? Luckily, I'd enjoyed some quality time with Jacs over the last month when both she and Nazrin had appeared at Wick House to have a rock on us. It was delightful, the two of them astride us, giggling away whilst we rocked happily together in our own little world.

Now Sebastian was deep in thought and with a serious face he confided in me, "I've decided, I can't put it off any longer, Blitz, I'm going to ask her the question. I'm not going to make her bolt by mentioning marriage; I'll just ask her if we can get engaged – that's not so frightening, is it? What d'ya think, old boy?"

Well, what could I say? I had my doubts but didn't wish to be negative, so I did what all of us do when in a tight spot...I nodded.

That went down well and Seb left the room feeling quite elated. Everyone had heard the conversation and no one else had any doubts. They were all delighted and Fireworks was jubilant. "What did I tell you lot? I bet my ginger stripes, if I'm not mistaken!"

Pasha voiced his opinion which had a worrying undertone because it echoed my inexplicable uneasy feeling. "The boy had better ask her soon. Procrastination is the thief of time."

A week later Wick House hosted their small get-together. All our favourite people gathered under one roof felt quite blissful. The evening started so well. Brenda came into our headquarters to admire the six of us, stroking each of us individually, exclaiming what a fine spectacle we made. She was followed in by June as she marvelled at the stallion and foal carved in India by Mali's son.

"Such wonderful workmanship," she'd said appreciatively. Turning to her friend, she added, "Who'd have guessed when we first met at that auction where we found Blitz all those years ago, that you'd end up a collector learning to restore and we'd be such great friends?"

June hugged her and replied, "I knew from the moment I bought good old Cobbers, that one rocking horse would never be enough. Who can ever get enough of drinking in their beauty every day of life? So, we have Blitziboy to thank for our friendship and because of all of them – this has happened." She waved her arm expansively to encompass and represent the whole estate and everybody who had somehow been brought together to live here. "These horses between them have literally been the saving and the making of us! Oh, and Fireworks of course, I'm sure he had a big paw in all this, too…"

Jacs then appeared at the door and the three of them continued reminiscing as she walked over and slipped on to my back for a gentle rock. She leaned forwards to reach Basculina and stroke her neck saying, "Brenda, have you noticed her eyes?"

The woman gazed into Lina's bright orbs and remarked, "Oh well done, June, your secret glass recipe worked then?"

June came to have a closer look and was quite astonished. "Nothing to do with me," she admitted, "I never found the stuff. Well, that's amazing, they've become completely clear! I hadn't noticed. However did that happen?"

Jacs laughed knowingly as they both looked at her and back to Lina's gleaming eyes.

"Go on then, give us your esoteric thoughts on this rocking horse mystery," Brenda demanded.

Jacs' answer was short and simple; she uttered one word: "Nazrin".

The two women smiled fondly at my clever and completely correct Jacs and said, "Well, who would dare argue with our rocking horse whisperer!"

Later, Manfri, Seb and Nazrin entered our room and smiled at us with deep affection.

"Oh, they're such a fabulous sight, a haze of dapples, a blur of outstretched legs and glistening eyes, just beautiful!" Nazrin remarked, sighing appreciatively.

Manfri laughed and said pointedly, "You'z changed yer tune, my gel! You 'az a touch o' the poet about ya today."

Nazrin just said, that was then but now, she wouldn't want to live without us. Seb predicted there was no chance of that happening; we were here to stay, adding that if June's plan worked out, this place wouldn't just be known as The Dapple Stud, it would become a famous rocking horse stud too! "Joby has already said he'll come full-time as they've got orders for rocking foals from several of our owners and requests for horses as Christmas presents!"

Just then, there was a soft knock on our door. We swung our gaze round to see Tehmi enter hesitantly and tell Nazrin she had something for her. She delved into her handbag and produced a small casket which she handed to her granddaughter. "This was my mama's box and it was given to her by our magician, Fu Ling Yoo. I only found it recently, just after you saw Basculina. I thought you should have it now. They've brought us such wonderful luck, I thought you'd like to hold on to them as a memento of your great-grand mama." With that, she smiled sweetly at us all and left to re-join the party.

Manfri stood back and watched as Seb and Nazrin opened the little casket, totally intrigued. There inside lay a small collection of the sacred saffron threads, their colour as vivid as the day they were placed there.

The young woman was thoughtful as she looked first at Lina and then at me. "I think we should join these two together properly, the way Fu Ling Yoo married Mumty and Pasha!" she declared happily.

"Oh, what about poor old Cobweb? He'll be the only one without a thread," Seb lamented.

"No, he won't. He can be their best man!" She laughed as she fished out two of the bright bracelets and proceeded to place them on our feet. It was such a generous thing to do and we were quite touched. "Only one person left in need of one now," she whispered to Seb as she pressed a third thread into his hand.

It was a tender moment and I fear Manfri was a bit embarrassed because he got up to leave. "All's lookin' good for the future, then!" he said cheerfully, giving me a knowing wink as he strode out, leaving the couple to themselves.

"Well, while you're in this romantic mood..." Seb started, turning to face Nazrin, speaking clearly and with confidence. "I want to ask you a serious question. What would you say to the idea of us getting engaged?"

We all held our breath but in the few seconds that elapsed, we didn't have time to gauge Nazrin's reaction because suddenly, all hell broke loose. The sitting room door flew open with Fireworks skidding in, Jacs close behind, tripping over to avoid the cat and landing sprawled at the shocked girl's feet. Jacs scrambled up and said as calmly as she could, "Now don't panic, Nazrin, but your father has been taken to hospital. Cyrus is on the phone to that little lad, Milou, right now. He's asked for you to speak to him because he can't understand him very well. You speak French fluently so go now..."

The poor girl blanched visibly as she rushed to the hall and grabbed the phone from Cyrus. After a brief conversation during which Nazrin remained level-headed, giving Milou calming direct orders and assurances, she replaced the receiver and turned to everybody muttering, "I'll have to go over tonight, he's had a terrible accident."

Seb comforted her and offered to accompany her to France, but she shrugged off everyone's offers of help, only requesting that Cyrus arrange her flight over as soon as possible.

*'Life is a series of bridges; be careful which you cross and which you burn.'*

By 10 o'clock that evening Nazrin had packed a small bag and Cyrus drove her and Seb to the airport for her to catch a late flight. They made hasty plans in the back of the car but despite Seb's insistence, she refused to allow him to go with her. Nazrin was adamant he should stay to help the stud cope in her absence as they'd be a member of staff short. He argued that she'd need him there to tend to her father's ranch and horses, but her parting words were, "I need to be on my own, I need time to think about what you've sprung on me tonight. I want to spend time alone with my father…" Without a backward glance she was off to catch her plane, leaving Cyrus and Sebastian feeling strangely empty and chilled. Nazrin was gone. Seb felt the warmth of his day had drained away as the sun in his life had set.

During the next week Seb was desolate. His thoughts raced around in his head. Had he driven Nazrin away with his proposition, had she fled to escape him? Had the most precious person in his life bolted for good? He attended to his work in a mechanical way, always listening out for the phone to ring. The trouble was that Gabriel had no phone. Nazrin could only call him from the hospital or from a neighbour's house. She was so pre-occupied that she'd only managed to talk briefly to him twice since she'd taken off and then she'd sounded detached and distant. The news that filtered down to us was vague; Gabriel had been nursing a sick horse that had thrashed about on the stable floor, kicking him badly. His leg and several ribs had been broken and he'd suffered a collapsed lung. He'd lain on the ground for hours until Milou had turned up after school as he often did, and had found the man struggling to breathe. His quick thinking and prompt actions had probably saved another life. He had run to alert Gabriel's neighbour who had transported the pair to the hospital where Milou had found a phone to inform Cyrus of the accident.

Nazrin landed at the local airport and took a taxi straight to the hospital in Arles. She had been shocked to see her father hooked up to breathing apparatus and drowsy from many drugs. Taking his hand gently, she comforted him; assuring him she was here for as long as needed and would take care of everything back at his ranch. He was to rest and recover and she'd visit him when he felt stronger. Once outside the ward, she leaned against the wall, slid to the floor and wept. A doctor had spotted her, taken her to a private room where he explained that Gabriel had been in grave danger but was now expected to make a full recovery, if he rested. "These gardiens are a tough breed and that's the danger," he warned. "He must take time to heal or it will leave him incapacitated." Milou had gone home earlier with his father but Gabriel's neighbour, Gerard, had stayed and now offered Nazrin a lift back to the ranch in his rickety truck.

It was after 2 o'clock in the morning when she alighted from Gerard's vehicle to stand solemnly outside the small-holding, her old childhood home. It was silhouetted against an inky night sky, a line of higgledy-piggledy rustic fencing, the small ancient stone hovel and charming dilapidated barn plus a few proud horses, outlined within their small corral. Their heads turned towards her expectantly as they whickered a grateful greeting. They marched up to her, manes ruffled by the chilly night breeze, and poked noses into her hand for a reassuring rub from the girl they recognised. Their dark liquid eyes spoke a welcome that touched her heart. This place and everything in it, was a world away from her usual life. The flashy stabling and refined thoroughbred horses of the racing world, the modernity and convenience of the twentieth century, the designer clothes and endless spending of money that came from a bottomless pit; it all seemed trite and meaningless. This earthy, honest place had meaning, deep meaning and purpose. She knew she was home; she'd smelled that tang of salty sea and caught a waft of the strange pungent sea wormwood, carried to her on the brisk breeze.

Her father's door was never locked so she entered the familiar dingy room and lit an oil lamp. Feeling ravenous, she poked about in his marble-shelved larder until she'd located a loaf of local crusty bread. Thickly buttering a sliced-off doorstep, she found some gnarled and fragrant home-grown tomatoes, hacked off a piece of 'black beef' from a cold joint and fashioned the ingredients into a delicious sandwich. Accompanied by a cold glass of her favourite local Vin de Sable wine, this simple feast was demolished, and with her hunger sated, Nazrin collapsed into her father's tatty armchair for a few hours of fitful sleep.

Dawn broke and the farm cockerel heralded the day with a lusty bout of crowing. Nazrin awoke, stretched her aching limbs and splashed her face with icy water. After changing into more suitable clothes, she started on the familiar routine of morning chores remembered from last summer. Why did she feel so peaceful and calm? Shouldn't she be panicking about the health of her father, the future of the ranch and his precious manade of beloved Camargue horses? Why did she not miss Sebastian or Wick Stud, her family and the horses back home? Suddenly it dawned on her; she was completely content here because *this* was home. That revelation started a huge internal battle, a conflict of confusing emotions that, for the moment, she threw to the back of her mind. Collecting Segolene from the corral, she saddled the mare in preparation for a long ride. She would search the marshes until she located her colt, Mistral, and after that she would check on the herd to see how the year's recent crop of foals had turned out. Feeling invigorated, Nazrin rode off without a care in the world.

Very soon she found Mistral living within a small group of young bachelor colts. This was nature's way of keeping them safe, away from the wrath of their father. The old stallion didn't tolerate young colts in the midst of his band of jealously guarded mares. Every male was a threat, even his own sons. In a few years they might try to challenge him for supremacy over the herd, but for now they were content in their little group, bonded to one another for friendship and security. They spent their days learning the lay of the land, where the best watering holes and succulent grasses were, where the dangerous bogs lurked, where it was safe to shelter from storms without encroaching on rival stallions' grounds. Turf wars were frequent; mature stallions often fought, and they'd learned to keep a good distance away from these spectacular but frightening displays of prowess. Mistral and his mates would mock-fight and play with each other without malice, but nevertheless, honing battle skills for the future. They would graze side by side, flick flies off one another with their tails, and indulge in mutual grooming. For now, they were the best of friends, living the natural life of wild horses.

Mistral had spotted her riding towards his secret clearing and had recognised her voice instantly when she'd called his name. He came trotting over and Nazrin dismounted to hug him and run her hands all over his stocky, well-muscled body. She traced her fingers over the newly applied brand he sported on his quarters, feeling proud he now wore his 'sous berceau' mark that he'd so deserved. He was tamer than the others, having been hand-reared, and in fact, he'd become quite bold and cheeky. Nazrin had to reprimand him for a few over-zealous nips and eventually shooed him away to join his surprised friends. "You'll be coming home for a few lessons in manners, my lad!" she warned, laughing as she re-mounted and headed home. As she neared the ranch, she spotted Milou who had arrived after his day at school and was standing by the barn, looking concerned.

"Hello! Oh, I'm glad it's you who took Segolene, I was worried when I saw she'd gone..." he shouted to her.

They headed indoors and the aroma of Nazrin's bubbling stew reached their noses. Before she'd left to ride in search of the horses, she'd lit the old Aga to warm the cold stone walls of the dwelling house. It had seemed sensible to throw meat and vegetables into her father's heavy iron creuset and place it in the lowest part of the oven, so she had a hot meal waiting for her that evening. Nazrin invited Milou to join her and they polished off the casserole with hunks of bread to mop up the gravy.

After the evening chores were done, the young boy told Nazrin how he'd found Gabriel the day before and how he'd run for help. Other neighbours had tended the sick horse and the night's jobs while he'd gone with Gabriel to the hospital. He explained that after the meeting back in April, he'd been unable to stay away; he'd visited every day. Milou stated with conviction that he wanted to learn everything there was to know about horses. He loved them and yearned to be a gardien one day. "Your father allows me to help and do many jobs so I'm learning. He taught me all about the mares and foals. I helped him with birthing this summer. I ride out with him at weekends to learn about the cattle too!" he exclaimed proudly with enthusiasm.

Nazrin was shocked that all this had taken place in her absence, but pleased that her father had the lad's company and was investing time in his education. At 7 o'clock, the young boy headed back to his family home at the nearby fishing village with a promise to help with chores the following day.

Life continued in this vein for the next few weeks. The previous summer, Nazrin had learned the idiosyncrasies of Gabriel's ancient Renault and could kick life into the reluctant engine. As she started up the old car, she smiled to herself; her father had declared that they were the only two people in the world who could start her. She'd relished those moments of closeness that had passed between them, over a silly car! Precious moments when she'd felt the ghost of Gabe was not haunting them both. Her twin was never mentioned but his memory always lingered here…

Nazrin would collect supplies from the local village and various produce stalls placed outside farmers' gates. She would prepare a meal for her and her little helper every evening. They shared the ranch work daily and Milou rode with her at weekends, mounted on the trustworthy old mare, Segolene. They both visited Gabriel in hospital and were delighted when he was eventually allowed home. It was the end of November before he limped back into his beloved dwelling, made more welcoming than he'd ever known it. Warm and cosy with a woman's touch gracing the shabby interior, a small posy of winter flowers in a clay vessel on the roughly hewn table and the aroma of a black beef stew in the Aga awaited him. His doctor had warned him he would have to refrain from physical labour for a while yet, but could do small jobs around the farm to build up his strength.

Gabriel watched Nazrin carefully, wondering at her total contentment. Did she not resent being here, away from the boy she so obviously loved? Did she not miss her comfortable lifestyle, mixing with the rich and famous racehorse folk? He didn't want her to stay out of duty, but he adored every minute spent with the daughter he'd missed badly for so many years.

Nazrin may have looked peaceful on the outside, but her inner torment had increased. Every night she wrestled with the chaotic battle of emotions that played out in her head. No, she didn't miss Seb, but thought about him constantly. She certainly wasn't ready to marry; cooking and cleaning for someone wasn't her style – yet here she was, enjoying every minute of caring for her father. Did she miss the cut and thrust of modern thoroughbred breeding, that challenge of producing the best racehorse to storm the tracks? Maybe not. Here in her wild Camargue, she still had the opportunity to breed the best stock, the toughest survivors to continue an un-broken lineage of a rare and ancient breed. She was so drawn to the natural way in which these horses were managed, left to breed in their tempestuous world with minimum human interference. Did she want to remain here out of a sense of duty; worse still – was there a niggling worry that Milou would usurp her position, replace her in her father's affections? That was ridiculous; a mean thought that she felt ashamed of having even considered. No, if she decided to stay, it would be because she loved her dad and he needed her here with him. And she adored this crazy place that time had forgotten...

*'Your decision to leave is correct if you are walking away, not running away.'*

Eventually, Nazrin decided what she should do. She'd thought hard about Milou. It seemed to her that the boy had helped Gabriel to leave behind the guilt and anger of losing his son, in the way that Basculina had helped her. The boy was not a substitute for her brother, but a comfort to her father who drew great satisfaction in schooling Milou to run his ranch as he may have enjoyed teaching Gabe. She had noticed the lad had innate talent, an instinctual way with the horses. That cannot be taught; one is born a horseman. Milou had the potential to be a great gardien and Gabriel had recognised that fact. Nazrin knew her father loved her more than he'd ever say and if she stayed here permanently, the three of them would get on wonderfully well. She'd even teach the lad how to start that temperamental car! But she missed Seb badly and longed to feel his arms around her...would he come out here to live? No, she would never ask him to abandon his career, but he could come for holidays; it was only a few hours away. Perhaps she could ask June if Basculina could be shipped over to live with her. She would soon get used to life without that lovely close partnership she'd enjoyed with Seb. Oh, it had been a tough decision but after much heartbreak, her mind was finally made up. Now she had the unenviable task of breaking the news to the people she loved.

During her long weeks of exile in France, Nazrin had longed to share her turmoil with someone, anyone who might understand. She hadn't the heart to write to Seb, it was just too painful – but there was one wise and compassionate friend whom she felt she could confide in and that was Manfri. She trusted him implicitly and knew he would never judge her harshly. She also knew he was unlikely to reply as writing letters had never come easily to the Romany man. Nazrin wrote down her worries, her fears and the conflict she was going through. She sent her letter to Manfri and felt a weight had lifted off her. Manfri had brought this secret correspondence with him when he'd visited Wick stud. While seated alone with us in our sitting room, he'd delved into an inner pocket and produced the missive which he'd read with a heavy heart, mumbling the words under his breath but loud enough for all of us to hear. We wished we hadn't listened.

Life at Wick Stud was unbearable. We all missed Nazrin so much. The sunshine had disappeared from our lives. We rocking horses felt so sad for Seb and for poor Lina, who grieved silently for her 'lovely girl' who she'd only just found again. The partners had lost a valuable member of staff and a friend they'd welcomed into their hearts and home. Jacs was angry with the girl who was causing her son so much pain. Sebastian was totally heart-broken and walked around like a lost soul, unable to eat or sleep. Such was his loyalty towards Nazrin, he defended her actions to the hilt and wouldn't have a harsh word said against her. He blamed himself for her not returning and I felt guilty that my premonition seemed to have played out. Pasha rarely spoke about Nazrin leaving, but one day he remarked glumly, "Misery loves company." It did seem appropriate. Even the weather had been gloomy since her departure; everyday had been sunless with immovable blankets of cloud shrouding the sky.

Come December, the annual Christmas tradition of having a huge extended party had been abandoned. No one felt like celebrating since Nazrin had phoned to tell the partners that her father was now out of hospital but needed nursing for the unforeseeable future. She had no plans to return yet, if ever. Tehmina and Teresita were angry too. If only they had refused to let her spend time with Gabriel, she may have resented them but they'd still have her in their lives. Old wounds prohibited them from even visiting her. They had let her spread her wings...but she'd chosen to fly away. Cyrus missed her almost as much as Seb. They both resisted the urge to fly out and turn up on Gabriel's doorstep. No one wanted to pressure the girl; the decision had to be hers alone.

Manfri had accompanied Joby to Wick House on one of his many visits to finish his rocking horse orders in time for Christmas. My wise old friend came to try and comfort Seb as he sat moping with us in our sitting room. The mood was dark and I remember Manfri telling us all that we must have faith. He said if Nazrin's love for Seb was strong enough, she'd be back. But if she was happier staying with her father, then we should respect that and try to be happy for her. He'd added that to truly love someone, you must be prepared to let them go and take comfort in their happiness. Love is hard because it's selfless. It was a lovely speech – but didn't help much. We concluded we must all be horribly selfish.

Christmas Day arrived and, frankly, we were dreading it. June and Jacs had planned a lovely but quiet lunch just for the family, but at the last minute, decided to invite Cyrus and Tehmina. The kitchen was cleared and the large scrubbed pine table was laid with June's best crockery, but nobody bothered to place any crackers out or put any tinsel up. Seb sat with us in our room, huddled despondently in the corner, trying not to think about the previous Christmas he'd enjoyed with the girl he loved. He took from his pocket the crumpled saffron thread that Nazrin had given him on that awful night of the phone call. He'd felt too angry to wear it after she'd gone without him and had stuffed it in his trouser pocket. Now, the pain of missing her made him want to wear it to feel close to her. Seb carefully untangled and stretched the jumbled threads out to form a string which he then wound around his wrist. It hadn't made him feel any less miserable but it had given him something to do.

On the dot of midday, Charlotte peered out of the window as the Ferozshah car arrived, but as Cyrus disembarked, he didn't approach the rear door to let his great- niece out. Nazrin was not coming. Pasha, who didn't speak much these days, decided to grace us with one of his sayings. He glanced out of the window and declared, "Fear not the storm for a rainbow is never far away… look, the sun has decided to make an appearance!" True enough, for the first time in weeks we noticed the sky had cleared and pale rays of sun tried to brighten the room. But it failed to lift our spirits.

Seb refused to join the others for lunch. He couldn't face Cyrus, today of all days. The Christmas feast was dished up and everyone began eating in near silence which was why they all heard it, the unmistakeable sound of a vehicle drawing up on the gravel drive. Then, there was a gentle knock at the front door. Slightly annoyed at being disturbed in the middle of a meal, David rose reluctantly to answer the unwelcomed caller. We all heard an exclamation of surprise and moments later, there was Nazrin standing in the kitchen doorway, scruffy and tired but still dazzlingly beautiful. The seemingly unfeeling and stand-offish girl was overcome with emotion as she joyfully accepted hugs and kisses with tears of relief flooding down her cheeks. She had been unsure of the reception she'd receive after the grief and pain she'd caused. "Where's Seb?" were the only words she whispered hoarsely. Jacs pointed towards the sitting room, and she hurried away to reunite with the love of her life.

I'll leave you to imagine that joyous meeting of kindred spirits. All the doubt, confusion and hurt of past months melted away during their embrace which seemed to fuse them together as one. After disentangling themselves from each other's arms, the pair sat and talked for a long time. Although I was feeling quite dizzy with happiness, I do remember snippets of their conversation.

"What made you decide to come back?" Seb had finally asked.

"My head told me to stay. My heart was split in two but my soul needed to be here with you," she'd answered.

At last, he braved the question he feared had made Nazrin run – "So after all this, shall we get engaged?"

With one of her most magnificently radiant smiles, she said simply, "Why not!"

**** THE END ****